Fashionably FAKE

MORGANA BEVAN

Cover Design by: Pretty Little Design Co.

Editing by Dayna Hart

ISBN: 978-1-916719-13-2

To the boss bitches who refuse to be tamed.

CHAPTER ONE

ROS

*J*ackson Levi was dead.

Not literally, but if he knew what was good for him, he'd delete my number and retract his stupid statement.

Us, in a relationship? No one would believe it.

I'd woken up to forty missed calls, a hundred or more texts, and countless voicemails. Most of them from Jackson fucking Levi.

A month ago, the Scottish actor had been fun. For a time, a very very short time, he was my friend. I could always count on him for a good laugh. Shit at work blew up? One text to Jackson and I'd laugh. Bad date? I'd open my phone to find a stupid meme waiting for me. I could enjoy myself, never feeling like he'd want something in return and be my normal dorky self.

I knew there would be no way he would ever be interested in me. Men only ever wanted to use me and, let's face the facts head on: I had no money, no fame.

Yes, I had connections, but they were all in the fashion realm and none of them would have the first clue how to help an Academy Award-winning actor.

Over the summer, he'd become the perfect distraction from my shitty, unpredictable life.

And then he'd ruined it all.

I lay in bed for over an hour, scrolling blurry-eyed through the messages and headlines. The more I read, the more my blood pressure spiralled.

JACKSON

We need to talk. ASAP.

ABI

Don't go to work today. The vultures are descending.

JACKSON

I panicked. I'm sorry, but we need to talk. Stop screening me.

I snorted.

Yes, Jackson, every time I miss a call, I'm screening you.

Couldn't possibly be that he was three hours behind, and I'd gone to sleep at a normal hour for the first time in weeks. My world totally revolved around the entitled asshole.

Okay, I didn't mean that.

Things were great until he'd asked me out and that wasn't a crime. Unfortunately.

I didn't like it, but I could forgive it. The awkwardness would fade out, maybe by the next time I saw him, and we'd go back to being friends. But telling the press I'd been his girlfriend for six months? That I couldn't forgive.

I dialled Abi, laying there with my eyes covered like some stupid childish game where it would all go away if I couldn't see it.

"What the fuck happened last night?" I asked the second she answered.

"I'm still getting all the facts but we can't find Jackson and he's not answering his phone," she said, her words almost drowned out by a sea of voices and low music in the background. "I'm still at the production company afterparty. Can you hear me?"

I grimaced, my ears straining. "Just about."

"Hold on."

I shifted onto my back and waited, staring at the ceiling like it might magic up a time turner. Shit, I'd give my favourite Gucci jacket for a way to go back in time and stop the idiot from opening his mouth.

A couple of seconds later, the party sounds cut off. "Better?"

"Much."

"Good. I've probably got five minutes before someone starts hammering on the bathroom door, so let's talk quick." She blew out a breath. "Are you okay?"

I pursed my lips and considered her question. "I don't know yet. I'm still in bed so I have no idea what's waiting for me outside the apartment."

I rubbed at my eyes, tiredness hitting hard. It was unusual for me to see this side of 7 AM after a gruelling month at Paris Fashion Week. The least I deserved was a week of long lie-ins and late starts. Instead, the universe threw a scandal at me the first chance it got.

"Why did he say it?"

"One of the magazines is claiming he had an affair with a married woman." Silence fell for a second and I could imagine my red-haired best friend chewing her lip, destroying whatever was left of her lipstick. "I think he panicked. Shaun and Nathan are pissed at him for not walking away."

My brow furrowed. "I might join them."

He had other options, but he'd chosen to drag me into it. Why? I'd have to return one of his many calls to find out. Or at least listen to his voicemails. Neither of which appealed.

I might do something stupid. *Like agree to play along.*

I shivered at the thought. Even pretend monogamy would be a step too far for me.

"The guys don't think it's true," Abi said. "The married woman, I mean. Not him saying you… you know."

I hummed in response.

What the hell was I meant to say to all this? Thanks for turning my life upside down for your own gain? Fat chance of that.

"But it's sweet though, right?" she continued, rambling through my silence. "You were the first person he thought of when he needed help."

"You're a terrible matchmaker. Don't even try it." I threw the covers back and climbed out of bed, scowling at the dark sky outside my window.

I had another two weeks before preparation chaos started for New York Fashion Week in December. As much as I'd love to throw the covers over my head and hide from the world, I couldn't and, honestly, I didn't want to be that person.

My mother had tried it for years – burying her head in the sand and ignoring my father's cheating, as if that would make it go away.

Abi went suspiciously silent.

"I might have pushed you at Finn, but that doesn't mean you need to return the favour, Abs. Jackson is my friend." I winced. "Was my friend. Remember when you tried to set me up with the guy from your agency?"

She groaned. "Don't remind me."

"Oh no, I think you need reminding."

I stepped into the silent kitchen and flipped the coffee machine on. It had been five months since Eva moved to LA in June to be closer to Abi and I still hadn't gotten used to it. Probably never would.

"The date went horribly. He threw every red flag in the book at me."

"I remember. You don't have to remi—"

"And then!" I said louder than necessary. "He turned into a stalker." I leaned against the counter, staring at the peeling off-white paint on the cabinet in the tiny kitchen. "So tell me again how great your matchmaking skills are?"

She sighed. "Fine. I'll keep it to myself."

I nodded. "Good choice."

"But that doesn't mean Jackson will."

"Abi!" I pinched the bridge of my nose, desperation leaking from me. "Can we not? He fucked up, and he needs to fix it before he turns my life upside down, but this changes nothing. I wasn't interested in ruining our friendship a month ago and I'm not interested now."

"I know. I know. I just think…"

"Stop." The coffee machine started spitting out my energy nectar, so I found the will to dig up some patience. "We're not doing this. He has a PR team or whatever, he can handle it."

"What if he can't?" she asked, her voice quiet.

Then he's royally fucked… but on his own. A pang of guilt sliced through me at the thought.

"Then it's not my problem."

If it's not your problem, why are you still talking about it?

"Even if you could help the guys salvage their launch?"

My eyes narrowed. "Wow! Abs, tell me you are not pulling the emergency card?"

"What if I am?"

"Then I haven't had enough coffee, alcohol, or sleep, and I need to hang up before you do it."

"No, don't hang up."

My head tilted at the panic in her voice. "You're avoiding something."

"Am not." Her voice hitched, giving her away.

"Hmm."

She sighed. "I'm avoiding Finn."

"Explain. Now."

Abi had been head over heels in love with the Irishman since before filming wrapped on Married Blind. The only time she'd avoided him was when they'd broken up before the show ended.

She couldn't say no to the man, and they were nauseously cute together.

"I've been nursing the same drink for the last few hours, and he's getting suspicious."

"Why would he get suspicious over a drink and why aren't you downing all the free booze like you're twenty-one again?" Then a lightbulb went off. "Oh my god! Abigail McCarthy, are you motherfucking pregnant?"

"Yes," she mumbled, her voice ridiculously low.

As if Finn would be eavesdropping on her in the bathroom. I almost laughed. Almost.

"That's amazing! Congrats!"

"Thank you," she whispered, her tone sheepish.

"Does Eva know?"

"No."

I grinned. "Oh, she won't let you live that down."

"Which is exactly why you're going to pretend I said nothing."

"Sure I am." I chuckled, but quickly sobered.

"But that settles it. I am not getting involved with Jackson Levi." Abi and Finn had only moved in together in August last year. Mona had a baby two months ago. Cat and Nathan just got engaged. I would not be rounding out the final piece in the Kings of Screen puzzle. No way.

"Ros!"

"No! Absolutely not. There's clearly something in the bloody water down there."

"Not every man is your dad."

"That would be impossible." I rolled my eyes, trying to shrug off the emotions thoughts of my father always elicited before they could fully settle again. "Doesn't mean I need to tempt fate though, does it?"

"I don't know, it might be nice."

I snorted. "Nice is not the word I would use."

Ulcer-inducing, definitely.

"I like my life. I don't need the man or the ring. I'll be the fun aunt who swoops in, spoils your kids, and then leaves you with a sugar-fuelled child with a slight addiction to Christian Louboutins."

"And I get that, but —"

The doorbell sung out, cutting her off.

"Hold that thought. Someone's asking to be murdered."

Before I could take two steps, the pounding started.

"I'm coming!" I scowled in the general direction of the front door.

Knocking on my door before 7 AM. Definite death wish.

The pounding continued, grating on my last nerve. *To Hell with stranger danger warnings.* I'd seen enough slasher films to know better, but I was ready to go full psycho on the idiot trying to bust down my door at the ass crack of dawn. Consequences be damned.

I swung open the door.

Just Jackson on my welcome mat, arm still raised to pound again.

For a split second, the last month ceased to exist, and a smile tried to claim my lips. Staring into his wide hazel eyes, I almost, *almost,* invited him in.

Then reality caught up.

I froze up while this war waged inside of me. Just stood there, mouth agape, emotions swirling from happy to annoyance to anger and back.

This is why I don't get up before the sun.

And that, ladies and gentleman, is why you check the peephole. You never know who is going to darken your door — axe murderers, religious zealots, the mob, or idiot actors who can't keep fiction separate from reality.

I needed a vat of coffee to deal with him. And maybe a getaway car on standby. Fuck.

Abi squawked in my ear through the phone I had mercifully not dropped, demanding to know who it was.

"I have to go."

"What? Why?"

"I'll talk to you later. Congrats again."

I hung up, never taking my eyes off the asshole smiling at me like he wasn't here to sweet-talk me into doing his bidding. Hell the fuck no.

"Why are you here?

··

CHAPTER TWO

··

JACKSON

*R*os stared at me from her doorway, her arms crossed, eyes spitting fire. Every time I saw her, I'd almost come to expect the gut punch panic that something amazing might slip through my fingers.

It didn't matter how long I went between sightings, how long it had been since she'd stopped responding to my calls and texts, that need to win her had never eased.

A couple of years ago, that might have worried me. Now, I was tired. Of the expectations placed on me, of the vice-like grip of my past failures, of watching my best friends couple up and suck me into their new realities.

A month ago, I asked Ros out. Let's just say I was still reeling from the rejection.

"We need to talk."

"So pick up the phone."

My eyes narrowed on the pixie haired menace. "I did. You screened me."

"I did not," she huffed and her eyes flashed with indignation.

"There's such a thing as time zones, Jackson. How about letting me wake up first?"

I crossed my arms and waited.

Last year, she might have gotten away with that lie. Now, I knew every tell. Her days of bullshitting me had come and gone.

Ros Butler avoided anything awkward or emotional. She never would have called because then she'd have to deal with what happened and that would make her feel awkward.

She sighed, her shoulders slumping. "Fine. I wouldn't have called you back."

I nodded, satisfied. "And that's why I'm here."

I glanced down the hallway, checking for prying eyes or the odd paparazzo who'd followed me into the building. Aside from an elderly neighbour shuffling towards the lifts with her little dog, it was thankfully deserted.

Didn't mean it would stay that way.

"Can we have this discussion inside?"

She stared at me, chewing on her lower lip.

"Ros, please."

Fuck, it felt weird, pleading with someone. It didn't matter that we had an odd sort of history; the words never came easy to me. But I didn't ditch my company's first film premiere, hijack our jet, and fly across the United States without a bodyguard in the suit I'd worn on the red carpet last night to give in easily.

"I know I screwed up." I held my hands out, trying to present a totally unthreatening image. "You wanted space, and I gave you that, but I need help, Ros. I need your help. Please."

She stepped back, gesturing me in. I didn't celebrate, couldn't until I had her on the jet back to Los Angeles. Still, I smiled and brushed past her. Despite me going for friendly, she scowled at me.

"Stop looking at me like that, pixie." I shook my head. "It's all going to be fine."

Her brow arched. "Are there paparazzi camped outside my door?"

"Not yet."

"*Yet* being the important word." She shut the door, but her hard expression didn't slip so much as an inch. Ros was the queen of bravado and, unfortunately for her, she'd handed over some of her keys this summer. "I have a life, Jackson. What the hell were you thinking?"

My smile turned sheepish as I scratched at my bearded jaw. "I might not have been."

"That's what I thought."

Shaking her head, she led the way into the living room. I couldn't stop myself from soaking in every eclectic piece of her flat. I'd missed it.

My house in LA was catalogue perfect. Whites, creams, and greys. Stark and sprawling. Ros's apartment was tiny in comparison, but it held so much life, so much colour.

It was rare that I'd need to be in New York. All of my business was in LA unless I was filming. Over the summer, I'd found every excuse under the sun to be here, to spend time with her. Just hanging out on her threadbare sofa filled me with more energy than an hour at the swankiest Los Angeles restaurant or bar.

She would never admit it, but she'd been grateful for my visits. Eva had just moved out West to be closer to her sister, my best friend's wife, Abi. That left Ros alone with a half-empty apartment. Now a clothes rack lined the wall in the living room, blocking the TV. Faded throws and pillows swallowed the single sofa, while art prints framed it.

Despite how in place everything seemed, it had all been pushed aside to make room for her true pride and joy. A black iron sewing machine.

She'd quickly claimed the space they left, but that didn't mean she'd taken it well. When asked, she'd put on a bright smile and wax poetic about all the benefits, knowing that no one would be able to see the dullness in her eyes or the pinch to her lips.

She hated it, and she stubbornly pushed through.

The first time I spotted it, I'd made up excuses to stay in New York for a full week and hung out with her every night. Then I'd returned periodically all through the summer. We'd tried out new bars, watched every cheesy film she loved, gone to shows and scouted every thrift store in New York City.

And I'd loved every second of it.

Living, laughing, breathing… without so much as a grain of concern that the person sharing all my time was faking their interest in me to further their career or would turn around and sell me out to the press.

Instead, everything we shared was raw and real.

A friendship I'd screwed up by letting my growing feelings and attachment to her get out of hand and control my mouth.

I bit my tongue at the urge to ask if the loneliness had gotten better. The answer wouldn't help. It might even make her more suspicious. She wouldn't appreciate me using our history to guilt her into a life-disrupting arrangement.

No, I needed to play this straight and cross my fingers she saw reason.

Ros took a seat in the only armchair in the room. She tucked her feet beneath her and fixed me with a hard stare. "When are you retracting your statement?"

I sat on the edge of the sofa, leaning forward and resting my elbows on my knees. Deep breath in. Here goes nothing.

"I'm not."

If I'd blinked, I would have missed the switch flipping in her eyes. She went from pleasantly irritated to incredulous in less than a second.

"I'm sorry." She laughed, the sound nervous. "I can't have heard you right."

"I'm not retracting my statement."

Her jaw shifted, my one and only warning before she shot to her feet.

"Yes, you are." She paced the tight confines of the living room, her pale face reddening. "I have a job, a career I'm working my ass off to build. This,"—she gestured at me, her eyes wild—"you, it's not in the plans, got it?"

"I know. If there were any other way, I'd take it."

"There is another way." She stopped in her tracks, staring at me. "Retract the statement. Admit you panicked. That's the other way."

"If I do that, they'll think I lied about the other story too." I shook my head. "I can't do that, Ros. It'll destroy all of my credibility right when I need it. And it won't just hurt me, but Shaun, Finn, and Nathan too. Your best friend —"

"Don't you dare bring Abi into this." She pointed at me, her expression shifting to deadly. "You don't get to fuck up and then emotionally blackmail me into going along with your bullshit."

"Shit!" I scrubbed a hand across my face. "Ros, I'm sorry…"

I'd barely started and already I was screwing this up. It wasn't a simple ask. If she agreed, she would have to uproot her life, I was fully aware of that.

"If you were sorry, you'd swallow your pride and do the right thing. Instead, you're here." She crossed her arms. "Not that I want you to, but you're terrible at grovelling."

I bit my cheek, holding in a grin before she read my reaction wrong.

"I can get on my knees, if it'll help?" I arched a brow at her and almost grinned when she blushed. "Or we could start with me ordering breakfast from your favourite diner down the street and pouring you an extra strength black coffee before we get into the details?"

"There won't be any details."

"Ros, please," I groaned. "Work with me. Just a little."

"No!" She started pacing again. "Not everyone is a big shot actor who can command people to do whatever the fuck he wants. I have a job, a boss, a life that didn't end just because my best friends skipped off to LA to follow you bloody celebrities."

"Maybe you wouldn't have to move."

She laughed mirthlessly. "Feed that line to someone who knows nothing about your life. I'm not stupid."

"Okay, so that probably wouldn't work." I held my hands out, trying to placate her. "But I'd pay you. Just name your price."

Her mouth dropped open. Her shoulders fell, the anger draining away as she blinked at me. Dread dug its claws into my stomach the longer the silence stretched.

"That way, you won't be out of pocket for taking some time off," I rushed on before she could formulate a response that would cement the destruction of my career and any chance of us rekindling our friendship. "I could pull some strings and find you an even better job in LA too if you didn't want to stop designing."

"I can't quit my job with no notice." She shook her head, muttering beneath her breath as she started pacing again. "And I definitely can't just pick up another job in LA. It doesn't work like that."

Then she went right back to muttering to herself. I couldn't make out more than snippets. Fashion Week, proving herself, a couple of unsavoury things about me that I'd begrudgingly allow. The vast majority of it was incoherent grumbling.

My grip on the sharp edges of my panic quickly started to wear off. Jimmy wanted us on a talk show as early as next week. No matter how many times I tried to reason with him on the flight here, he refused to be logical.

She hadn't even agreed yet, and he and Audra, my publicist, had already packed her schedule with dress fittings, red carpets, conveniently public dates where at least two paparazzi would be ready and waiting to snap photos of us.

She'd always made fun of me for my fame, claimed to not want so much as a grain of it. It had been one of the many things that drew me to her, even if it was contradictory. How could she be a fashion designer with her own label and not be famous?

I should have conceded defeat, apologised, and walked out the door. Returned to keeping my distance until Christmas when Abi and Eva would force her to join us in LA. If I had any other choice, I would have. But there were no other choices. She was my only hope.

Her rant cut off as I stood. Hope flickered across her face, making my resolve falter for all of a moment. Only I couldn't afford even an ounce of weakness. Not now.

So I squared my shoulders and brushed past her. Such a brief touch but I had to clench my fists to stop myself from reaching for her.

"What are you doing?" she asked, as I walked past her and into her kitchen.

I froze on the threshold. I always forgot how tiny this bloody kitchen was. How had the three of them shared such a small flat and not killed each other?

The cabinetry created a cramped U-shape but two people wouldn't have been able to pass each other. Especially not if the fridge or oven doors were open.

She deserved so much better.

"Jackson!" Ros shouted, tearing my focus from the outdated and inadequate space. "What are you doing?"

"I was going to make you breakfast," I said as I opened her fridge. Nothing but a bottle of vodka, a packet of shitty American cheese and a few mouldy tomatoes. Not even slightly surprised. "But maybe I should just order in."

I shut the door and started opening cupboards. If I couldn't make her breakfast, at least I could make coffee.

"What are you looking for?"

"Your coffee stash."

She snorted. "Why the hell would I keep coffee in the apartment when the better coffee is at the street cart down the road?"

"Good point. Safer than you burning down the flat first thing in the morning."

We both laughed. The first real, genuine laugh between us in a month.

Fuck, it felt good.

If she just said yes, we could have this every day.

"Did you make it to that immersive Great Gatsby show?" I asked.

"No. I didn't go."

I wanted to ask why, but held the question in.

"Did Abi invite you to the premiere?" I asked, knowing full well that she had and Ros had refused. "I was surprised you weren't there last night, at least for the catch up time with Abi and Eva. Minus the drama, you would have loved it."

"She did, but I had things I needed to do here." She shrugged.

"Why don't I believe you?"

"What's not to believe? Work keeps me busy. I live in the best city in the world." She planted her hands on her hips, staring me down like she could actually cow me.

It was an oddly endearing sight.

"There's no one in the apartment to complain about my machine running or to get annoyed when I miss dinner because I'm focused on my latest project. Life is great."

"Right."

Sighing, she relented. "Fine, it's been lonely here and if you hadn't pulled your shit, I would have been there, enjoying all the free booze and critiquing all the outfits. Happy?" She glared at the cabinet behind my head.

That pang of guilt returned to stab me in the chest. "I'm sorry."

"It's not your problem. I manage perfectly well on my own, like always."

"I never said you didn't."

Her brows climbed.

"What? I didn't." I took a deep breath, getting my voice under control before I made this worse. "It is my problem. I know you well enough, Ros. Being away from your friends is making you crazy and, if it wasn't for me, you would be in LA right now, enjoying time with them and getting a break from feeling lonely."

"Don't start."

"If you accepted my offer, you'd be in LA, with Abi and Eva within easy reach at all times and zero concerns about money." He leaned forward, resting his elbows on the table. "Would accepting my offer be so bad?"

She glared at me. "You can't buy me off."

"You'd enjoy it. You know you would." I smirked. "All the red carpet events, talk shows, galas, private parties. A personal stylist and easy access to the latest fashions."

She pulled a face that confirmed I was right.

Never one to quit while I was ahead, I leaned closer and dropped my voice. "You want to wear haute couture to a premiere? Met Gala? No problem. Want to grill a particular designer for industry secrets? I'll set it up."

Her eyes fell shut on a shiver of delight.

"You hate being sensible, Ros, so stop trying." I took a step, closing the distance between us. Her eyes narrowed, but she didn't back up. Minor success. "Let me help you escape. Just for a little while."

"Hypothetically, if I said yes," she held her hand out, silently cautioning me to keep my mouth shut when excitement shot through me. "*If* I said yes, how long would our arrangement last?"

"A year."

"A year!"

"I tried. I promise I did." I shot her an apologetic smile. "They think anything less would look suspicious."

I thought I finally had her. I took a step towards her, forcing my most charming smile to my lips.

"We would— No!" She shut her eyes, shaking her head. "I don't need to know. I'm not doing it."

"Just think about it."

"I don't need to."

I fixed her with a 'get real' look. "Forget the last month." I stared into her face, willing her to hear the truth in my words. "I can't handle this on my own. As my friend, I'm begging you to help me."

CHAPTER THREE

ROS

As my friend, I'm begging you to help me.

I'd give it to the asshole, he knew how to make me listen. How to dig himself so deep into my psyche the thought of *not* helping him hurt.

But how could I? I'd meant it when I'd said I couldn't just pick up and leave. An adult — as much as I despised calling myself one — didn't abandon her responsibilities on a whim.

Not even when that whim involved saving her *friend* from being massacred by the press.

Of course, knowing all of that didn't lessen the sickly ache of guilt.

I wish I could say my day righted itself after Jackson left. Somehow I went from running early to panic-inducingly late.

"What happened to you?" The receptionist at Dakota Reed asked when I finally stepped out of the elevator.

I glanced down, wincing as I took in my soaked Alexander McQueen wool pants and stained Balenciaga blouse. I'd barely made it halfway to my local subway station when the skies opened, emptying almost a bucket of water on my head.

I'd never been more grateful for my pixie cut than that moment. Unlike all the other unlucky souls around me, my hair had dried out by the time I reached my stop and it didn't matter that it stuck up in places. It matched my aesthetic.

I stopped at the crosswalk outside the subway station because I didn't have a death wish, a car jumped the light, and I watched in slow motion as it drove through a puddle.

"You don't want to know," I muttered, walking past the reception desk. "Is the she-dragon in yet?"

The last thing I needed was to run into Dakota Reed before I'd erased the evidence of my disastrous commute.

"No. Her assistant said she's stuck in traffic." She glanced at the clock on her desk, her lips pursed. "You've probably only got ten minutes though." She flashed a concerned smile.

I waved her off. "Ten minutes is all I need."

I rushed across the open plan space, dodging mannequins, spools of fabric, and interns too focused on their tasks to look where they were going. Barely containing a sigh, I made it to my office without further destruction and drew the blinds.

I made a beeline for the closet of backup clothing I kept just in case Dakota flipped out over a particular piece in the show. One day I'd find it amusing that I now needed to use it to save myself from her potential wrath.

For now, I cared about one thing, and one thing only. Getting rid of my destroyed outfit.

Five minutes later, I dumped that carefully thrifted outfit in the trash.

I stared down at it, a pile of once perfectly stitched fabrics. It felt callous to throw them out without at least mourning their loss for a second. Maybe thanking them for their service... not that I was into that mumbo jumbo crap.

The phone rang, saving me from making a decision.

"Roseline, good, you're in," Dakota said, her tone almost disappointed.

I winced at her use of my full name.

I'd told her once six years ago that I preferred Ros and she'd ignored me.

"Do you have a minute to chat?"

Oh, this could not be good. Dakota only called when there was an emergency.

"Of course," I said, somehow keeping my voice even.

Everything's fine. I have nothing to worry about. I aced fashion week. She probably just wants to congratulate me…

"I have to say I'm surprised you were able to keep a lid on it for so long."

"I'm sorry?"

"I hope you are." She tutted. "Don't play coy. I know about Jackson. I'd wager the entire office does."

Well, yeah. None of them lived under a rock and Jackson's bullshit had pretty much blanketed every gossip rag on the planet overnight.

"Okay."

Deafening silence followed my response.

"Honestly, it's kind of a relief," she said, her tone sympathetic for some bizarre reason. "You've been distracted the last few months. Now it all makes sense. Of course, it would have been good to know before now. Those kinds of connections come in handy."

"Do they?"

"Well yes, he and his friends have proven themselves quite popular. Do you think he'd walk for the New York show?"

"Uh I don't think so."

"But if you asked him, he would say yes."

"I highly doubt that."

"You can't ask your boyfriend to do you a favour?" she asked, her tone dripping with disbelief. "I'm afraid your position has become untenable."

She couldn't mean it.

"Don't worry about finishing out the day. You can leave your keycard on your desk," she said, amusement tinging the words. "And I'm sure one of the interns can take over your clean up tasks from Paris."

White hot anger pulsed through me, wiping out the shock. Firing me because I refused to exploit a relationship was one thing, suggesting an intern could handle my workload was very much another.

I couldn't even focus on the fact she'd fired me. My brain just fixated on the insult.

"*R*os. I wasn't expecting to hear from you so soon," Jackson said, his surprise audible through the phone. "Is everything okay?"

I couldn't answer the question truthfully, so I didn't even try.

"We'd have separate rooms?"

For a second, silence reigned and I worried that maybe he'd changed his mind. Maybe he didn't need the favour anymore.

"Yes," he choked out. "Are you—"

"I'd have to kiss you… in public?"

Another beat of silence, but he recovered faster this time. "Yes, but not senselessly. My team will insist on strategic PDAs and they'll orchestrate the moments for them so we'll be prepared." He cleared his throat. "If you're uncomfortable at any point, you can tell me and I'll do what I can to limit those instances."

"I can do that."

"Are you… agreeing to help me?" Jackson asked, barely restrained excitement in his voice.

That was… good. Right?

Every time I thought of Jackson kissing me, my brain blared alarms at me. As if thinking it would somehow push *me* over that line and place the destruction of our friendship on me.

I didn't have many friends, especially not guy friends. Keeping them was important to me, more than any relationship ever could be. Friends wouldn't abandon me because I couldn't give them something. Boyfriends, now those were an entirely different ballgame.

He'd admitted he'd screwed up, he knew asking me out was a terrible idea that had temporarily put a blip in our friendship. So the risks were minimal, right?

I needed the money. He needed the image repair. I'd get to spend more time with Abi and Eva. I'd escape the guilt of leaving one of my friends to fend for themselves.

It was a win-win for all of us.

I just needed to say the words…

"You said the compensation was up to me?"

"Name a figure and it's yours."

My eyes widened. "Just like that?"

"Aye."

"I could say something stupid like a million."

"You could," he said, a smile in his voice. "Do you want a million? We could build a monthly payment into the contract and, of course, I'd pay your rent for the next year so you'd have the option to return to your old apartment."

"You can't be serious?"

"Deadly serious." Jackson laughed as my jaw dropped. "You're giving up your life to save my career, Ros. I'll give you anything you want."

I chewed my lip. This whole situation was insane. One minute I had a normal life, a good job, friends and family nearby. The next, the rug got yanked out from under me and I was left scrambling to pick up the pieces.

It was ridiculous. Outrageous. The type of wild, impulsive nonsense I usually avoided at all costs. My reckless little heart pounded, begging me to dive in head first and screw the consequences.

And I was inclined to agree with it.

Where had playing it safe gotten me recently? Jobless, lonely, worrying about money and the future. If I said no to this, what other options did I have? I'd almost certainly be evicted if I didn't figure out another source of income quickly. My student loans ate up most of my salary and my vintage fashion addiction took the rest of it. My savings were non-existent.

So say yes!

"You know this is crazy, right?" I narrowed my eyes at the office wall that I still needed to strip of personal effects. "I could ask for five million and you'd just whip out your cheque book?"

He chuckled. "Probably. But a million seems fair."

"Fair," I muttered. As if a million wasn't also an extreme exaggeration. As if any of this was normal.

It was temporary, I reminded myself. One year of the Hollywood circus to get my feet back under me. Was my pride really worth more than that?

"Fine," I huffed. "One year. But I want it in writing that I can back out anytime, no penalties, and I get the full one mil if I do."

"You can back out within reason, and your fee will be prorated."

My mouth dropped open. Why the hell was he pushing back? He wanted me to agree. I chewed my lip, staying silent, willing him to buckle to my terms, but he didn't so much as sigh. No sweating on his part. The bastard knew he had me.

"Fine," I huffed.

"Good. I'll have my team prepare everything."

"And I know your reputation, loverboy. Keep it in your pants."

I needed him to stay a friend. Friends stuck around. Boyfriends left, eventually.

"I'll be a perfect gentleman, scout's honour."

"You were never a scout."

Despite myself, I smiled at his ridiculousness. I let out a breath. This was happening. I was really doing this.

"How soon can you leave?"

"How soon do you need me to leave?"

"The jet can be ready by 6 PM. Would that work?"

That gave me less than two hours to get home and pack. "Can I bring my sewing machine?"

"Sure." He didn't even sound surprised. "I'll pick you and your many bags up at six."

Pick me up to move to LA.

To his house.

Where, every time we went out, every eye would be fixated on us and the gossip rags would dissect my every action and outfit.

But at least my money worries were over and I'd have my friends back. Right?

Fuck.

❄

I stepped onto the private jet, my Docs sunk into plush carpet.

This was fancier than any five-star hotel I'd ever stayed in.

"Champagne, Ms Butler?" A steward in a crisp uniform appeared as if by magic, offering me a crystal flute.

I accepted it automatically, unable to tear my gaze from the jet's interior. Cream leather seats, polished wood accents, mood lighting... It was straight out of a magazine shoot.

Jackson chuckled as he sank into a seat, amused by my awe. "It's just a plane."

Just a plane? Was he kidding?

If I had his money, I'd be in awe of all the pretty things around me every single day. I would fill my life with any excuse to get on this jet and luxuriate in comfort on my way to the next exclusive experience.

Instead of doing any of that, he closed his eyes and relaxed. It was wasted on him.

I sat across from him. "Maybe for you. The rest of us aren't accustomed to flying around in the lap of luxury." I took a sip of champagne, savouring the dry bubbles. "I mean, we have a guy whose only job is to bring us champagne and nibbles!"

Jackson smiled, opening his eyes to study me while he reclined lazily in his seat. "Perks of the job, I suppose."

"You suppose?" I shook my head in disbelief. "This is incredible. The seats are so comfy!" I wriggled deeper into the leather. Though I'd be worried about putting my Doc Martens on the seat, no matter how new and clean they were.

"I'm glad you approve." Jackson's gaze turned soft. "Make yourself at home. We've got a few hours before we land in LA."

LA. I gulped more champagne to steady my nerves. In a few hours, we'd be starting our crazy charade as a couple. Of course, the promise of the first instalment of eighty large hitting my starving bank account within the next week helped settle them a little.

"Don't look so worried." Jackson reached over and gave my hand a reassuring squeeze. "You'll love it there, I promise. Sunshine, beaches, easy access to Abi and Eva. My assistant will be on hand to help you with anything you need too."

I sighed, setting down my champagne flute carefully before I dropped it. "That does sound pretty nice." Not as nice as the buttery soft leather under my hands, but lovely all the same. "What happens when we land?"

Jackson took a swift sip of his champagne before responding. "The usual media circus, I'm afraid. Paparazzi will be camped out on the tarmac, clamouring for shots of us together."

I tensed. "Seriously? They're allowed to just wait there and ambush people?"

"Who knows. It's a nightmare either way." He fixed me with a serious look. "It'll be loud and very bright. You'll be tempted to respond to their ridiculous questions. It's important that you don't."

Like he shouldn't have when he falsely announced to the world we were a couple?

Right.

He patted my hand reassuringly. "I have a team who will escort us safely to the car. Tinted windows, the works. Once we're inside, my driver will get us home quickly."

Home. His home. I took a bracing gulp of champagne.

"My assistant Jen will meet us there," Jackson continued. "She's fully briefed and ready to help you get settled. Anything you need — groceries, salon appointments, bank errands — she'll take care of it."

I nodded, already compiling a mental list. New wardrobe suitable for sunny LA and whatever fancy events he needed me to attend. A wine fest with Abi and Eva at the first available moment. Scout out some new thrift stores…

"Before I forget, the contract." Jackson rummaged in his briefcase, pulling out some stapled documents. "Had my lawyer draw these up. Standard stuff, but let me know if you have any questions."

I took the contract, skimming through the legalese. A lot of privacy clauses, payments scheduled monthly, one-year term... everything we'd agreed to.

Wait. "An NDA too?" I frowned at the non-disclosure agreement. "You don't trust me to keep my mouth shut?"

Jackson winced. "It's not personal. My team insists, that's all."

"Of course they do." I tossed the NDA back on the table. "I'm not signing that. You'll just have to trust me."

"Ros…"

"No." I crossed my arms stubbornly. "If we're doing this, it's on equal ground. I'm not some employee you can bully into silence."

Jackson sighed, raking a hand through his hair. "I know it seems unnecessary between friends. But in my world, NDAs are standard procedure. It protects us both."

I bristled, hackles raising. "Protects you, you mean."

"That's part of it, yes," he admitted. "But it also means I can relax and be myself around you. No second-guessing if something private will end up as a tabloid headline."

I bit my lip. When he put it that way, it almost sounded reasonable.

Jackson leaned forward, holding my gaze earnestly. "This past year hasn't been easy, Ros. My life splashed across the gossip rags constantly." His jaw tightened. "I believe I'm safe opening up with you and I could never imagine you selling my secrets, but my instincts have been proven wrong before."

I looked down at the document, chewing my lip. "I still don't like it. But... fine. If it means that much, I'll sign."

It's not like I ever planned to sell him out anyway. Reckless I might be, but a traitor? Never.

Jackson's shoulders sagged in relief. "Thank you. Truly." He raised his glass to me. "Here's to a fresh start for both of us."

I clinked his glass. The champagne bubbles fizzed like the butterflies in my stomach.

Here goes nothing.

JACKSON

The six hour flight back to LA passed far too quickly for my liking. I would never get enough of Ros's enjoyment.

When we'd first met at Finn and Abi's wedding for the reality TV show, Married Blind, she'd been an excited force of life. Rubbing her hands together for the potential between her friend and mine, happy that Abi would finally have her life shaken up. Part of me thought she'd jump on the opportunity to instil some of that chaos into her own life when I made my offer.

Still, it didn't faze me that it took half a day for her to agree. Life-changing decisions should be considered properly, no matter how odd it seemed for rebel Ros.

But something did faze me for the first time in my career. Getting off the plane and inflicting a pack of rabid paparazzi on an innocent woman. Not once had I hesitated to open a door knowing they were outside, impatiently clamouring for *the shot.* Until now.

"Are we getting off or going back to New York, Jackson?" she asked, her tone amused but the undertones of exasperation leaked through.

I glanced down at her, wishing for the first time that I wasn't an actor. Wishing she could see my concern and believe it, truly understand that if there had been another way, I wouldn't have involved her. But she expected pretty words from me. Whenever I chose to be authentically honest with her, she assumed it was nothing more than an act. This would be no different.

"Of course we're getting off." I forced a smile. "Just bracing myself for the madness."

Still I didn't exit the plane. I turned back and took her hand, tugging until she looked into my eyes, her brow puckered in confusion.

"Remember what I said." I leaned down, ensuring I had her full attention. "Don't give them anything. Don't react. Don't even flinch at their questions. You stay tucked under my arm until we get to the car and say nothing. Got it?"

She bit her lip, a thread of concern flickering in her eyes before nodding.

I stood there for a second longer, studying her. What I planned to do if she couldn't handle it, I had no clue. I couldn't exactly smuggle her off the plane.

In the end, I put our fate in the hands of the universe. I'd done all I could.

Taking her hand, I led her out the plane door, placing my body in front of hers instinctually. I paused at the top of the stairs, absorbing the chaos below. A pack of at least twenty paparazzi waited on the tarmac, jostling like ants and unleashing a barrage of blinding camera flashes into the fading pink sunset light. Black-suited security guards grappled to hold them back as the pack pressed towards the plane, trampling each other recklessly for the money shot. Their shouted questions echoed around the private airfield.

"Jackson! Over here!"

"Is Ros Butler behind you?"

"Why were you in New York?"

"Where have you been hiding her?"

"Why haven't we seen you together until now?"

"How did you keep your relationship secret for so long?"

"Is this another fake relationship for PR?"

She flinched behind me but I squeezed her hand, silently reminding her to keep her game face on. I plastered on a grin, waving as my security pushed back the crowd.

"No comment today, lads!"

The cameras continued to flash blindingly as we made our way down the steps. A bodyguard met us at the base of the stairs, his face set in severe lines.

"This way, Mr Levi." He gestured to the SUV waiting in the opposite direction of the cameras.

I nodded and took off towards the car, pulling a stunned Ros along. The paparazzi got louder, screaming their questions until they blended in a cacophony of sound I had no chance of deciphering.

Finally reaching the car, I opened the door and guided her in first, catching a glimpse of her stunned expression.

Guilt swamped me. She didn't deserve the nightmare I had dragged her into.

I slid in after her, taking my first deep breath since we'd landed. The door slammed shut behind me, blocking out the chaos. My heart pounded as we pulled away, the tinted windows concealing us from their intrusive lenses.

"You okay?"

She nodded, eyes wide. "That was... full on."

"I know, and I'm so sorry." I couldn't let go of her hand; my fingers had almost seized around hers. The whole thing had triggered an instinctual need to keep her safe and turning that off proved difficult. Fuck. "I never wanted this for you."

"It's fine," Ros said, pretending to be confident while she stared back at me with an unnaturally pale face and her voice shook. "I knew what I signed up for."

Even if she had, it didn't make it right.

Christ. What had I done?

CHAPTER FOUR

ROS

The SUV crawled through wrought iron security gates and turned down a long driveway lined with manicured tropical gardens. At the end sat a sleek modern house straight out of Architectural Digest. Floor-to-ceiling windows overlooked the crashing Pacific below. Definitely not the urban jungle I was used to.

I let out a low whistle as I stepped out of the car, craning my neck up at Jackson's house. "Swanky digs you got here."

It was all sharp angles, cantilevered over the cliff's edge. The ocean breeze rippled through palm trees down below.

"It's no palace, but make yourself at home," Jackson said, grabbing our bags from the trunk.

I tore my gaze away and raised an eyebrow at him. "I don't think I want to know what your definition of a palace is."

He laughed and led me inside. The interior was just as sleek — polished concrete floors, abstract art, cosy oversized sofas. The back opened directly onto the ocean vista, the sun sparkling on the endless Pacific.

"Yep, fame's gone to your head," I muttered, staring out at the never ending blue, awestruck. Seagulls floated on thermals below. "This is fucking incredible. How can you say this isn't a palace?"

He shrugged, but that smirk still claimed his lips.

"It's even better at sunset."

I frowned at him, confused and wishing I could read him just a little. With anyone else, I'd think he was uncomfortable, but Jackson only showed people what he wanted them to see. The curse of dating actors.

Not that I'm dating him… that warm fuzzy feeling? Yeah that's just gas. Nothing important.

With that disconcerting thought circling inside my mind, I turned my attention back to the view. I had to admit, I could get used to this. Waking up to that view, ocean breezes, the rhythmic waves — it beat sirens and honking horns in the city.

Maybe this year wouldn't be so bad after all. A pause button from real life and all its problems.

"Tell me something." I turned towards him, planting my hands on my hips and fixing him with an annoyed look. "Why exactly did we spend the summer hanging out in my cramped apartment when you could have flown me out here for weekends?"

He laughed. "It was a great summer though."

"It was, but it would have been better here, laid out on a sun lounger beneath the California sun."

"I might have been craving a little taste of normal." Jackson gripped the nape of his neck and stared at me, a sheepish glint in his hazel eyes. "And you just seemed in your element in New York. What kind of friend would I have been to pull you out of it?"

"Jackie! You're back!" an upbeat female voice called out, interrupting me before I could bring out the thumbscrews and make Jackson sing all his secrets.

My head tilted at the almost identical Scottish brogue. Why did they sound alike? I turned to find a petite, stylish blonde bounding down the glass stairs. Before I could so much as smile in greeting, she threw her arms around Jackson in an enthusiastic hug.

A little too enthusiastic for an assistant.

Jackson laughed and spun her around. "Good to see you too, Jen."

As he set her down, the blonde — Jen — kept a hand resting casually on his arm. I tensed.

Was his assistant hitting on him right in front of me knowing I was meant to be his girlfriend? Fake or otherwise.

They chatted quietly, their heads bent together while my heart raced and my mouth went try. Jackson seemed completely unfazed by her closeness, responding to her friendly flirtations with an easy grace. I couldn't believe the nerve of him, forcing me into a contract when he—

Wait.

Why the fuck was I jealous over this? I forced a smile and stepped forward, offering my hand. "Hi, I'm Ros."

Jennifer turned to me with a bright grin, her hazel eyes appraising me with something akin to excitement as we shook hands.

"Ros, meet Jennifer, my assistant," Jackson said, oblivious to my tension.

Jen's smile grew even brighter as she pulled away. "So nice to finally meet you." She shot Jackson an annoyed look. "I can't believe Jackie kept you a secret. I'm shocked he managed it honestly, but it doesn't matter now."

She reached for my hands, catching me by surprise. She held them tight, swaying us from side-to-side like some weird bloody reunion. Who the hell did this chick think she was?

"I'll forgive him eventually, but I'm just so excited to finally meet a girlfriend of Jackson's." She winced. "You'd swear the man took an oath of celibacy only I know that's not true because—"

"Enough, Jen," Jackson snapped, a panicked edge to the words.

He inserted his surfer build between us, breaking Jen's hold on me. I backed away until I could see the pair of them clearly.

"Sorry," Jen mouthed to him. "Anyway, Mam's going to flip when she finds out Jackie's been hiding you from us."

I shot Jackson a bewildered look. Mam?

Sensing my confusion, he clarified. "She's also my baby sister."

Jen nodded eagerly. "So that makes us future sister-in-laws."

The blood drained from my face at that word and I caught Jackson smirking behind her.

"And oh my god, have I missed normal company. He's an amazing big brother," She hooked a thump at Jackson, "but a girl needs a little grounding surrounded by him and his friends, you know?"

"Jennifer," Jackson groaned, rubbing at his eyes.

"What? It's true. Your life's not normal, bro. You know that."

She winked at me then, a mischievous light sparkling in her eyes. "But I'm so happy he found a girl who can make him appreciate the little things again. You know how these celebrity types get, right?"

"Jesus, Jen. Stop talking."

"But I want to hear all the details. How did you meet? Was it love at first—"

Jackson clamped a hand over her mouth, silencing her with a glare that only seemed to amuse her further. She broke out of his hold and backed away, grinning.

"Don't worry, Ros. I won't pester you for details. Yet." She gave me an encouraging smile before shooting him a pointed look. "Anyway, I should go and check in with Audra."

"Good idea," Jackson said, his tone dry.

"Well, she's a force of nature," I said wryly after Jennifer disappeared down a hallway.

Jackson laughed, rubbing the back of his neck. "That's one way to describe my sister. Sorry about the ambush."

I waved it off. "Don't worry about it." Meeting his family had thrown me, but it could've been worse.

"Here, let me show you around, so you can escape Hurricane

Jen if needed."

He led me through the open living spaces and sleek kitchen, before bringing me upstairs. He opened a door to reveal a spacious guest suite, gesturing for me to enter. I gasped as I took in the view.

Windows made up the far wall, making it seem as if the room was floating in mid-air. All I could see was endless blue ocean meeting pink-and-white streaked sky.

"Wow," I breathed, walking up to the windows. Below, waves frothed white against the rocky shore.

"Not bad, huh?" Jackson said. "I figured you'd like this one. This is your room."

I tore my gaze away to find him watching me with a soft smile.

"You're not serious," I whispered in awe.

"Of course I'm serious." Jackson turned back to me, his brows furrowed in confusion. "Why wouldn't —"

"It's just so gorgeous. I can't believe…" I trailed off, my gaze returning to the ocean below.

I'd get to wake up to that view every day for a year. How was I going to make myself leave it in the end?

*A*fter unpacking my bags, I wandered back downstairs in search of Jackson. The living room was now bathed in darkness, only the lights from the kitchen and a screen illuminating the sleek space. I found Jackson seated at the kitchen island, laptop open in front of him.

A woman's face filled the screen, her sharp jaw that models would envy accentuated by her severe black bob. Blue eyes raked over me as I approached.

"…now that she's finally here, we can start getting ahead of this thing."

Jackson glanced up at my approach and gestured to the stool beside him. "Ros, perfect timing. Come meet Audra, my publicist."

I slid onto the seat, waving awkwardly at the screen. "Hi."

Audra's hawk-like gaze narrowed on me. "So you're the girlfriend we've heard so little about until now."

I bristled at her accusatory tone. "That's because I'm not actually his girlfriend. I'm just helping him clean up the mess he got himself into."

"Details," Audra said with an impatient flick of her hand. "And the sooner you start answering that question with a cute story about wanting your privacy, the better. This entire operation depends on you selling the woman who's spent six months keeping one of Hollywood's hottest bachelors to herself. Got it?"

I bit my tongue to refrain from snapping that this whole disaster was her client's fault, not mine. Instead, I nodded.

"Good. Now let's get to work."

I struggled to keep my expression neutral as Audra rattled off suggestions. I could barely keep up with her and very little of it made sense. It might have also rubbed me the wrong way that she didn't once stop to check my opinion.

"We need to get you two out and seen together immediately. Nice start at the airport, shielding her. The housewives will melt over that, but we need more." She tapped her chin, considering us with pursed lips. She smirked as if a light bulb had gone off in her head. "Tomorrow morning, I want you on Rodeo Drive, hitting up the boutiques while you grab some suitable clothing to integrate Ros into your world."

Her gaze raked over what she could see of me. I'd left my leather jacket and Doc Martens upstairs, but she couldn't stop grimacing at my vintage AC/DC t-shirt and collection of vintage pendants.

"Something wrong?" I asked, my tone sugar-sweet even though I wanted to tear into this bitch.

"Try to go for something a little less… alternative."

I ground my teeth, holding my temper in check by a thread. I was here to help Jackson and helping my idiot friend meant doing what this woman said.

"Followed by being papped grabbing takeout from Eataly in Beverly Hills and, when you're appropriately dressed, dinner tomorrow night at Catch — make sure you're seated by the window. Then Friday afternoon, stroll the Santa Monica pier holding hands. It will need to look candid so dress casual."

Audra glanced down, scanning her notes. "Saturday, hit up Runyon Canyon in coordinated athleisure outfits. There's always photographers around that trail. Make sure you look sweaty and affectionate when you reach the summit."

My head spun.

"We'll also need some Instagram stories of cosy domestic moments around the house. Bake cookies together, lazy Sunday morning coffee on the patio, that sort of thing."

I struggled to keep my expression neutral as indignation thrummed inside me. She clearly saw me as nothing more than a prop.

What did you expect when you agreed to be a fake girlfriend?

Touché.

Jackson nodded along. "That all sounds great. I'm sure we can make it work, right, Ros?"

He turned his charming grin on me. I wanted to scowl but Audra's laser focus made me uneasy.

"Of course," I said through gritted teeth. "But Jackson will need to be the one doing the baking in those cosy domestic moments," I spat the words like they gave me hives. They probably would. "I can't bake for shit."

Audra rolled her eyes. "Noted, but it's settled then." She glanced at her diamond encrusted watch. "I have another client to update. We'll reconvene tomorrow to talk about the press release."

The screen went dark before I had the chance to answer. Audra had already hung up. I stared blankly at the dark screen, her rapid-fire instructions echoing in my mind. The full weight of what I'd agreed to pressed down on me. What had I been thinking? I couldn't pull this off.

I slumped against the counter. "Please tell me it won't always be that intense."

Jackson winced and I groaned.

"You'll get used to it," he said, his tone soft, trying to be comforting.

Somehow I doubted that.

I'd known faking it wouldn't be easy. Of course I did.

Now my stomach churned at the thought of setting the wheels in motion.

"You okay?" Jackson's brow furrowed in concern. "You've gone white as a sheet."

"Yeah," I squeaked. "Perfectly fine. What could possibly be wrong with this situation?"

He shook his head. In an instant he was on his feet, gripping my shoulders and swivelling my stool to face him. I blinked up at him, pulse pounding in my ears.

"Hey, listen to me." His voice was low and urgent. "I know this seems like a lot right now. But I promise, I've got your back. We're in this together, okay?"

My panic must have shown on my face because he moved even closer, hands warm on my arms.

"If at any point you feel overwhelmed, just give me a signal and I'll get you out of there. No questions asked."

I stared up into his concerned, gorgeous hazel eyes. They bored into mine, sincere and imploring me to trust him.

I could get lost in those eyes.

It really wasn't fair for him to be that good looking. With the mussed, dirty blond surf curls and bearded jaw, I had no issues understanding why women all over the world drooled over him.

He squeezed my arms, and I stiffened.

Shit! Bad Ros!

I shook off his grip. "I, uh, I should call Abi and Eva. Tell them I got here fine and all that," I mumbled, slipping off the stool. "We'll talk tomorrow, yeah?"

CHAPTER FIVE

ROS

Cameras flashed as Jackson stepped onto the sidewalk. He turned back and offered me his hand, smiling like there wasn't a rabid pack of paparazzi outside the store, shouting questions. I stared at it for a beat too long before taking it, pretending not to notice the shutters going wild.

He kept promising me it would get easier, but I couldn't see how.

We strolled up the boutique steps arm in arm, pretending to ignore the camera flashes capturing our every move. My lips twitched with the effort to act natural. Inside, my heart hammered against my ribs.

I wasn't made for this fishbowl lifestyle, but I'd made a promise and I'd be damned if a photographer with no sense of boundaries turned me into a quitter.

Jackson gave my hand a reassuring squeeze before pushing open the door. The cool, perfume-scented air washed over me.

We were barely through the doors when the staff swarmed us.

"Mr. Levi! We just received the new collection, haven't even put it out yet..."

They spoke rapidly, vying for Jackson's attention. He held up a hand.

"We're here for my girl today." He smiled down at me warmly. "Ros needs a whole new wardrobe."

Their eyes raked over my ripped jeans and vintage tee critically. Their plastic smiles slipped for a second, poorly hid disgust in their eyes.

Typical Hollywood types. They wanted glitz, not someone like me.

I felt every inch the Pretty Woman beneath their eyes.

Well screw them. Their disdain didn't faze me one bit. I didn't need their approval.

I clapped loudly, making them jump. "Chop chop, ladies. I don't have all day."

They blinked at me in surprise. I gestured at the racks impatiently.

"Come on, let's get moving. I wear a size four, or a six if it doesn't stretch." I snapped my fingers. I strode towards the racks before they could dismiss me, my senses attuned to the hunt. I could dig up treasures anywhere.

I began pulling items and shoving them into the assistants' arms, rattling off demands. Silk blouses, cashmere sweaters, leather pants — they piled up quickly.

"I'll need this in red, too. And that one in a deep blue." I barked orders like a drill sergeant.

They scrambled to keep up.

"And I'll need some edgy heels to go with these." I held up a leather mini skirt. "None of that spindly stiletto crap. Something badass." I flashed a tight smile at the wilting shop girls staggering under my selections. "Well? Hop to it!"

They scurried off in search of my specifications. I smirked, adrenaline pumping through me. Beside me, Jackson bit back an amused grin.

"Remind me never to get on your bad side." He chuckled.

I smoothed a hand over my black pixie cut. "Please. They have no idea who they're dealing with."

His laughter rang out, turning heads and sending warmth through me.

"I'd pay to see you unleash on someone for real," he said, eyes dancing.

I lifted my chin. "Careful what you wish for, Levi."

Jackson trailed behind, grinning as the flustered staff tripped over themselves to meet my demands. Part of me thrilled at his amusement. The other part cringed at how over the top and awful I had to act just to get a grain of respect from these women.

Finally, with a small mountain of clothes gathered, I herded the assistants towards the fitting rooms. As we walked, Jackson fell into step beside me.

"Quite a show you're putting on," he murmured. "Seems like you're getting into the Hollywood spirit after all."

I rolled my eyes. "The second we're out that door I'm donating it all."

He shook his head. "No, you won't. You'd never waste money like that."

I huffed, annoyed that he could see through me so easily. "Fine, but don't get used to this. As soon as I can get my hands on some fabric, I'll be wearing Ros Butler originals."

"I look forward to it," he said.

And I believed him.

I stared at the heap of clothing before me, wondering what had possessed me to grab so much stuff. The over-sized fitting room suddenly felt claustrophobic.

A knock interrupted my spiralling thoughts. "I have the additional items you requested," called out one of the assistants.

"Come in."

She scurried inside and hung a dozen more outfits on the rack, keeping up bubbly chatter about flattering colours for my skin tone and styles to highlight my best assets.

I tuned her out, critically assessing the pieces she'd picked. A blush pink mini dress with ruffles. Slim cut jeans paired with a cropped tank top that would show off my midriff. Cute wedges with bows.

It was all so... basic. The kind of outfit you'd see on an aspiring influencer. Not exactly my style.

The assistant finally finished her spiel. "Let me know if you need anything else!"

"Will do," I said dismissively, already shoving hangers across the rack.

The door had barely shut behind her when Jackson's voice sounded.

"Everything alright in there?"

I smiled despite myself. "Just peachy," I called back. "Unless you count being surrounded by clothes that aren't really me."

The door cracked open and Jackson slipped inside, an understanding smile on his face. "Not up to your usual impeccable standards?" He stepped closer, his eyes searching my face. "I can run interference if those harpies are too much."

"I'm fine. I don't need you to rescue me."

Jackson held up his hands. "Wasn't suggesting that. Just want to make sure you have whatever you need."

His sincerity softened my defensiveness. I sighed, shoulders slumping.

"I appreciate that. But honestly, their attitude is nothing new. I can handle a few snobby shop girls."

Jackson frowned. "You shouldn't have to. No one should make you feel 'less than' for being yourself."

Warmth bloomed in my chest at his words. I bumped his shoulder lightly with mine. "Look at you getting all righteous on my behalf."

He smiled crookedly. "What can I say? I've got your back, pixie."

I leaned in close so only he could hear. "Look, I'm sorry. Can we just pretend to be the happy couple and get through this?"

He smirked. "If that's what you want."

I nodded. "I do."

I turned to the array of clothing, studying it all like I could magic a solution that would please both me and Audra. Which would be next to impossible.

"Never thought I'd see the day you, of all people, would look unhappy surrounded by designer clothes," Jackson said, his deep Scottish accent laced with amusement. He picked up a beaded gown that probably cost more than my entire wardrobe and dangled it in front of me.

"Very funny." I gestured in despair at the fluffy dresses. "I can't pull this stuff off. It's too... perky."

Jackson chuckled. "I don't know, I think you could rock a cropped tank or mini dress." His eyes glinted playfully. "Might inspire some new fantasies in fact."

I tossed a balled up top at his head. "You're terrible."

Laughing, he ducked and held his hands up in surrender. "Kidding, kidding. You look stunning in anything." His smile softened. "Especially when you're being yourself."

Warmth rushed through me at the sincerity in his voice. I busied myself hanging up rejects to hide it.

"Yeah, well, no amount of fluff and bows can turn me into a Rodeo Drive clone."

"No arguments here." Jackson leaned casually against the wall. "But in all seriousness, I thought you wanted the designer life, the fashion label with the stores on three continents."

I rolled my eyes at his naivety. "As if. My dream isn't about hoity-toity boutiques with the same repackaged stuff."

He looked puzzled. "What do you mean?"

I gestured at the interior with disdain. "All this. The whole image and vibe. It's so... fake."

Understanding started dawning on his pretty face.

"I don't care about massive corporate brands or whatever's on trend," I picked up a white dress with bows and winced. That had *not* been in my picks. "I want to make real clothes that help people feel comfortable in their own skin." I placed the dress back on the rack and poked a finger at his rock solid abs. "Not squeeze into some itchy getup that looks good on Instagram but you can't breathe in."

Jackson barked out a laugh. "Duly noted. No corsets in your collections."

I cracked a smile before growing serious again. "I just want my work to mean something, you know? To create an experience."

He considered this, brow furrowed adorably. "But isn't that what these designers do?"

I shook my head firmly. "Their goal is money and prestige and getting celebrities to wear their stuff. For me, it's about the artistry. The feeling. The human experience. Does that make sense?"

He fell silent, clearly mulling it over. I shifted nervously, unsure why I was confessing so much. But a new warmth filled his eyes, like he was truly seeing me for the first time.

"It makes perfect sense," he said finally. "I think I'm starting to get you, Roseline Butler."

Hearing him say my full name so tenderly made me shiver. I focused on the rack in front of me; anything to stop me staring into his eyes.

Friend. He's your friend.

I picked up a dress, desperately trying to ignore the burn of his gaze on me, but I failed miserably. I snuck a glance at him and caught him studying me with a mix of amusement and curiosity.

"What?"

"Nothing," he said, shaking his head. "Just... you're full of surprises."

"Shouldn't that be obvious by now?"

"Maybe." He chuckled, shaking his head. "Alright then." He picked up another dress. "Tell me, how does this make you feel?"

"Like I'm being interrogated by a Scotsman with too much time on his hands."

"Sounds about right." He smiled, his eyes shining. And just like that, the tension between us eased.

I sighed. "As much as I'd love to duck out, I guess I'd better try some more things on." I shot him a hard look. "But I'm getting some things that match my style. I'll wear the expensive clothes, but not at the expense of me. Got it?"

He smiled. "I'd expect nothing less." Then he crossed his arms and settled in. "Out, Jackson."

"Sure you don't need help?"

I nodded hard. "Out." I pointed at the door to the room.

He backed out, his hands held up.

When the door shut, I turned back to the ridiculously plush dressing room, smiling despite myself.

The space was bigger than my apartment back home, with floor-to-ceiling mirrors and a sitting area. Who needed so much space to try on clothing? Not this New Yorker.

I eyed the mound of clothes they'd pulled, wrinkling my nose. It was all so expected — the latest trends and designer logos, but little heart or originality.

With a sigh, I shimmied out of my dress and reached for the first option. A slinky bandage dress in fire engine red. As I slid it on, the fabric gripped every curve. It was sexy, but almost too revealing for my taste.

I studied my reflection, turning this way and that. Had to admit it looked damn good. Maybe I'd underestimated these Hollywood stylists. They might dress vapid starlets every day, but they knew how to make a woman look hot.

Now if only I had a pair of leather boots and a battered vintage leather jacket…

❄

I strained and tugged at the zipper on a slinky black dress, but couldn't get it to budge. After fighting for a few futile minutes, I sighed in defeat.

"Jackson?" I called out, pausing as my voice echoed in the cavernous dressing room. "You still there?"

"Still here," came his muffled reply from outside. "Everything okay?"

I bit my lip. But what choice did I have?

"I'm stuck in this dress. The zipper's jammed. Can you... give me a hand?"

There was a pause. For a second, I thought he'd left. The door creaked open and he poked his head in, a teasing grin on his lips. But as his gaze landed on me, the smile faded. His eyes widened as they travelled over the snug black dress.

For a moment, he just stared, seeming to forget what he was going to say. A flush crept up his neck.

"Just help me with the zipper please." I turned my back to him and swept my hair aside.

"Of course," he whispered just before his fingers grazed my skin as he worked the zipper free, making me shiver.

I sucked in a sharp breath. His tall frame towered over me, and I could feel the heat radiating off his body. His warm breath tickled the hairs on the back of my neck. I tried to steady my racing heart as he gently grasped the zipper and pulled it up, his fingers brushing against my spine in the process.

When it was done, his hands lingered on my shoulders. Our eyes met in the mirror, and for a moment, the air crackled between us.

"Thanks," I said, my voice hoarse.

"You look amazing."

"Thank you."

His gaze made a blush creep up my neck, a mix of pride and vulnerability washing over me.

I fidgeted with the dress, smoothing invisible wrinkles. "Well, I should change out of this. Don't want to stretch the fabric."

I glanced up and found him still staring, eyes dark and intense. Heat rushed up my neck.

"Or did you need help unfastening it?" He smirked, cocky as ever. The ass.

I rolled my eyes, trying to ignore the butterflies his teasing brought to life. "Get out, Casanova. I've got it."

His grin only widened. "As you wish."

With a final wink, he slipped out. The door clicked shut, and I let out a breath.

Friends.

We were just friends.

I reached around, grasping for the zipper, but it was stuck tight again. Great. After a few moments of fruitless tugging, I sighed.

"Jackson?" My voice came out tentative. I shook my head. Since when did I hesitate around him?

No response. Was he really not going to help me after that whole production?

"Jackson!"

I strained again with the zipper, contorting myself awkwardly, but it wouldn't budge. Finally, I huffed in defeat.

"Jackson Levi, get your Scottish ass in here and help me out of this bloody dress!"

The door opened again and he peered in, eyes dancing with laughter.

"Well if you insist."

He slipped inside, closing the door behind him.

"Just help me." I turned my back to him.

He did as I asked, only his touch lingering longer than necessary. My breath hitched at the contact.

What was I saying about us being friends?

When the dress hung loose again, neither of us moved away. Our eyes met in the mirror, the air suddenly charged between us.

"Thanks," I choked out.

"Anytime." His voice was rough, filled with an emotion I couldn't name. I shivered as his fingers skimmed up my spine to rest on my shoulders.

We stood frozen, neither speaking as the tension mounted. I wet my lips unconsciously. Jackson tracked the movement, his eyes darkening further. I couldn't look away, my skin burning everywhere we touched.

Slowly, he leaned down, his minty breath fanning my cheek. I swayed closer, my lashes fluttering shut...

A knock shattered the moment. We jumped apart as a muffled voice called out.

"Everything okay in there?"

No, everything was not okay. I'd nearly kissed my friend. Fuck.

Jackson cleared his throat. "We're fine!"

He shot me a heated look I felt down to my core.

"I'll let you change," he murmured before slipping out.

I sagged against the wall, pulse racing wildly. That had been... intense. Too intense. I couldn't let it happen again.

With shaky hands, I shrugged out of the dress, hanging it up. But my skin still tingled everywhere Jackson had touched me. No matter how I tried to deny it, he was getting under my skin. And it terrified me.

CHAPTER SIX

JACKSON

J pulled the sports car up to the large iron gates, putting it in park. The guards seemed extra vigilant tonight, and no wonder. I could hear the paparazzi on the other side of the gate even through the closed car windows.

Ros presented the picture of serenity in her green-chequered dress. But no matter how good a mask she presented to the world, I could see through her. Nerves radiated off her in waves as she stared out the window. Her hands twisted together in her lap and fuck did I wish she'd give her lip a rest. One more tug and I wouldn't be able to fight off thoughts of kissing her.

You promised her you'd be her friend only.

And I meant it. I just didn't expect it to be so fucking hard.

I reached over and took her small hand in mine, drawing her gaze to me. "You alright?"

She gave me a shaky smile that didn't reach her eyes. "Just ready to get this over with."

"Remember what I said." I squeezed her hand. "The second you want to bail, say the word and I'll put an end to this date."

A small chuckle escaped her. "Somehow I don't think Audra'll like that."

"I don't give a damn what she likes." A scowl overtook my face and I forced it to relax. "I'm not going to let you be any more uncomfortable than you have to be doing this. You're doing me a favour."

"A favour you're paying me for."

"Doesn't matter."

Appreciation shone in Ros's eyes. It killed me that she seemed so unused to having someone stick up for her. She deserved so much more.

A large black SUV pulled up behind us with two large body-guards in dark suits up front, idling in wait. She turned, peering at it over her shoulder. Her grip on my hand loosened as she took them in, seemingly drawing some security from their presence.

The large iron gates started to open, slowly swinging outward. As the gap widened, the muted sounds of the horde outside grew louder.

Ros tensed beside me.

Dozens of photographers packed haphazardly behind perma-nent barriers started snapping pictures wildly, their flashes temporarily blinding through the windshield.

She let out a small squeak of surprise, her hands flying up to shield her face from the onslaught of light and noise. I reached over, taking one of her hands. She'd done so well this afternoon at the boutiques, but that lot had maintained a distance, while this bunch were chaotic, even with the barrier holding them back.

"It's alright, I've got you," I said in as calm a tone as I could muster over the bedlam outside. She nodded shakily but didn't lower her other arm from her eyes yet.

I gave her hand a gentle, reassuring squeeze. "Breathe, Ros. They're always ten times worse right outside the gates like this. But it'll die down once we get going, I promise."

One or two scrambled into the road, blocking the car and pissing off the security guards.

"Oi! Get behind the line!" one of them shouted, prowling towards the paparazzo with his night stick in hand. "Move it!"

The overzealous idiots backed away, clearly not willing to try their luck with our burly security guards.

Ros took a steadying breath, dropping her arm to peer out nervously at the mass of people. Nodding again, she looked over at me and managed a small smile. "Okay. Let's get this over with then."

I smiled back, hoping she saw the pride in my eyes. Many people craved fame, seeing only the money and the luxuries. Very few were strong enough to handle the attention that came with it.

When I'd first met Ros, I'd known she'd be one of the rare exceptions. She just needed a minute to find her feet.

I pressed down on the accelerator slowly, steering us through the openings and into the chaotic fray.

*H*alf an hour later, we arrived at Catch, Malibu's hottest restaurant. The small lobby immediately opened up into a large dining room with wide, floor-to-ceiling windows. Crystal hung around the light fixtures, refracting colours around the crisp, bright space as the sun set outside.

I watched Ros take in the spacious interior, her eyes wide. Plushly furnished and dimly lit, the restaurant was bursting with people, some more famous than me, all of them here to be seen.

Some of them, I unfortunately recognised. The Sanderson brothers.

The maître d' recognised me instantly and ushered us to our table in the window, perfectly positioned for the cameraman in the trees to get every shot he could possibly want. Audra would be pleased.

I braced myself for the torture of the next two hours. I hated this part of the job, the feeling of sitting in a fish tank while everyone around me took photos and gossiped.

It served a purpose. No one inside the building would be there if they didn't want to be seen for one strategic reason or another. That knowledge didn't make the anticipation any easier.

The only upside would be spending two hours with good food and Ros's undivided attention.

As soon as we sat down, she started scanning the restaurant curiously. Her eyes jumped from table to table.

"Holy shit." she whispered, practically leaning over the table to make sure I could hear her. She glanced between me and then back to a grey haired guy a few tables over. "Is that Michele Durand?" She nodded towards the old director.

I laughed, but she barely noticed, her gaze already somewhere else.

"No way. I didn't know she was in LA." Her eyes went huge and only continued getting bigger as she recognised more and more faces.

There was something endearing about her unrestrained fangirling. It made me wistful for my younger days, before I realised just how shallow this all was. Until her gaze landed on a certain table and her mouth dropped open. I knew right away who she saw. Damn Sanderson brothers. I tried getting the waiter's attention to take our drinks order, hoping it would distract her.

It didn't work.

"This is too good. They always look miserable in photos together."

I sighed internally when I looked over at our rivals enjoying themselves as usual. Their supermodel dates hung all over them.

"Do you know them?" Ros asked, eyes still glued to the brothers' table across the room.

"We've worked together a few times," I said, trying to keep my voice balanced so the topic wouldn't stretch on. My history with the Sandersons was complicated, to say the least.

Ros peered at me, sensing there was more to the story. Her brows rose as she fixed me with those green eyes that could drag state secrets out of a spy. "Come on, dish. Who are their dates?

Why do they always look so miserable in photos if they're happy now?"

I leaned towards her, admitting defeat before we'd really begun. She wasn't one to let things go easily once curiosity struck.

Lowering my voice, I said, "The blonde is Mason's girlfriend of the month. Can't keep up with who he's with these days."

"And the brunette?"

"Chris's fiancée, Allegra. Third one this year if rumours are true."

"Ha, I knew it. They always look annoyed as hell in photos." Ros grinned mischievously. "Abi and I had the biggest crushes on them in college. Used to cut out all their magazine covers, paste them to our dorm room walls."

I choked on my water, almost spraying it across the table. "Please don't tell Finn that."

He'd never let Abi forget it. We'd been rivals with the Sanderson Brothers ever since we landed in LA. Our careers took off at the same time, and it was always a toss up for directors and producers on whether their project would go further with the Kings stamp or the Aussie Brothers. It got old fast for us, but the assholes shit-talked us any chance they got in interviews.

Ros just laughed. "Don't worry, she already swore me to secrecy. Besides," she shot a pointed look at the Sandersons, "they don't seem worth the hassle."

I couldn't help but smile as she settled her opinion of them firmly on my side of the table.

Thankfully, the waiter appeared with a bottle of champagne. Who ordered it, I had no clue — probably Audra — but I would not look a gift horse in the mouth. Ros clapped her hands together in excitement, completely forgetting about my rivals.

"This looks amazing!" Her eyes widened. "That's a crazy expensive bottle," she mouthed at me.

When the waiter moved away, I said, "Only the best for you, baby."

She winced.

"What is it?"

"One, that was such a corny thing to say, and two, I hate being called baby."

"Shit, I'm sorry. I didn't know."

"It's okay." Ros waved it off but she still shifted uncomfortably. "It's just I dated this guy through college and his mother called him baby even though he was a grown ass man. It was cringe."

"I can imagine." I winced.

"He dumped me when I refused to call him it." She shuddered. "I got off lightly with that one."

I winced. "Aye, good thing you dodged that bullet."

It had been years since I had seriously used a pet name with a woman. I'd once called my childhood sweetheart 'dove', back when we were engaged. But those days were long gone now.

I would have to be desperate to use that term with Ros. I never wanted to taint what we had by dragging old history into it. She was her own unique person, not a replacement for anyone from my past.

"So what should I call you then, if not baby?" I pursed my lips, considering the safe options. "How about darling? Or sweetheart, maybe?"

She scrunched her nose sceptically. "Darling sounds old-fashioned. And sweetheart makes me think of cotton candy."

We both cracked up at that image. The tension broke as I said, "Alright, no darling or sweetheart then. What do you suggest?"

Ros tapped her chin in thought. "What about... honey?"

I wrinkled my nose. "Honey's too cutesy."

"Tough crowd." Her eyes lit up as if struck by inspiration. "I've got it — what about 'hot stuff'?"

We dissolved into laughter, hearing the ridiculous pet name said aloud. A passing waiter shot us a curious look that only made us laugh harder.

Wiping tears from her eyes, she sighed, "Okay, no hot stuff. We'll keep working on it…"

I smiled, enjoying this rare easy humour between us. It was refreshing amid the unfamiliar tension of our new relationship. Being with Ros had always felt light and fun, but ever since my slip, I hadn't been able to enjoy it.

She swirled her glass, her gaze shifting to the window next to us. "I thought this was one of those photo-op dates," she said, her tone confused. "Where are the cameras?"

"Oh they're out there." I leaned across the table and took her hand, drawing her attention back to me. "This restaurant has high security protocols. Only a select handful of trusted photographers are allowed onto the grounds. And they have strict rules about staying back by the treeline."

Ros searched my face. I gave her a small, comforting smile.

"So it's still for publicity, just more controlled."

"Exactly." I winked. "See, you're getting the hang of it already."

She shook her head. "You people are fucking mental."

I chuckled. "I couldn't agree more."

She glanced towards the bar, doing a double take. "Wasn't that the guy Finn was on Married Blind with? The LA Stingers goalie?"

I followed her gaze to where Anders Olofsson stood chatting with friends. "Aye. That's him."

She observed him, no doubt assessing his body language from afar.

"He seems nice enough," she finally said. "More relaxed than most of the guys here."

I nodded. "Anders is down to earth compared to a lot of play-ers. We grabbed beers sometimes before he moved to Toronto."

"That's good. You need more normal friends."

I laughed. "Can't argue with that."

I considered Nathan, Finn and Shaun normal, but I could see how that might be a lie these days.

And they'd all married or gotten into relationships with strong-willed women who wouldn't let them float off in their egos any more.

I needed that.

I needed Ros to take me seriously.

CHAPTER SEVEN

JACKSON

"I'm never blindly following you again," Ros said with a huff. She groaned as she shifted the ice pack on her swollen ankle. "No one who knows me would believe I'd hike up a dry, dusty mountain in LA heat for you." Her brow furrowed and she shot a dark look at me. "In fact, I wouldn't do it for any man."

Audra had put a Runyon Canyon hike on the calendar for this morning. It had all gone well and we'd almost — *almost* — been able to ignore the roar of the helicopter blades while the paparazzi snapped even more pictures of us. We'd laughed; she'd berated me as she puffed up the hill, unfit despite her petite frame. For a while, it was fun.

Until she slipped and tweaked her ankle.

"I heard you the first time, angel."

Her face darkened. "Do I look like an angel?"

Right now? Definitely not.

"Point taken." I busied myself pulling wine glasses from the kitchen cupboard. Ros's gaze burned on my back, watching every move. "Audra will be happy with the shots coming down the mountain."

"Don't remind me," she said, her voice muffled, but full of despair. I turned to find her face down on the counter, her head buried in her folded arms. "I am never going to live that down."

"There's nothing wrong with needing help once in a while."

"You can't be serious." She propped her head up and glared at me. "You carried me down the trek bridal style. The gossip rags aren't going to give a shit that we were wearing matching outfits. All they'll see is the damsel in distress being saved by the action hero. Just you wait."

I bit my cheek, holding back a smile. I'd never get tired of this, of her berating me, all passionate and fiery. "You were injured, Ros. No one is going to hold a moment of weakness against your punk rock image."

I straightened the flower arrangement on the kitchen island, ensuring it sat perfectly centre. Then I moved on to the sofa cushions, fluffing them and rearranging them even though the cleaning staff had already done it yesterday morning.

"What is wrong with you?" she asked, shock dripping from her tone.

"Nothing."

I glanced up at her just as her brows rose.

"I've been here for three days. I have never seen you tidy."

Turns out surprising someone you care about is nerve-wracking.

"I've been busy. This is perfectly normal for me."

Her suspicious expression didn't relax. "Why don't I believe you?"

The doorbell rang before I could respond. Ros tensed, her brows knitting together as she glanced from me to the hallway.

"Who rings your doorbell at 8 PM on a Saturday night?" An edge of panic slipped into her voice.

Panic? Why was she panicked? Had I screwed up? Shit.

Before I could take more than a step, the front door opened

and Finn called out. "Jackson, boyo, we grabbed some pizzas and beers. I know you wanted it to be a classy evening, but I am not drinking wine if..." He trailed off as he rounded the corner. "What the bleeding hell did you do to her?"

Abi and Eva followed him, their expressions amused until they spotted Ros and her ice pack.

"I didn't do anything. She fell."

Finn smirked. "And you're sticking with that story, are you?"

Laughter filled the room at my expense. Abi and Eva hugged me briefly before joining Ros at the breakfast bar.

"Is that really what happened?" Eva asked her.

"Oh my god," I muttered as the doorbell rang again.

Ros's eyes widened. "Tell me that's a courier and not the rest of your rag-tag group?"

I frowned. "Why would that be a problem?"

"For such a smart man, you're fucking clueless." She dropped the ice pack on the counter before shuffling to the edge of her chair. "Help me!" She shouted at Abi and Eva, her hands flying out for them.

I glanced from Ros to Finn, pure confusion consuming me. "What am I missing here?"

"I'm in sweats, and I haven't showered, jackass." Ros limped slowly towards the stairs, Abi and Eva holding an elbow each. "Would it have killed you to warn me?"

My gaze dipped to the midnight blue fabric hugging her lovely ass. She'd seemed so comfortable sitting there with me, it hadn't occurred to me she wouldn't want to be seen like that.

"Ah, I just wanted to surprise you." I rubbed the back of my neck sheepishly.

"Well for the record, I hate surprises." She glared at me over her shoulder. "Especially this kind."

Damn.

Bree, my ex, never took an interest in my friends. She'd always made excuses to avoid seeing them no matter the occasion. So it never occurred to me that a woman would care enough to worry about their appearance around them. She would have demanded they all leave while Ros just nodded at them with a smile and tugged Abi and Eva along with her.

When she disappeared up the stairs, Finn clapped me on the shoulder, his body shaking.

"Laugh it up, asshole."

"It didn't occur to you that a fashion designer would want to be put together with other people around?"

No, unfortunately, it hadn't.

"Jesus." He dragged a hand across his jaw, his lips twitching. "This fake relationship of yours is going to be fun."

$\mathcal{B}$y the time Ros returned, the sun had sunk lower over the Pacific, casting the living room in a hazy orange glow. Rock music filtered quietly through the speakers, almost drowned out by my friends' laughter.

Finn, Shaun, and his wife, Mona, Nathan, and his girlfriend, Cat, hung around the kitchen island, digging into an assortment of pizzas. Finn had filled them in on my failures of the day, eliciting odd sniggers from each of them as their amusement rose again.

Despite their teasing, I wouldn't change this for the world. Our lives were filled to the brim with superficial things and connections. This little group held my sanity in their hands and it warmed my heart to see everyone so at ease. Their laughter and lively banter filled the space, smiles coming easily as they shared amusing stories and playful teases.

"Better?" I asked Ros when she returned wearing black leggings, a red blouse and Docs.

She nodded as I offered her a glass of red wine. "Though, keep those coming and I'll forgive everything."

I chuckled. "Deal."

Despite the disastrous start, my purpose still remained. I wanted to give her a relaxed night in with our friends where she didn't have to worry about our every little action or look. There were no photographers in the bushes and the position of the property meant they couldn't set themselves up with a long-range lens. Hopefully she would feel more settled here, surrounded by familiar, friendly faces.

So far, it seemed to be working. Ros curled up on the sofa with Abi and Eva at either side of her, their heads bent together. Her smile lit up her whole face, eyes shining. She looked more at home than I'd seen her since arriving in LA.

"So Ros," Nathan called out, signature smirk in place. "Has our boy properly wooed you yet? Private jets, diamonds, the whole nine yards? You know, sold the image properly?"

She rolled her eyes, but laughed. "Oh yes, it's been non-stop roses, serenades, and fawning declarations of love."

"Sounds exhausting." Nathan grinned, dodging the pillow I threw at him. "In all seriousness, you let me know if you need a break from this brooding asshole. I promise a night out with us lads will set you right."

I chuckled at the offer, he didn't mean a word of it. Nathan had mellowed considerably since dating Catrina. He'd replaced his cocky arrogance with an easygoing smile.

Cat laughed. "Too right. Can't have you burning out on us already."

"Good to know I have options." Ros smiled into her wine glass.

I scoffed in mock offence. "As if I'd let you steal her away that easily." I tossed another pillow at Nathan. "Find your own fake girlfriend."

"No need, I've got the real deal right here." He smiled down at Cat like a man who'd gone to battle and won. Which he had. She kissed his cheek, her eyes shining with a love I craved.

Nathan and Cat had fallen into bed after a chance meeting in a bar. What was meant to be a one night stand ended with him walking into her office to discover he'd slept with his new lawyer. Most people would have conceded defeat. Not Nathan. He knew what he had and he refused to let it go.

Ros made a show of glancing between them. "Clearly, you two have this relationship thing figured out. Any tips you can offer?"

Cat laughed. "Oh no, we're just as much a disaster as anyone else. Right, babe?"

"Without question," Nathan agreed.

I shook my head. Considering Nathan had once believed his only worth came from his successes, I'd say they were being humble. Cat had almost transformed him into a new man. Gone were his arrogant womanising days and fears that all women wanted from him was his fame and money.

Cat had given Nathan the gift of seeing his own self-worth, and in return he cherished her with his whole heart. I wanted what Nathan and Cat had, that easy, all-accepting love that bolsters you when life tries to knock you down. If only Ros would see reason and realise we could be so much more than fake or just friends.

I sighed under my breath, raking a hand through my hair. This constant resistance wore on me more each day. The urge to give in to my feelings was becoming impossible to ignore and we'd barely even begun. Somehow I had to find a way to hold it in. I couldn't risk scaring Ros off again when she'd already forgiven me for slipping up once. Our friendship meant too much to her.

✳

When the conversation lulled, I slipped through the open glass doors onto the moonlit balcony, hoping the fresh air would clear my head.

Out over the cliffs, the crashing waves filled the silence, a soothing rhythm. I closed my eyes, focusing on the salty breeze brushing my skin. Slow footsteps followed, but I didn't turn.

"Alright there, mate?" Nathan leaned against the railing next to me. His voice was subdued now, the cockiness replaced by concern.

I let out a long breath. "Honestly? I'm struggling."

"Because the last woman you were serious about fucked you over and skipped town?" His brows rose emphasising his question.

"No, but thanks for adding that to the fucking pile." I scrubbed at my jaw.

The others gathered around, faces solemn now. Shaun clasped my shoulder, while Finn hovered close, their expressions open, but patient.

"Ros isn't Bree. She's got more integrity in her little finger than Bree had in her entire body." I shook my head. "I'm more than over that woman. A year in a fake relationship with Ros will feel more like a real relationship than we had in the end."

"Then what is it?" Shaun asked.

"I didn't think it would be this hard." I crossed my arms and leaned back against the balcony. "Being with her, even pretending, it... might be more than I bargained for."

Nathan rested a hand on my shoulder. "What do you mean?"

"At first it was just a role, you know? Put on a show for the cameras and change my public image." I gazed through the glass at Ros smiling amidst our group. "But playing her boyfriend... it feels less and less like acting and it's only been a couple of days."

"Did she ever explain why she rejected you?" Shaun asked, rubbing his jaw.

I shook my head.

Finn winced. All of our eyes narrowed on the Irishman.

I straightened and took a step towards him. "What do you know, Finn?"

"Nothing. Absolutely bleeding nothing." He backed away.

"I call bullshit. Try again."

He sighed. "Fine, but if Abi finds out, I'm a dead man." He pointed at me, a severe look in his eyes. "Got it?"

"My lips are sealed. Now talk."

"Few years back, when Ros first moved to Brooklyn for Uni, she had a string of bleeding awful boyfriends. All time wasters, going nowhere in life," Finn said. "Wankers who only cared about using her and tossing her aside."

Nathan swore under his breath. "Pricks."

Finn nodded grimly. "One after the other, they'd sweet talk her until they got what they wanted, then toss her out like yesterday's trash. Broke her heart over and over."

My stomach turned at the thought of anyone treating Ros so callously. She deserved the world.

"Couple of the bastards stole designs right from under her, passed them off as their own at big shows. Really did a number on her trust in people."

Shaun clenched his fists, expression stony. "Fuckers. I hope karma caught up with them tenfold."

Finn huffed in dark agreement before continuing. "After that, she swore off dating and closed herself off. Figured the risk of heartbreak outweighed any reward."

It all made so much sense — her hesitancy around vulnerability, her scepticism of the smallest sign of affection.

"That's why last year, when you came sniffing round all shiny and charming, she bolted quicker than a rabbit from a fox," Finn concluded solemnly.

It had taken me a good couple of months to convince Ros to meet me for coffee and I'd been nothing but friendly towards her. I hadn't hit on her at the wedding, as much as I desperately wanted to ask her out.

"It probably didn't help that Audra had me "dating" a new model every week." I raked a hand through my hair, frustrated beyond belief.

Nathan squeezed my shoulder. "Don't beat yourself up over the past. It's an unfortunate part of the business, but you know you're nothing like the losers she was attracted to."

I nodded, taking comfort in his reassurance.

"So the question remains, how does Ros actually feel about you?" Shaun asked. "Could she ever see past the celebrity?"

"Or the fact you're a man who could leave her one day," Nathan added, wincing.

"If I could answer that, I wouldn't be out here, torn between playing the gentleman and pushing her."

Finn snorted. "As if you could keep that act up much longer."

I sighed wearily, hating how right he was. "Half the time, I think she tolerates me. The other half..."

"Maybe you need to test her," Nathan said before taking a swig of his beer.

"Or maybe I should back off and accept that I've been friend-zoned." As bad as I wanted her, maybe space was best for now. "Re-evaluate in a year when our agreement is done."

Nathan burst out laughing. "Good luck laying off Ros for a whole year, mate. We all know you're as patient as a toddler."

He wasn't wrong — my willpower tended to crumble around her. But fully committing to the role might help earn her trust to see beyond the hype to the real me.

"Not a whole year," I conceded. "But backing off for a bit could do us good. Give her space to see that I'm here to stay and not what she thinks."

Shaun nodded thoughtfully. "Show her who you are when the cameras aren't rolling. Prove you value more than the glitz of fame."

Finn grunted in agreement. "And stop letting Audra pull your strings. Be your own man for once."

"Not saying it'll work, but it's worth a shot, right?" Nathan said with a soft smile.

I squared my shoulders, meeting their eyes with renewed determination. "Alright. It's a plan."

CHAPTER EIGHT

ROS

I swirled the wine in my glass, watching the way it sloshed against the sides. Not long after the guys disappeared onto the patio, Eva, Abi and I had reconvened to a small nook receding into the wall of the living room. It was private and cosy with the soft glow of the fireplace warming us and casting flickering shadows on the walls, making our little nook feel like a sanctuary.

"Have you told Finn the news yet, Abi?" I asked.

She spluttered, tearing my focus from my glass. Her wide-eyed gaze shifted between me and Eva, her panic easy to read.

"Oh, c'mon. You told me a week ago. How have you still not told your own sister?"

"Told me what?" Eva asked, her voice deepening with suspicion.

Abi pulled a face, her pale skin turning beet red and almost blending in with her auburn hair. "I've been busy."

"That's a terrible excuse."

"It's true!" She glanced down at the wine glass she'd spent the last hour nursing like no one would notice the liquid level only decreased when she walked into the kitchen. "No point holding this any more." She placed it on the coffee table and met her sister's curious gaze. "I'm pregnant."

Silence fell. I waited on tenterhooks for Eva to react.

"Oh my god! Really?" She finally shrieked, throwing herself at Abi when she nodded. After a moment, Eva leaned back to take Abi's almost identical face in her hands. "I can't believe you're having a baby! I'm going to be an auntie."

Abi's eyes shone with happy tears. "I know, I'm still processing it myself."

"How far along are you?" I asked.

"Almost eight weeks." Her hands settled protectively over her still-flat stomach.

Eva tutted disapprovingly. "And you've kept this from me for how long?"

Abi laughed nervously. "About a week, give or take." She threw up her hands defensively. "I wanted to wait until the first trimester was over before telling anyone!"

"Except the father?"

Abi sighed, cheeks colouring again. "I was going to tell Finn tonight, I swear! I just haven't found the right moment."

I laughed aloud at that. "You? At a loss for words? Now that's a first."

She nudged my shoulder playfully, eyes still dancing with happiness. "Oh shut it, you. I'm allowed to be nervous!"

Eva squeezed her hand reassuringly. "He's going to be over the moon, Abs. You two are going to be amazing parents."

Abi smiled, the sheer joy in her eyes radiating through me. Even with her worries, I knew she was absolutely thrilled to start this new chapter in her life with Finn.

A loud laugh broke through the glass, snaring my attention and tugging it towards the patio. Jackson, Shaun, Nathan and Finn were laughing and smiling, their faces alive with joy and excitement. But really, I didn't have eyes for anyone but Jackson.

I should have looked away, shouldn't have let myself study his handsome face like it belonged to me. It didn't. We were nothing more than pretend. Part of me wondered what it would be like, if he were truly mine, that I could be lucky enough to have a guy like him.

We were friends. Just friends. And that was better than any relationship because it would last forever.

Right.

"Did you guys ever think we'd end up like this?" I asked, taking a sip of my drink. "Navigating the wild world of Hollywood?"

"Can't say I did." Eva hooked a finger at Abi. "Though I should have expected it the second you got this one on Married Blind." Her eyes twinkled in amusement. "I've learned that life doesn't always go according to plan, but let's be honest, when Abs decided to stick with Finn, our normal went up in flames."

"Tell me about it," I muttered.

"How is the glamorous Hollywood lifestyle treating you so far?" Eva's tone danced between gentle teasing and true curiosity.

I considered the question, absently nibbling my lower lip. How did I say batshit crazy without sounding like I was complaining?

"It's been... an experience for sure," I said finally. "Definitely way outside my usual scene."

"How are you really feeling about this whole Jackson and fake girlfriend part of the equation? Any regrets?"

I shook my head, but held my tongue. Nobody needed to know I found Jackson attractive, and saying it aloud would only make it a problem. Right?

"Seriously, Ros." Abi leaned forward, her red hair framing her disbelieving expression. "It's been three days. We know you. You must have regrets by now."

"It's not like I had much choice in the matter." I sighed, setting my glass down on the coffee table. "It's been intense, that's for sure. Some days it feels like I've stumbled through the looking glass into some weird alternate reality."

"But there are things bothering you?" Abi asked, concern etched on her face.

"I can't even walk down the street without someone shoving a camera in my face or asking if I'm going to marry Jackson next week," I grumbled. "I can't aimlessly scroll social media anymore."

I hadn't made it to a single thrift store yet. What the hell was happening to me? Nothing kept me from a good thrift store.

I shrugged. "But what's the point of wallowing? I couldn't have changed any of it. I didn't tell a press line full of cameras that I was in a six-month-long serious relationship." Then a thought occurred to me. "Actually, I do have one regret."

Eva and Abi exchanged worried glances before turning their attention back to me.

"Not pitching a fit when Dakota Reed fired me for refusing to exploit my non-existent relationship with Jackson to benefit her brand."

They gasped in unison.

"She did what?" Eva screeched.

I sighed. "It's fine, it was days ago. I'm over it."

"That bitch fired you?" Abi seethed, eyes blazing.

"Said my work ethic had slipped, which was utter bullshit. I'd just saved her neck at Paris Fashion week." She wouldn't have had a show without me.

"I'm so sorry, Ros." Eva placed a comforting hand on my arm. "Why didn't you tell us sooner?"

"I don't know." I stared at the dancing flames in the fireplace, anything to not take in their pitying expressions. "I guess I didn't want to admit how much this fake relationship has consumed my life. I already feel like all anyone sees is 'Jackson's girlfriend,' not the person I've worked so hard to become. Like, what's next? Am I going to lose everything that makes me who I am just because of some stupid lie?"

Eva took my hand. "We would never think that. We're here for you, no matter what."

"You're not going to lose yourself," Abi said, her voice firm but gentle. "We won't let you. And neither will Jackson. You should talk to him about it."

"God, no," I groaned. "The last thing I need is for him to think I can't handle this whole charade."

"It's not about whether you can handle it or not." Eva fixed me with her sternest look. For someone two years younger than me, she'd mastered the older sibling act. "He turned your world upside down, and the least he can do is support you when you need it."

Eva topped up my glass and handed it back, gesturing for me to drink. I gladly listened. "You're still the same strong, independent woman we know and love. This situation is tough, but it doesn't define you. And it won't, unless you let it."

"Exactly," Abi said, accepting her own refreshed glass. "You're more than just a label or a role. You're Roseline fucking Butler, high fashion queen in waiting, and no fake relationship can change that."

"Maybe it's time you put your big girl panties on and talk to the man." Eva swirled the ice cubes in her glass, smirking.

"Even if it's just a fake relationship, communication is key, right?" Abi tilted her head, studying me with more clarity than I'd like. I shifted in my seat, fidgeting despite the half a bottle of wine sloshing around inside of me.

"Ugh," I groaned, rubbing my temples. "I know you're right, but it feels like surrendering if I tell him he was my only lifeline."

"Ros, you can't carry all of this on your own." Eva's eyes filled with concern. "You should talk to him. He might surprise you."

"Besides," Abi added with a grin, "even though it started out as something fake, who says it can't become something real? There's definitely chemistry between you two."

"Abi!"

Absolutely not. We were just friends.

"She's got a point," Eva added with a grin, "you two make quite the convincing couple. Maybe there's some truth behind all this make-believe."

"Hardly," I scoffed, but couldn't help the small smile that tugged at my lips. "He's Hollywood's golden boy, and I'm... well, me."

"Exactly," Abi chimed in, her eyes twinkling with mischief. "Opposites attract, remember?"

My cheeks heated up at just the thought of giving him a chance to prove he wouldn't be like every other man. Last month, I'd sworn blind he wasn't my type. A total lie, but a necessary one.

"Alright, enough of that,"

I huffed, rolling my eyes. But their words lingered in the back of my mind, stirring a whirlwind of thoughts I'd been trying to ignore. "Cheers to surviving this crazy town," I said, raising my glass in a toast and hoping to distract the pair of them.

"Cheers!" they chimed in unison, clinking glasses with me.

CHAPTER NINE

ROS

By the time Monday rolled around, I thought I'd seen it all, prepared myself for every aspect of this weird alternate reality I'd found myself in.

Out of control swarm of paparazzi? Hated it.

Sitting in a fish bowl of a car while strangers photograph and scream questions at you? No thanks.

Fans stopping you on a pier in the middle of the afternoon, mid-conversation to ask for selfies? Too weird to comprehend.

Spending an evening celebrity spotting with orgasmically good food while someone photographs you from the trees? Weird, but I didn't hate it.

The deafening roar enveloped us as Jackson and I made our way through the stadium. Flashing lights illuminated the sea of fans waving glowing sticks and cheering for the opening band. I tugged my leather jacket tighter, already overwhelmed by the scale of it all. This spectacle set my teeth on edge.

Jackson smiled and waved to the crowd while the security team led us towards the fenced-off VIP section in the centre of the main floor. I forced my face to relax, all the while wishing I could disappear into the shadows rather than be paraded in full view.

Tucked beneath Jackson's arm, I should have been sheltered from the brunt of it.

Jackson leaned in, lips brushing my ear. "You're doing great. Stay close."

I nodded tightly. One foot in front of the other.

"Look at that," I said under my breath, never one to shy away from a sarcastic comment. "We get our very own welcoming committee."

"Welcome to my world." Jackson grinned, taking it all in stride. It was clear he'd done this a hundred times before.

As we entered the VIP section, the cheers grew deafening, and camera flashes went off, overly bright in the darkened space. I squinted, fighting the impulse to cover my face.

Thankfully, there wasn't a horde of salivating vultures hammering us with questions. One photographer stood at the entrance, catching the VIPs as they entered while another wandered around the fenced off area. I focused hard on not letting my shoulders drop or show even a glimmer of my disappointment at that.

There would be no off switch tonight. I needed to be on for the next three hours; if I so much as grimaced a camera might catch it.

The crowd went wild, and the lights flashed as one of the opening acts took to the stage. We were late, fashionably late because we couldn't just be fashionably fake. I had no idea which band stood up there. We'd come to see Marable. One part of this deal I actually was excited about. The lead singer came into view, his face plastered across screens dotted around the stadium, confirming that we weren't so late we'd missed all of the opening acts.

"How ya doing, Los Angeles? We're Mania 465. Are you ready to experience the rock gods that are Marable for the final time?"

A third of the crowd cheered, another third screamed no and

the rest booed. Somehow I had missed that this was Marable's farewell show. I'd been following the Welsh band since I was a teenager. I'd never seen them live.

Had you not agreed to be Jackson's fake girlfriend, you never would have seen them.

Okay, so maybe that made me feel slightly thankful for Jackson's fuck up. Not that I'd ever tell him that.

Beside me, he effortlessly shook hands and exchanged greetings with fellow celebrities. All the while, my shoulders itched under the weight of thousands of eyes trained on us.

My discomfort must have been written all over my face.

"Smile, Lovebug," Jackson whispered, his lips brushing against my ear. "They can smell fear."

My gaze snapped to his, eyes narrowing. "What the hell is a Lovebug?"

He bit back a grin. "Just testing how it sounds."

"Well strike it from your vocabulary, Levi." I scowled, but warmth crept up my neck. His teasing let me forget the cameras for a moment, reminding me it was still just us beneath the act.

Jackson chuckled, the sound low and smooth. "As you wish." He steered us towards another celebrity, winking. "Shall we mingle?"

I smothered a groan, plastering on a smile. The sooner we gave the vultures their shots, the sooner I could lose myself in the music and just enjoy the show.

Nodding, I took his offered hand and let him lead me over to a couple in the corner, nursing wine glasses. I recognised the actress from countless period dramas but blanked on the producer's name.

Plastering on a smile, I listened as Jackson made introductions, exchanging pleasantries about projects and plans. I let their conversation wash over me, observing the subtle power plays between industry forces disguised as small talk.

Sipping my drink, I feigned interest while scanning the room covertly. But surprisingly, as the minutes passed, the tension slowly began seeping from my shoulders.

These normal moments reminded me it was all just an act — we were really just along for the ride like everyone else.

Catching my dazed expression, Jackson leaned close. "Thinking of making a break for it?" he murmured, amusement dancing in his eyes.

No, but god, wouldn't that be great. Or you know, to just be able to watch the band without feeling like I couldn't so much as twitch in case someone took my reaction the wrong way.

I shot him a sour look. "And miss all the fun?"

Before he could reply, a lively voice cut in. "Too right she wants to escape you, you miserable sod."

I turned to find a sandy-haired man grinning roguishly, eyes twinkling with mirth. His wiry frame was draped in a Marable T-shirt and worn jeans, a stark contrast to the designer suits around us.

"Fraser," Jackson said, his surprise audible for once. "Come to torture me, have you?"

"Aye, someone has to keep that ego in check." The newcomer pulled Jackson into a back-slapping but familiar hug before turning to me with a grin. "And you must be the wee lassie putting up with this pillock. Pleased to meet ya. I'm Fraser, his brother."

I found myself smiling. "Ros. And believe me, it's no easy task."

Fraser threw back his head and laughed. "I like her already, Jackie!" Turning to me, he said confidingly, "Jen and I have years of ammo against this one, if you'd care to compare notes."

"My place or yours?" I smirked at Jackson. "I could use dirt on tall, blond, and full of himself over here."

Jackson groaned good-naturedly. "I see how it is. Gang up on me, why don't you."

"Has he told you about how he used to fancy himself as a pro-skateboarder?"

I shook my head and Fraser sniggered, a mischievous glint in his hazel eyes. "He was a cocky bastard growing up. Swore blind to his friends he could jump the backyard fence on his skateboard and didn't have the sense to duck out when they bet him he couldn't do it."

Jackson groaned. "Please stop."

But Fraser ploughed on, undeterred. "Really, he was showing off for some girls at the next door party. He snapped up their dare. Grabbed his skateboard, his friends set up a makeshift ramp and off he went. Took a flying leap..." He chuckled, clearly relishing the memory. "Only problem was, he never actually made it over. Got his foot caught and slammed into the fence, breaking two boards."

I stifled a laugh, picturing a teenaged Jackson sprawled inelegantly among the splinters. "Oh please, go on."

"Don't encourage him," Jackson grumbled, though I noticed the corners of his mouth twitching in reluctant amusement.

"Or the time he had us all in stitches mimicking Mam during Sunday dinner. Didn't know she was standing right behind him!"

By now, I was openly grinning, my surroundings forgotten, enjoying Jackson's visible discomfort. It was gratifying to see this untouchable movie star be humanised through family embarrassments.

Fraser cocked an eyebrow, gears turning. "I remember another one—"

"Alright, that's enough," Jackson cut in, throwing an arm around both our shoulders and steering us away from the crowd. "You've tortured me to the limit, brother. Don't you have people to see backstage?"

Fraser snorted. "Yes, but—"

"Then you'd best not keep them waiting." Jackson gave him a gentle shove towards the VIP exit.

I shot Fraser a conspiratorial look. "We'll have to continue this later."

He winked. "I'll save the best for when his royal highness isn't around."

As he ducked under the ropes with a final cheeky wave, I turned to Jackson with a grin. "Your brother is quite something."

He sighed in mock exasperation. "Don't I know it. Now you see why I try to keep him away from parties."

"Oh, I'm glad he crashed this one."

Before he could respond, his phone pinged. He fished it out of his jeans and glanced at the screen before cursing under his breath.

"Audra. She's demanding to know why there are no shots of our kiss online yet."

My mouth went dry and I swallowed hard.

Jackson met my eyes apologetically. "We need to give them something to talk about, or she'll have my head." He searched my face hesitantly, awaiting permission. "Only if you're okay with it."

I took a steadying breath, steeling myself. This was all part of the agreement, no different than anything else we'd done. Still, my pulse raced as Jackson cupped my cheek gently.

Time seemed to slow down. I stared into his eyes and tried to remind myself that one kiss wouldn't change our relationship. I didn't want things getting weird between us just because of a staged kiss.

My gaze dropped to his mouth, making me wonder what those full lips would feel like pressed against mine. How long the kiss would last — we hadn't agreed on that, maybe we should have. Would there be tongue? Would sparks fly or would it just be awkward?

Heat rushed to my cheeks and I quickly glanced away, clearing my throat like I hadn't just had inappropriate thoughts about my friend.

"Okay, let's get it over with." I took a step forward, closing the distance between our bodies.

It's all fake, for the cameras.

No point letting myself get carried away with silly fantasies.

Still, curiosity lingered. Was Jackson a good kisser? The confident way he watched me said he knew what he was doing. Knew how to please a woman.

Stop it! I gave myself a mental shake. We were friends, that's all. I couldn't afford to blur that line. This kiss had to stay strictly business.

"You sure?" He wrapped an arm around my waist, squeezing me ever closer.

My heart hammered in my chest. Whether because of our audience or the fact it felt so good to be pressed against him like this, I couldn't say. I resisted the urge to squirm away from the intimacy. Instead, I plastered a fake smile on my face, hoping it looked genuine enough to fool the photographers snapping our every move, hoping it looked fake enough that Jackson wouldn't see through to the flutter of butterflies in my stomach.

"Just shut up and kiss me, Hollywood Hunk."

He blinked. "You think I'm a hunk?" His smirk grew.

"It was a joke, jackass."

"Sure it was," he said, his voice low as he leaned in, his lips brushing against my ear. I couldn't help but shiver at the contact, cursing myself for being so affected by his easy charm.

He tilted my chin up, his eyes searching mine for any hint of resistance. I knew what was coming, and I hated how much I wanted it.

The tension between us mounted, becoming nearly unbearable. Heat radiated from his body, the steady rhythm of his breath mingling with mine. It was intoxicating, disorienting — and terrifying.

"Ready?" Jackson whispered, his eyes flicking briefly to the cameras surrounding us before returning to mine, filled with determination and just a hint of vulnerability. I nodded, swallowing hard as I braced myself for the moment our lips would finally meet.

To anyone watching, we must have appeared like any other star-crossed couple, lost in a passionate embrace as the world around us faded away. No one would suspect that this was nothing more than an act.

His lips met mine and warmth instantly flooded through me. His mouth moved slowly yet purposefully over mine, his beard tickling my skin. I sank into it and let all of my concerns fade away. His arms tightened around me, crushing my body against his, sending an unexpected rush of desire through me.

My lips parted and our tongues met tentatively at first. Then the kiss deepened, growing hungrier, more urgent. I clutched at his shoulders, barely holding back a moan as my knees nearly buckled.

I lost all sense of our surroundings, consumed only by Jackson and the intoxicating slide of his mouth on mine. A hungry noise rumbled in his chest that made me melt further against him. My skin burned everywhere we touched.

When we finally broke for air, lips swollen and chests heaving, I found myself wishing the kiss could have lasted forever. I stared up at Jackson, pulse racing wildly.

Jackson stared into my eyes. I tried to hold on to my indifference, my conviction that a man would only make my life needlessly complicated before he got what he wanted and left me, but all I could think about was the way his lips had felt against mine, and how desperately I wanted to feel them again.

The moment our lips parted, camera flashes blinded us, leaving spots in my vision as I tried to regain my bearings. Jackson's hand lingered on my waist for a second longer than necessary before he released me, his smile flawless even as I struggled to maintain my composure.

"Are you alright, Ros?" he asked, genuine concern colouring his voice.

"Fine," I snapped, irritated by the heat that still burned my cheeks and the way my heart pounded in my chest. "Just peachy."

For a moment, he stared at me, seeing far too much.

Please don't force me to talk about it. Please don't…

"Let's get a fresh drink."

Relieved, I let him guide me through the throng of celebrities towards the private bar at the back. I could feel their gazes on us, scrutinising every move, every expression as they whispered amongst themselves. It was suffocating, and despite my annoyance with the entire situation, I couldn't help but be grateful for Jackson's steady presence beside me.

As we sipped our drinks, I couldn't shake the feeling that something had shifted between us.

"Ros," Jackson said, drawing me out of my thoughts. "I know this is all... a lot. But thank you. For going along with this."

"Whatever," I muttered, taking another sip of my drink and ignoring the way my fingers trembled ever so slightly. "It's not like I have much of a choice, do I?"

I instantly wished I could take the words back.

"You do have a choice, and I'll never stop being grateful to you for not exercising it." His earnest gaze fixed on me, intense and uncomfortably open. "But I want you to know, I don't take this for granted. And if there's anything I can do to make it easier for you…"

"Don't fall in love with me for real?" I suggested dryly, but the words came out more vulnerable than I'd intended.

Jackson chuckled softly, his eyes crinkling at the corners. "I'll do my best."

What I really needed to worry about was me. I couldn't stop staring at his lips. What the fuck was I going to do if *I* fell for *him*?

CHAPTER TEN

ROS

The racks of glittering gowns threatened to swallow me whole. I'd crafted the most complicated, haute-couture dresses. I'd hand-stitched many lines of sequins. Hot glued diamonds to yards and yards of corsets. Bedazzled far too many shoes and belts. It shouldn't have felt any different to my pre-Jackson normal.

Yet it did.

For the sake of moving things along, I agreed, still not entirely convinced.

We moved through the dresses quickly. None of them hit that instinctual yes button inside of me. Instead, I obsessed over the details – the way the fabric draped just so over my hips, if the slit revealed too much or not enough, and whether I could walk in it without tripping over myself.

"See, this one is perfect for showing off your legs!" Jen said, snapping me out of my thoughts. "You look like a total bombshell!"

"Thanks," I mumbled. A flush crept up my neck. "But what if

I snag the material on something? This one feels even more delicate than the last."

Seriously, a split nail could tear a hole in it, the fabric was that
thin. I vetoed it before they could gush anymore and marched
back into the ensuite with the next pick.

"Ugh, this one's even worse." I stepped out of the bathroom a
few minutes later in a deep red gown. The neckline plunged so low
that it made me feel exposed and uncomfortable. There would be
no wearing a bra with this one. "I look like a wannabe Hollywood
starlet who got lost on her way to an audition."

"You're being too hard on yourself." Amelia smiled, stepping
forward to examine the fit of the dress. "You look stunning, but if
you don't like this one, we'll just keep looking. There are plenty
more to try."

"None of them are going to work." I glared at my reflection,
anxiety spiralling. "These dresses aren't made for people like me.
They're for tall, willowy actresses and models."

Not short, punky label-less fashion designers who should've
stayed hidden behind the curtain, making sure the real stars
sparkled under the lights.

Jen stepped forward, brow furrowed. "Don't be ridiculous.
You've got an amazing figure, any of these would look killer."

I shot her a withering glance. "I feel like a little girl playing
pretend."

Jen just laughed and rifled through the remaining options,
relentless as always. "The day I see you as a wallflower is the day I
go skydiving naked."

Despite myself, I cracked a smile at the image. Leave it to Jen
to pull me from the brink with her outrageous words.

I grimaced at the heavy beading. "I feel like I got run over by
an aggressive graphic designer."

Jen bit back a smile. "Less bling, got it."

Even the simpler dresses left me dissatisfied. The clock ticked
past noon, then one o' clock. My smiles grew tighter, comments
more clipped.

Finally, Amelia intervened. "Let's take a little break."

I nearly agreed when Jen gasped. "Wait, try this one!" She held up a flowing midnight blue gown that looked like an exact replica of the Anastasia velvet opera dress. A small glimmer of excitement bloomed in my chest, but I refused to give it space to grow.

Too tired to argue, I carefully shimmied into it. The cool velvet slid smoothly over my skin. I stepped back into the bedroom without even looking in the mirror.

They both fell silent, eyes widening.

"It's perfect!" Jen declared.

I turned to the big mirror Amelia had set up in my bedroom, braced for a barrage of negative thoughts.

None came.

I gasped at the sight of it — a deep midnight blue that shimmered like the sea under moonlight. The designer had taken the Anastasia inspiration and elevated it, adding delicate beading across the bodice. My heart raced just looking at it.

I studied myself in the full-length mirror, my eyes darting from one detail to another – the way the neckline hugged my collarbones, how the beading caught the light just so, and whether the tightness around my waist was too much or not enough.

"That colour is perfect on you!" Amelia said.

"Wow. You look like a goddess!" Jen clapped her hands together excitedly. "What do you think?"

I stared at my reflection. "It's beautiful, but..."

I bit my lip, torn, unable to stop thinking about damaging it.

"Seriously, my brother knows how to pick 'em." Jen picked up the hem of the gown to examine the intricate beadwork. "You're going to blow everyone away at the premiere tomorrow."

"Am I though?" I asked, my voice wavering slightly. "I mean, I don't know how to walk a red carpet or pose for photos. This all feels so strange."

"You might not be used to this world yet." She joined me in front of the mirror, her hazel eyes meeting mine in our reflection.

She placed a comforting hand on my arm. "But you've got what it takes to shine here. You're talented, smart, and absolutely stunning. Don't doubt yourself for a second."

"How much is it?"

Amelia and Jen shared a look, one that screamed *bite your tongue*.

"I'm not leaving the house in a dress of an unknown value. How much is it?"

Amelia sighed. "Twenty thousand."

I blinked, my voice momentarily lost. Then, my heart started thundering for an entirely new reason.

"You want me to wear a twenty thousand dollar dress?"

"It's okay. We have insurance," Jen said, brushing my concern off like insurance removed the possibility of my destroying someone's work of art.

"A torn hem isn't the worst I've seen." Amelia smiled, a glimmer of sympathy in her eyes. "But I have some friends who are absolute magicians with repairs. I promise you no one will throw out one of these masterpieces if you ruin it. You'll be fine." She patted my shoulder gently, seeing straight through me. "This is what these dresses are made for — to be worn and admired. Trust me, you're doing this gown justice just by wearing it."

I managed a shaky smile, wishing I shared her confidence.

Before I could spiral further, the bedroom door burst open. We all turned to see Jackson stride in.

"Jen, I need you to…" He halted mid-step, words dying on his lips as his gaze landed on me.

I flushed as his eyes darkened, our kiss still fresh in my mind. He stepped closer, and for a moment, the world around us melted away. His attention was entirely fixed on me, like he hadn't seen me in days instead of hours. His gaze roamed over every inch of my face and body, lingering on each detail until desire burned through me.

"Speechless, are we?" Jen teased her brother after a too-long silence. "Well? What do you think?"

He blinked hard, seeming to gather himself. "You look... incredible. Absolutely beautiful."

My stomach flipped at the awe in his tone.

"Told you so." Jen shot me a playful wink.

"This is definitely the one. No question," he said, his voice brimming with certainty. His eyes never left me as I stood there, shifting uncomfortably under his intense attention. "Jen, you've really outdone yourself," Jackson continued, still trying to regain his composure. "I mean, I knew Ros would look good, but this is... wow."

"Right?" Jen chimed in, her eyes sparkling with pride.

"You're going to steal the show."

"Doubtful, but thanks," I muttered, still struggling to push away the doubts that clawed at the edges of my mind.

"Hey," Jackson said gently, catching my attention once more. "Don't doubt yourself, alright? You're going to do great."

"Really?" I asked, more than a little surprised by the conviction in his words.

"Absolutely," he confirmed, nodding vigorously. "You look like you were born for the red carpet, Ros. I can't imagine anyone else wearing that dress."

In any other situation, I would have been able to shrug it off as a friend pumping up and supporting a friend. But there was a glimmer in his eyes I couldn't ignore. Especially when I could still feel the ghost of his lips against mine.

It was surreal, to say the least. An odd warmth grew in my chest at his praise, like the first flicker of a flame catching fire.

"Seriously, this dress was made for you," Jen added, barely able to stand still in her desperation. "I mean, look how it shows off your curves!" She leaned in conspiratorially.

"I think the verdict is in, pixie. You look gorgeous." The awe in his eyes stole my breath for a moment.

Jackson moved to stand beside me, his gaze never leaving me. "Everything about this is perfect, from the neckline to the colour. You look..." He trailed off, at a loss for words.

I shifted, uncomfortable under such intense focus. "Like I'm playing dress up?"

He frowned. "What? No. I was going to say you look elegant. Sophisticated."

"Oh please." I fought the urge to cross my arms over my chest. Instead, I rolled my eyes. "I look about as sophisticated as a duck in stilettos."

"Have you seen a duck walk in heels?" Jen piped up. "Those feathery bitches have grace."

Jackson and I both turned to stare at her.

She grinned. "What? It's true."

I bit my lip to contain a wholly inappropriate giggle. Only Jen.

Jackson just sighed, shaking his head. "The point is, you're stunning. Trust me on this."

I turned back to the mirror and studied my reflection again, only this time I focused on seeing myself through his eyes. The way the dress hugged my body, emphasising my curves. How the colour made my skin glow. The elegant beading that accented, not overwhelmed me.

Looking closer, I saw what he did. I looked... right. Not like a dress someone else should be wearing, but one that belonged on me.

Warmth bloomed in my chest and I met Jackson's gaze in the mirror. "You really think so?"

"I know so." His eyes roamed my figure appreciatively and he swallowed.

I flushed, unused to such open admiration from him. I didn't know what to make of this version of him. Was it genuine, or just another role? And which scared me more?

Jackson was still watching me, waiting. Our gazes remained locked in the mirror, a thousand unspoken words passing between us. What I wouldn't give to know his thoughts.

Jen's voice broke the spell. "Down boy." Jen smacked his shoulder. "That's my future sister-in-law you're ogling."

I jerked back, cheeks flaming. Jackson shook his head at Jen, his lips twisting in amusement. Despite the burn of embarrass-ment, their playful banter eased some of the tension knotting my shoulders.

Predictably, I gave in. What else could I do? Audra would eat me alive if I attended a red carpet event in vintage.

Or at least, that's the excuse I comforted myself with to smother the reality.

Jackson thinks I'm stunning.

CHAPTER ELEVEN

ROS

I stared at the blank sketchpad on my lap, pencil poised but unmoving. A week ago, I lost my job. How had so much time passed and I still hadn't figured out what to do with my life for the next year?

In normal circumstances, I would have figured out my game plan by now. Instead, I'd wasted seven days flitting around on his arm, making googly eyes at a man I'd spent months building one of the realest friendships with. I'd almost gone stir crazy that month I'd cut him off.

I needed to figure out what to do with my time, and stat. Just because I'd signed my life away for a year didn't mean I had to sit pretty and not work on my goals.

Or endlessly daydream about that kiss.

Frustrated, I dropped my sketchbook on my bed and got up. I needed to do something. Anything. Or I might lose my mind.

I headed towards the kitchen for a glass of water, my mind working overtime assessing the options available to me.

Should I look for another fashion designer job or take some of the money Jackson was paying me and launch my own label? Launching the label would barely put a dent in it. Plus I wanted to be someone other than Jackson Levi's fake girlfriend.

And the next time some piece of shit tried to exploit me and my friends, I wanted to be able to tell them to go fuck themselves without a concern for my livelihood.

The only way I could imagine achieving any of that would be through my own label.

I passed the open door of the home gym. My gaze landed on an unexpected sight: Jackson, bare-chested and glistening with sweat, bench-pressing like a Greek god come to life. His muscles bulged with each grunt, and my feet rooted to the spot. My breath hitched while my eyes traced his defined muscles, absorbing every fluid movement of his toned body.

This wasn't the charismatic, polished actor the world knew; this was raw, unfiltered Jackson. Heat suffused me, pooling low in my core, threatening to engulf me.

I needed warning for this kind of eye-gasm.

When he'd mentioned the gym, I'd assumed he'd be leaving the house, getting into a competition with Finn and Jackson and coming back complaining that he'd pulled a muscle.

You know, like he normally did.

Not setting thirst traps for me.

Too many seconds ticked by with me staring at him. My heart hammered in my chest. What was wrong with me? I wasn't supposed to react like this – not to him.

"Enjoying the view, sweetheart?" Jackson asked, startling me.

I met his amused gaze and wished I had backed away immediately. He smirked, flexing exaggeratedly as he racked the weights, confident he'd rattled me.

"You wish, pretty boy." I scoffed, crossing my arms. "I've seen better pecs on an 80-year-old at the Y."

He chuckled, clearly enjoying getting a rise out of me. "If you stuck around, I could give you an up close examination." He shot me a flirty wink.

I rolled my eyes, refusing to acknowledge the way my pulse quickened. "I think I'll pass, Hercules. Wouldn't want you to throw out your back trying to impress little old me."

"Is that a challenge?" He sat up. I bit my lip, unable to tear my eyes from his sweat-slicked muscles.

"Some other time, showboat." I shrugged a shoulder, forcing an air of nonchalance I'd forgotten how to feel. "Wouldn't want you hurting yourself on my account."

He grinned, clearly seeing right through me. "Oh I won't hurt anything. But I do like seeing that fire in your eyes."

Heat rushed to my cheeks. "Keep dreaming, Levi." I turned on my heel, calling over my shoulder, "Have fun with your testosterone fest!"

"See you later, firecracker."

His voice followed me out onto the balcony. I didn't even have the wherewithal to process the absurd nickname — all I could do was stumble away, my cheeks burning.

I burst onto the patio, my mind running in circles and my body feeling like it was on fire. Leaning against the cool stucco wall, I pressed a hand to my flushed face, wishing for an ice pack or the water I'd completely forgotten to grab on my way through the kitchen. Not even the sea air could cool me.

This was not the reaction of someone disinterested.

"This... this isn't happening," I muttered. "So the guy's got abs. Whoop-de-do."

But no amount of sarcasm could wipe the image of those sculpted muscles from my mind. With a huff, I gave up and fished out my phone, dialling Abi.

She picked up on the second ring. "Hey. We were just talking about you."

I started pacing the balcony, too wound up to stand still. "Yeah? That's... great."

If Abi noticed my distracted tone, she didn't let on. "You'll never believe what just happened. Emma went into labour right in Charlie's office!"

"Whoa," I said vaguely, still seeing Jackson's muscles flexing in my mind's eye.

"I know, right? Charlie looked ready to pass out. Kept mumbling 'the carpet, the carpet.' Finn had to take over calling the ambulance." Abi chuckled. "I bet he never thought he'd have to talk his agent into breathing."

I forced a hollow laugh, trying desperately to focus on her voice, on the story. But my thoughts kept circling back to the gym, replaying the scene on an endless mortifying loop.

What would those muscles feel like above me if we…

No. Red alert.

Do not step out of the friend zone, Butler. Don't do it.

After a few more failed responses from me, Abi's tone sharpened. "Alright, what's going on with you? You're clearly not listening to a word I'm saying."

I winced, knowing I'd been caught. "Sorry. Just distracted I guess."

"By a certain charming Scot?" Eva shouted from the background, a knowing edge to her tone.

My cheeks flamed. "What? No!"

"Uh huh. Sure, Jan," Abi said wryly. "Face it, our fearless Ros has finally fallen for those Levi charms."

I bristled at the implication. "You're delusional. It was just a temporary lapse in judgement."

Eva laughed. "Keep telling yourself that, honey."

I scowled, even as doubt trickled in. They didn't understand — this was just physical attraction. I wasn't falling for Jackson… was I?

No. I couldn't afford to. He'd leave me eventually if I did. This little crush would pass. It had to.

"Cut the crap, Ros," Eva shouted. "Dish the details!"

I scowled, knowing I was cornered. "Ugh, fine! I walked in on him working out shirtless, alright? He decided having a home gym meant he didn't need to leave the house."

I started pacing again, ranting to cover my flustered state.

"Who even lifts weights alone like that? He couldn't go to Finn's fancy gym with his equally jacked buddies? No, he had to be half naked and sweaty right where I'd see."

My cheeks heated just picturing those flexing muscles again. I definitely didn't need that mental image seared into my brain.

Deafening squeals sounded through the phone. I yanked it from my ear with a scowl until the shrieking subsided.

"This is not exciting news!" I snapped.

"Are you kidding? This is huge!" Abi shouted. "Our ultra-resistant Ros is finally falling for the Scottish heartthrob."

"I am not!" My denial sounded weak even to me. "He's my friend. It was just hormones. A completely normal physical reaction."

Eva cackled gleefully. "Whatever helps you sleep at night."

Their delighted shouts continued as I fumed. They didn't get it. This changed nothing.

I wasn't falling for Jackson Levi. And I'd prove it, no matter what it took.

Abi hummed sceptically. "Maybe you're fighting this so hard because deep down, you want it to happen."

I bristled. "What's that supposed to mean?"

"It means this reaction is coming from somewhere," Eva said gently. "Have you thought about embracing it?"

My eyes widened in disbelief. "Embrace it? Are you nuts?"

Abi sighed. "Why not enjoy yourself? You're playing the part of Jackson's girlfriend already. What's the harm in making it real?"

Something in me snapped. "You know why I can't do that! I refuse to be just another conquest for a man who will forget I exist once the next pretty thing catches his eye." I tried to swallow the words, tried to hold it in, but I couldn't stop it. "Every guy I've cared about has either cheated or found someone better eventually. You think Jackson will be any different?" I shook my head bitterly. "I can't go through that again. I won't."

A heavy silence followed. I meant what I said — I wouldn't

survive Jackson using me and tossing me aside in the end. No matter how intriguing our attraction felt in the moment.

Some risks were too great, even for me.

Finally, Abi spoke up, keeping her voice level and gentle. "I know you've been hurt badly in the past. But have you considered Jackson might be different?"

I scoffed half-heartedly. "All men are the same."

"You don't really believe that," Eva said. "Jackson spent over a year trying to get close to you, just as a friend. And when you rejected him, he accepted it and backed off. Does that sound like the jerks you used to date?"

I fell silent, turning her words over. She had a point — Jackson had respected my boundaries.

"I've never seen him look at anyone the way he looks at you."

My automatic denial wavered. Jackson did treat me like I was special. But that didn't guarantee forever.

"I get that you're scared," Eva said gently. "That's normal after what you've been through. But don't let fear hold you back from something that could be amazing."

I slumped against the balcony railing, my swirling emotions making me dizzy. Maybe Crazy and Crazier had a point. Jackson wasn't like those losers. I could admit that, but admitting it didn't mean I wanted nor needed to full-on dive into coupledom.

CHAPTER TWELVE

JACKSON

The limo glided down the street towards the madness waiting at the end of the red carpet. Ros sat rigid beside me, fidgeting with her dress and staring out the tinted window. I watched her from the corner of my eye, sensing the nerves coming off her in waves.

"So Audra thinks this new project could get some buzz come awards season," I said, blurting out the first thing that came to mind in the hope that it would distract her. "More of a gritty character piece than my usual action fare."

"Mhm," she murmured, gaze still fixed outside.

"Should be a nice change of pace. Sink my teeth into some real acting challenges again."

"Yeah."

I rambled on about my next project, the indie drama I couldn't wait to try after years of action flicks and sappy rom-coms. No matter how much I talked, Ros remained lost in her own world, offering only vague hums and one-word replies as I prattled on.

I was normally so good at this — putting people at ease. But none of my usual tricks were working on her. I sighed and leaned my head back against the leather seat.

As the limo slowed to a stop, the sounds of the awaiting spectacle filtered through — shouted questions, camera shutters, screams from overzealous fans. Showtime. At the sound of it, Ros caught her bottom lip between her teeth, her body tensing up even more.

"You look beautiful, by the way," I said, making one last ditch to ease her mind. "That dress is stunning on you."

A faint smile touched her lips. "Thanks."

Her gaze flickered to me briefly before skittering away. She went back to fussing with her skirt, though her shoulders lowered slightly.

I resisted the urge to grasp her hand. Until she explicitly welcomed it, I'd keep my hands to myself in private.

"I know this is a lot," I said. "But I have total faith in you. You're going to be amazing tonight, pixie."

"Easy for you to say," she said, her voice barely above a whisper. "You're used to all this chaos."

"Trust me, it's never easy." I smiled at her honesty, so rare in my world of glittering fakery. "But I promise you, once you step out there, you'll shine brighter than any star on that carpet."

I turned my palm up in invitation. She glanced down, hesitation in her eyes. She had always been unapologetically herself with me, flaws and all, but she hated anyone, including me, seeing her vulnerable in any way.

I let the moment stretch on. She needed time to gather her courage. And I'll admit, it felt good being the one to reassure and support her for a change.

Moments ticked by, but finally, she placed her hand in mine and lifted her chin a fraction. I smiled and gave it an encouraging squeeze.

That's my girl.

"It all seems terrifying right now, but I know you can do this. You belong by my side, that's all they need to know."

She bit her lip. "But what if I trip or say something stupid?"

I squeezed her hand. "Doesn't matter. You're with me, and we're in this together."

She took a shaky breath. "It's just... the power they have, to judge every little thing about me..."

"Only if you let them." My voice was gentle but firm. "No matter what anyone says or writes, you know who you are. Their opinions don't change that."

Ros stared at me. The hard lines of her face had softened. Seeing her like this, every instinct screamed to pull her close and kiss away all her fears. Our faces were mere inches apart, and her lips parted slightly...

Her gaze flickered down to my mouth. Yet she made no move to pull away or break the spell wrapping around us.

For a blissful moment, nothing existed but the two of us and our temporary sanctuary in the back of the limo. There were no screaming fans outside the car, no line of photographers and reporters waiting to grill us.

The intercom buzzed to life. "We're up next, Mr Levi."

I jolted upright, knocking heads with Ros. So much for the cosy moment.

I rubbed my temple. "Are you ready for the madness, lass?"

She gave me a wry smile. "What if I said no? Not like you can turn this thing around now."

"Do you want me to try? Just say the word, and I'll tell the driver to circle around. We could make a run for it."

She barked out a surprised laugh. "What, bail completely?"

"Sure, why not? We'll sneak out the back, grab some burgers..."

Amusement sparkled in her eyes. "As tempting as that sounds, I'm pretty sure your publicist would hunt us down."

I shrugged. "Worth it to see you smile."

She ducked her head, blushing. After a moment she looked back up.

"Thanks, but I was joking. I can handle it." She paused, holding my gaze. "But thank you. For offering."

"Any time, firefly."

She winced. "No."

I nodded, filing that rejection away.

She squeezed my hand, bracing herself. "Just don't leave me alone out there, okay?"

"Never." I brought our joined hands to my lips, brushing a feather-light kiss over her knuckles. "We've got this, firecracker."

Her lips quirked. "You're ridiculous. Now let's go give these vultures a show before Audra sends out a search party," she said with forced bravado.

As the door opened, an explosion of camera flashes and deafening cheers enveloped us. I blinked against the glare, trying to get my bearings. It felt like stepping into a hurricane — the chaotic atmosphere of the red carpet was a force to be reckoned with. The flashing cameras were blinding, each one vying for the perfect shot of the newest celebrity couple. Shouting reporters clamoured for our attention, eager to secure an exclusive quote or soundbite. Fans straining against the barriers, desperate for an autograph or just a glance.

And above it all, Ros's name rang out over and over. They shouted it, pleaded it, demanded it. Everyone wanted a piece of her.

I glance over to find her looking a bit shellshocked. She plastered on a smile but it didn't reach her eyes. The chaos was getting to her, threatening to crack that tough exterior she armoured herself with.

The crowd surged against the barriers, desperate for a glimpse.

I paused, extending a hand to Ros. Cameras zoomed in, capturing every moment. For a second, she hesitated. Her attention flitted between my hand and the sea of cameras.

What if this was too much for her? What if she'd decided she'd made a mistake? Would she see this through after all or leave me stranded alone on the carpet in another media shitstorm?

Then her small hand slid into mine and squeezed tight, her grip warm and firm.

Relief and something that felt strangely like joy washed over me. I gave her a nod and a genuine smile as we began our first walk together down the red carpet.

I matched my strides to hers, shielding her as much as I could with my body. We waved and smiled for the cameras, a united front.

"Jackson! Ros! Over here!"

The questions came rapid-fire. "Tell us how you two met!"

"Any wedding bells in the future?"

"Ros, how did he sweep you off your feet?"

The camera flashes increased to a blinding degree as we paused for photos. Ros leaned into me unconsciously. I pulled her closer, struck by how natural it felt to have her pressed against my side. The roar of the crowd and the reporters' incessant questioning faded to background noise. She glanced up at me, a vulnerable glint in her eyes that stole my breath.

Then she pushed her shoulders back and lifted her chin, defiance bleeding in, smothering the softened edges.

Fuck, was she beautiful.

No matter how insane things got, I wouldn't let go of her hand. She gave me strength and courage I'd never found with anyone else.

"Any plans for the future?" Another reporter shoved a mic in my face. "Wedding bells, maybe?"

The last time someone had asked me that question, a different woman wore my ring. I forced a chuckle.

"Let's just focus on tonight, aye?" My voice came out hoarser than intended. The reporter laughed at my pain, just as I'd intended. "We're here to celebrate the fantastic work done by everyone involved in this film, and that's what we should be talking about."

"Come on, give us something! Your fans are dying to know."

Her grip on my hand tightened slightly. Every protective

instinct flared inside me. It wasn't right for these vultures to keep prying into our personal lives.

Before I could snarl at the rude reporter, Ros jumped in. "Our main focus right now is our careers," she said smoothly. "We both love our work, and support each other in that."

I gazed down at her, amazed. My little warrior.

"The future is unknown." She shrugged. "Who knows what comes next?"

The reporter looked disappointed, but moved on. I resisted the urge to stick my tongue out at the leech.

"Nicely done," I murmured to her through my smile. "Definitely never getting on your bad side."

She smirked. "Please. You wouldn't last a day."

I laughed.

We paused for another barrage of flashing bulbs before continuing down the carpet. I noticed the glint of something in the bodice of her gown. Leaning in, I spotted a cluster of safety pins hidden amongst the beading.

"You've got something stuck in your dress," I whispered against her ear.

"No, leave them!" Ros grabbed my hand before I could touch them, surprising me with her vehemence. Lifting up on her toes, she leaned in close to explain and whispered, "They're for... insurance. I need them." Red burned along her cheeks as she pulled back even as her tone remained firm.

"Alright, alright," I said, taken aback by her sudden defensiveness. "I just figured they were left behind from adjustments or something."

"They're there on purpose." She glanced down, taking a deep breath before staring up at me through her lashes. "It's a superstition of mine. It's silly, I know, but if I don't have them, I feel like something will go wrong."

She held my gaze unflinchingly, probably expecting me to laugh at her. I could never.

"Nothing silly about it," I assured her. "We all have our rituals."

And I didn't know an actor who didn't follow some complicated system to ensure a good take or a good show.

Still, I removed a single pin, tucking it into my pocket. Ros started to protest, but I squeezed her hand and leaned in again, pressing my face to the side of hers. The action made the press go crazy.

"But if it makes you feel better, I'll wear one too so you always have a backup." I pressed a soft kiss to her cheek. "I promise I won't let anything happen to you tonight. You're safe with me, pixie."

I'd said the nickname to her countless times over the last year, and she'd never reacted. Now her eyes widened. I braced myself expecting her to finally reject it. Instead, her lips curved and joy rushed through me.

Finally, we reached the end of the carpet. As we posed for final photos under the theatre marquee, I leaned in close.

"Almost there. You're doing amazing."

Ros met my gaze, relief and gratitude shining through. Staring into her vibrant green eyes, conviction settled in my bones and I knew, whatever this was between us, it was real. If only she'd give it a chance.

The deafening roar faded as we stepped into the cool, dim theatre. No more cameras, no more questions. Just her hand, still clasped in mine.

CHAPTER THIRTEEN

JACKSON

"What's Jackson's favourite colour?" Jen asked, smiling encouragingly.

Ros didn't even blink before responding, "Forest green."

I had to bite my cheek to keep from laughing. What a load of rubbish.

I leaned back on the sofa, stretching my arm along the top behind her shoulders. We were practising for the talk show interview that would finally — hopefully — put a stop to the constant questioning of our relationship. The sceptics had diminished in the last two weeks, but there was still too much speculation for me to fully relax.

Not that Ros hadn't tried. Considering I'd thrown her in the deep end, I couldn't be prouder of her. Very few people could have pulled it off at all, let alone at short notice.

My ex from back home definitely wouldn't have. She would have booked herself on the first available flight out to escape me and the attention.

Audra and Jen sat across from us, the pair of them night and day in more than appearance. They fired question after question t, but Jen had fun and tried to laugh through the awkwardness, while Audra hit us like a drill Sergeant.

"And Ros's favourite flower?"

"White roses." I tried to sound as in love as possible, emulating my best friends without being sappy. Or so I hoped. Jen nodded encouragingly. "They remind her of her grandmother's garden."

Total bull, but it flowed off my tongue better than the truth: she hates flowers and thinks they're wasteful and better left in a field for the insects and bees to enjoy. Audra had also vetoed that truth when we'd first tried to use it.

Ros winced but nodded, committing to our fabricated history.

"Enough of the easy questions." Audra shifted in her seat while scrolling through her tablet with a perpetual furrow between her brows. "What do you love most about each other?"

My mouth went dry at the L-word. Stupid, I know, but I'd avoided saying it to anyone since… I got into acting. If the cameras weren't rolling, that word did not come out of my mouth.

"His kindness," Ros said. "Jackson is always thinking of others. He goes out of his way to help people and I love that about him."

Did I? Were we still pretending or did she mean it?

Audra nodded, pleased for the first time since we sat down. Had I fallen into an alternate universe in the last five minutes?

"Examples?"

"He'd do anything for his friends and family." Ros chewed her lip in indecision. "Whenever they need anything, a confidant or a getaway house to hide from the press, he's ready to step in." She side-eyed me and my heart just about stopped.

Was that admiration? I daren't believe it.

"I'd do the same for my friends, so it's only right that my perfect match would think the same."

I stared at her, struggling to find the tells that usually gave away her lies. She had a habit of maintaining eye contact at every turn, watching for signs that she'd been figured out. Now she could barely look at Audra, let alone me.

"Jackson?"

"Right. Uh…" I scrambled for an answer. Trust Audra to go off-book. "Her passion and her honesty. If she doesn't like something, she'll tell you."

My lips twitched, remembering how she'd laid down the law at Abi and Finn's wedding, making it clear that faking it for a show or not, he wasn't allowed to hurt her. Only she hadn't ranted at Finn, she'd focused all of that manic energy on me. I might have fallen in love with her that day.

Wait! No. No love. Jesus, get a grip, man.

I cleared my throat, forcing that paralysing possibility away. "When she cares about something or someone, she's unstoppable."

Audra's mouth twisted, but she moved right along to the next question. "What annoying habits does Jackson have?"

Before Ros could open her mouth, Jennifer held her hand up. "Ooh, tell them how he always leaves his wet towel on the floor!" She leaned forward, an eager glint in her eyes.

I shot her a warning look while Ros tried not to laugh. Leave it to my baby sister to put ideas in her head that would show me up on national television.

"Thanks, Jen," I said dryly. "Any other bad habits you want to share?"

Her eyes lit up and I braced myself.

"As much as I'd love to hear every single one, I've got this." Ros threw me a teasing glare. "Leaving the kitchen a mess after baking cookies."

My brow rose. Of all the things she could have picked from Audra's list, she went with that? I shook my head.

I gasped dramatically. "I do not!"

I really didn't. I didn't know the first thing about baking, but Audra decided it would soften the housewives of America. My argument that I'd never be able to back that up if someone invited me onto a cooking show — which wasn't a stretch of the imagination, I'd received and rejected invitations in the past — went ignored.

"There's always flour everywhere!" Ros continued, her tone indignant.

"Lies!"

Her lips twitched as she stared at me, her eyes bright.

"No," Audra snapped, dragging our attention back to her. She scowled at us. "Less bickering, more sweet nothings." Then her gaze tracked over us. "Let's practise your body language. Jackson, put your arm around Ros."

I lifted my arm off the back of the sofa and placed it around her, expecting her to tuck herself against my side. This wasn't much different to how we spent our film nights, tucked up on the sofa with her leaning more and more against me before she eventually fell asleep before the credits.

Instead, she turned to stone, every muscle tense.

Audra clicked her tongue. "Relax, Ros. You look like you're sitting next to a stranger."

She shot me an apologetic glance before forcing herself to lean against me. But her back remained ramrod straight, muscles tense.

"Remember, you're madly in love. Try it again." Audra frowned.

She shifted closer, attempting to appear casual. But I could feel the unease rolling off her.

Audra let out an impatient huff. "No, that's still not right. Once more, from the top."

Ros grimaced and I shot her a sympathetic smile. She tried again to mould herself to my side, but couldn't fully disguise her discomfort. She kept fidgeting, unable to settle.

I'd been so sure that she'd come around, that there had been a reason for her rejections. What if there wasn't? What if I'd let wishful thinking colour my vision and had locked us together for a year for nothing?

Not nothing. You still need a reputation overhaul.

Finally, I'd had enough of watching her squirm. Pushing aside the awkward discomfort of knowing I might have got this whole thing drastically wrong, I leaned in and whispered in her ear while Audra barked more useless instructions.

"Just tune her out, pixie. Focus on me, breathe nice and slow. Imagine there's a film playing and it's just a normal night." I rubbed her arm gently, hoping the reassurance would help. Audra's demands only added more stress to an uncomfortable situation. She needed a softer touch. "Don't give her the satisfaction of getting under your skin."

Ros stared into my eyes, every secret vulnerability laid bare. I didn't like it one bit. She wasn't the type to show weakness. Sure she'd been making progress with me but she would never leave herself open with other people around.

"I've seen you saunter into an exclusive NYC club in head-to-toe vintage and convince the bouncer you were a foreign princess. You can handle this and more."

At my murmured words, her muscles loosened slightly and a grin ghosted across her lips. I kept whispering encouragement, reminding her to breathe and that we were in this together. She leaned into me, head coming to rest naturally on my shoulder. My pulse kicked up a notch.

I wished I could freeze this moment and flip the script. Pretend it was just me and Ros together because we wanted to be. No acting, no cameras, no made-up story we had to sell.

But she didn't really want this. The second Audra called time, she'd pull away again.

Still, I couldn't resist enjoying how she felt pressed against my side. Warm, soft... like she belonged next to me. It was all pretend, but a guy could dream, right?

Audra finally nodded in approval. "Better, but keep practising."

I hid a smile. I'd take any excuse to hold Ros close while I could.

"What's your favourite thing to do together?" Audra asked.

I squeezed Ros closer. "Easy. Curled up watching a film, just the two of us."

I hoped it sounded convincingly in love. Audra's loud huff suggested it did not.

"How about cuddling by the fire?" Ros offered. "So romantic."

She blinked innocently while I fought back a smile. Well played. Audra seemed pacified, for now.

"Were you worried, Jackson, when you had to film overseas?"

"Yes," I sighed. "Going two months without seeing my girl's smile? Torture."

Ros patted my chest, her smile brittle. "But absence makes the heart grow fonder, right snookums?"

I choked on a laugh. Audra looked one jab away from throttling us, but pressed on.

"Why didn't Ros visit you on set in Hungary?"

"I wanted to." Ros took my hand and smiled up at me like Audra had instructed her to do for this question. "But work was crazy with fashion week, and I couldn't get away."

Audra nodded, her expression barely shifting before she glanced at her list and her lips pursed.

"Alright, the one everyone wants to know — tell us about that first meeting," she said, staring at Ros.

"Well, uh, it was at this fancy Hollywood party," she stammered. "I didn't know anyone. Then I saw Jackson across the room."

She told the made-up story about noticing me from afar and cheesy sparks flying. But her heart wasn't in it at all. She rushed through it, cheeks red, not meeting anyone's eyes.

"We just clicked right away. It was like magic," Ros mumbled. Then she clamped her mouth shut, clearly done.

"You can do better than that." Audra shook her head, frowning.

"I know I can, but only if we're telling the truth." Ros met my gaze, a question I couldn't decipher in her eyes. Whatever she saw made her straighten her spine and turn back to Audra with steel in her expression and tone. "We're not doing the fake story. I'm not an actor. The less made up, cheesy crap I have to remember the better. We're using our actual story."

"Now wait a —" Fire slashed in Audra's eyes.

"I think Ros has it right," I said, cutting my publicist off. "We're friends, Audra. We know enough about each other to sell a relationship with real facts."

"Besides, our meet cute is way cooler than some pretentious party." Ros shrugged. She lifted her chin and stared Audra down. "We met at our friends' arranged wedding for a reality TV show. I was a bridesmaid for Abi, Jackson was one of Finn's best men."

Then she told it honestly, how we'd chatted at the reception, then saw each other again at another wedding months later. With each real detail she shared, Ros seemed to relax, getting more confident.

"That's the truth," she finished firmly. "We don't need some made-up first meeting."

Audra definitely didn't like that. Her lips disappeared in a thin line. "The public wants romance and drama. Not boring weddings."

Ros laughed. "What's more cavity-inducingly sweet than a couple meeting for the first time at a wedding?" Her brows rose. "That's every woman's dream: go to a wedding, leave with a future husband. It's why every single reception ends with single women falling over each other trying to catch the bouquet." She glanced up at me, using her eyes to plead with me as if I would ever deny her anything. "It's important to me. I'm already faking enough, I won't pretend to be someone else."

A tense pause followed. Audra glared at me, expecting me to get my fake girlfriend in line. A few days ago, I might've agreed with her to keep the peace. But something in Ros's eyes stopped me. She needed this one real piece in the middle of all the play-acting. And I found I needed it too.

"Ros is right," I said finally. "Let's keep it honest."

Audra looked fit to explode, but miraculously held her tongue.

"I agree," Jen said. "You guys should tell it like it really happened."

I shot her a grateful look. Having my sister stand up for Ros meant a lot.

Audra pursed her lips. "Don't you want your love story to be exciting and memorable?"

"What's more exciting than falling for the guy you spent your best friend's wedding dancing with?" She shrugged her shoulders. "I mean, it would have been better had we walked down the aisle together, but it's still pretty spectacular."

My mind latched onto her words, filling my head with images of her gliding towards me in a white dress instead of walking next to me. Her smile lit up the room, all for me. Promising to love each other forever — for real, not just for the cameras.

"Ros already does everything you ask without complaint. Give her this one thing."

Audra's glare sharpened. "We need buzz to sell this story."

I shook my head. "My mind's made up."

A tense beat passed as we stared at each other. What would happen if she didn't give in, I wasn't sure. I had no interest in firing Audra. As difficult as she could be at times, she was good at her job.

Finally Audra sighed, relenting. "Fine. We'll try it your way, just this once."

Ros smiled at me, her expression so warm and grateful it made my chest ache.

Audra ploughed forward with more questions, undeterred.

"Why reveal your relationship now?"

"Well, uh, it was time?" Ros asked, faltering slightly.

"With my life constantly in the spotlight, it felt impossible to keep something so important private any longer."

Audra hummed, unsatisfied. "And what about claims this is all fabricated for publicity?"

Now it was my turn to stumble. "That's simply not true. Our love is real." Even I winced at how stilted and fake that sounded.

A sly gleam entered Audra's eye. She'd caught us off guard and was relishing it.

"Not very convincing," she tutted. "We need to get your stories straight."

I resisted the urge to throttle her. Of course our fumbling was unconvincing — this whole thing was a bloody sham!

"What Jackson means is, we wanted to keep things just between us at first." Ros slid her hand into mine. "But we're tired of hiding how we feel and having to plan every second of our lives to avoid the cameras."

Her voice rang with such sincerity even I almost believed it. She held Audra's gaze evenly until the publicist blinked first.

"Well then." Audra shuffled her notes, flustered. "I suppose that will suffice."

Ros and I exchanged a relieved look. Surviving Audra's interrogation felt like a sweet victory.

We powered through the remaining questions, falling into an easy rhythm. With each coy glance or casual touch, our chemistry grew more palpable. Lingering looks replaced awkwardness, and Ros relaxed into my side like she belonged there.

I couldn't keep my eyes off her. The way her nose crinkled when she laughed. How she picked at her nail polish between questions. My fingers itched to reach out and touch her, but I resisted. With her so close, distraction came easily. The floral scent of her shampoo flooded my senses. Her arm pressed against mine, warmth seeping through. I shifted in my seat, pulse quickening.

Focus, Levi.

This was all pretend, I reminded myself sternly. Ros did not actually want boyfriend me. She wanted friend me.

Finally, Audra checked her watch. "I think that's enough for today. Well done." As she gathered her things, she added, "One more thing. I think you two should announce your engagement on the talk show tomorrow."

"Absolutely not."

"It's the next logical step. You've supposedly been together for six months." Audra just lifted a brow. "I've known celebs who get engaged after a week, so it wouldn't be unusual, and we need a big splash."

Ros shrugged. "I'm game if you are."

I gaped at her. I searched her face, finding only excitement and mischief.

Cursing inwardly, I said, "Alright, let's do it. Ros and I will announce our engagement on air."

When Audra left, I turned to Ros uncertainly. "Are you sure about this?"

"In for a penny, in for a pound." She lifted her chin, eyes sparkling. "She's right, it makes sense."

Her bravery left me in awe. I wanted to give this maddening, captivating woman everything she desired. Even if it was just a reckless charade.

I took her hand, a misplaced thrill rushing through me. "Okay, I'd better find you a ring then."

She would be the death of me, no doubt. But part of me hoped that having her by my side, even temporarily, would make all the craziness that came with fame a little easier to handle.

CHAPTER FOURTEEN

ROS

"What if she sees through me?" My eyes widened as I spun back to Jackson. "Oh my god, what if I slip up?"

I didn't wait for his reply, just started pacing again, my heart pounding in my chest like it was seconds away from making a break for it.

A clock ticked on the wall, the sound of it stupidly loud for the confines of what I'm sure would be a perfectly lovely dressing room on any other day, with another couple in it. In ten minutes, Jackson and I would sit on a garish talk show couch and spin the biggest lie of our lives.

A live studio audience waited to dissect our every word and gesture like vultures. What if I slipped up? Froze under the hot stage lights? Tripped over my tongue or these ridiculous stilettos? *Why couldn't I wear my boots?* A cold sweat broke out down my spine.

A warm hand grasped my shoulder. I spun to face Jackson, taking in his easy smile. How could he be so calm?

"It's going to be fine, pixie," he said, his Scottish accent soothing, yet not. "We're sticking as close to the truth as possible. You know me. You've got this. Just follow my lead out there."

I shrugged off his hand, my panic shifting to irritation. "Follow your lead? This whole fake relationship was your harebrained idea. Maybe you should follow mine and call this whole thing off!"

I didn't mean that.

Jackson just chuckled. "Cold feet already? Can't back out now. Don't worry — you look stunning, you know what to say. It'll be a breeze."

"But what if I mess up?" My hands balled into fists. He didn't get it. "What if I trip over their rugs and faceplant? What if no one believes us and this just makes the rumours worse? What if they ask something we haven't rehearsed? What if they see right through us?"

Jackson's hazel eyes softened. He squeezed my shoulders gently. "Doesn't matter what they believe. I believe in you — in us."

My protests died on my lips. I searched Jackson's gaze and found only sincerity shining back. Slowly, my frayed nerves settled.

"There's nothing for you to worry about. We've been through every possible scenario. Just trust yourself, and trust me. We'll be fine."

Then Jackson's lips curved into a teasing grin. "Well, there is one thing missing."

Before I could ask, he pulled a small blue satin box from his pocket. My eyes widened as he cracked it open, revealing a monstrous pink diamond ring.

I stared at the gaudy thing, unable to tear my gaze away.

"Oh wow," I said, somehow keeping the revulsion from my voice.

The ring was vintage at least, with a central diamond the size of a Skittle flanked by smaller stones that would put the Hope Diamond to shame. Definitely not my style.

Jackson watched me closely. "What do you think?"

He said it lightly, but I could hear the underlying tension in his voice. My gaze bounced from the glittering jewels to his uncertain eyes.

Oddly, the sight of that ring and all it symbolised didn't send me bolting for the exit. How far would we push this charade? Would I have to plan a wedding? Go through with it? Even that didn't scare me, which should have been a red flag.

But then, I'd agreed to this scheme with clear eyes, knowing the stakes. I had to remember that.

I met his gaze again, seeing my own rattled emotions reflected back. "It's very... flashy," I said eventually. "Perfect Hollywood engagement ring."

Jackson barked out a surprised laugh, the tension shattering. "High praise, coming from you." His eyes crinkled at the corners. "Shall we see if it fits?"

I nodded, struck mute. Jackson lifted the ring from the box without so much as a tremor in his hand. Time seemed to slow, the air charging between us. He took my left hand in his, pausing before sliding the ring into place.

In that moment, my world narrowed down to Jackson's skin against mine. My heart wouldn't stop pounding, even though I kept reminding myself that it was all fake, that it meant nothing.

"There." His voice came out gruff when the ring settled against my skin, his Scottish brogue raking across my nerve endings and making me shiver.

I stared down at my hand. The weight of the ring felt as foreign as the reality: I was wearing Jackson Levi's engagement ring. We were doing this. And I felt... good. Strong. Ready.

I smiled up at him, a grin stealing over my face. "Not too bad, Levi."

The responding light in his eyes warmed me more than any shiny jewels could. And his smile... a girl could get addicted to those slow, easy smiles. My attention drifted to his lips, fixating there while my mind helpfully reminded me just how good our kiss had been at the Marable show.

We were standing so close, it would take barely anything for me to rise up and press my lips to his. For a fleeting moment, I imagined what it would feel like to kiss him in celebration, like a real engaged couple would.

As much as I tried to deny it, there was an irresistible attraction simmering between us. But acting on it would only make things messy.

Jackson was my friend. My very hot, very platonic friend who I wanted to keep forever.

What about friends with benefits?

A sharp knock made me jump. I backed away from Jackson, as a production assistant poked her head in. "It's time!" she said, her expression both excited and oddly nervous.

What did *she* have to be nervous about? She wasn't going to sit in front of a studio audience and have her life dissected for entertainment. "Thanks, we'll be right there," Jackson said. Once the assistant closed the door, he took my hands again and leaned down, placing himself at my eye level. "What do you say, pixie? Ready to share our love with the world?"

His lips twitched and I chuckled.

I stared down at the ring pinching my skin where Jackson held me. The sight of it grounded me, forcing the purpose of this charade to the forefront of my mind.

This was going to be easy. We were mostly sticking to the truth, and I knew him, almost as well as I knew myself. I could answer anything as long as I remembered to throw some loved-up looks his way.

Plus, I was a born and bred New Yorker. I'd faced down giant rats, lawless cyclists, murderous taxi drivers and soulless landlords. If I could survive New York, I could handle one interview.

And with Jackson looking at me like that, like his world rotated around me, I felt strong enough to face anything — even a thousand prying eyes.

I met Jackson's steady gaze again and nodded. "Let's do this."

❄

"*I*'ve got a special surprise for you today," Mira Jacks, the host of the aptly named Mira Jacks Show said.

She stood in the middle of her set, her trademark smile firmly fixed in place and arms flung out with more enthusiasm than the situation necessarily needed.

"He's been the talk of the town for years, but more recently this Hollywood transplant has claimed all of our focus for a more *romantic* reason." She grinned as the audience responded with enthusiastic screams and clapping.

My grip on Jackson's hand tightened. My heart beat so fast, I could swear I was going into cardiac arrest. I glanced over at him, trying to find some reassurance in his steady gaze.

"Please welcome our guests, everyone's favourite Scottish heartthrob, Jackson Levi and his secret girlfriend, Ros Butler!" Mira shouted before I was ready.

The audience erupted in raucous cheers and applause. I gulped. This was really happening.

Jackson gave my hand a reassuring squeeze before we stepped from the relative safety of the backstage area and into the glare of spotlights. I blinked against the sudden brightness, gripped by the surreal sight of hundreds of shadowy faces whooping at the mere sight of us.

Of Jackson, rather.

To them I was still a faceless name.

He waved to the crowd, completely at home in the spotlight, though his thumb continued rubbing soothing circles over my knuckles, silently reminding me I wasn't alone up here. I managed a passable imitation of his natural grin, struggling not to squint against the heat of a thousand lights.

We crossed the plush carpet punctuated by zebra print throw rugs. Clearly, Mira tried a little too hard embracing that Hollywood glam decor. I fought not to trip over them in my spindly heels while Jackson guided us towards the cosy interview nook set before a kitschy fake backdrop displaying the Hollywood sign.

"Welcome, welcome!" Mira beamed at us, shaking first Jackson's hand, then mine. Up close, her age showed through the caked on makeup and dyed hair. But genuine warmth shone in her eyes as she gestured to the loveseat. "Make yourselves comfortable."

I perched stiffly on the edge beside Jackson, keeping our thighs pressed together per Audra's explicit instructions. As I mentally ran through Audra's checklist — hold his hand, sit close, do not tense up at any point — I tried to keep my breathing steady. This was it. The moment of truth.

His large palm settled on my knee while Mira settled into a matching wingback chair.

"So lovely to have you both," she said. "Ros, what an honour to have you on our show. That dress is gorgeous!"

"Thank you. It's vintage Dior."

Another point I'd won against Audra. She got the shoes, I got the dress. One day, I'd take all the wins.

"You've been quite the Hollywood bachelor, yet here you sit, head over heels at last!"

Right on cue, Jackson lifted our joined hands to his lips. "What can I say, my Ros stole this weary heart. I'm a lucky man."

Despite the cheesy line, warmth sparked through me at his words. Our gazes caught, something genuine passing between us.

Her eyes widened as they landed on the diamond adorning my finger. "What a beautiful ring. Did someone give it to you?"

The studio fell silent, the audience straining to see the engagement ring.

Jackson and I shared a coy glance, giving the appearance that we were silently discussing whether to share our "news" with the world. Then, I turned back to Mira and smiled.

"Actually, we do have some exciting news..."

Mira gasped dramatically. "No! Don't tell me Hollywood's most eligible bachelor is off the market?"

The audience began murmuring excitedly.

Jackson grinned. "I'm afraid so. Ros makes me the happiest

I've ever been. So…" He lifted my hand, showing off the gigantic engagement ring. "I asked her to marry me."

The audience erupted into deafening cheers and applause. A couple of people burst into tears, or screamed no. I fought the urge to cringe, overwhelmed by the scale of the lie we'd just told the world.

Mira pretended to fan herself. "This is wonderful! Oh, congratulations!"

I forced an embarrassed smile. "Thank you. I'm still getting used to it."

Understatement of the year.

"And how did he propose? I want all the romantic details!" Mira pressed.

I glanced uncertainly at Jackson.

"Well, I wanted it to be special for my Ros," Jackson said. He leaned back, wrapping his arm around my shoulders and cuddling me into his side. I smiled up at him, channelling every memory I had of my parents. "So I planned a private dinner on the beach, with flowers and candles everywhere…"

As he droned on describing the fictional scenario, I shifted in my seat, extremely aware of his thumb lightly caressing my waist. I struggled to focus on his words, but those gentle strokes kept sending delicious sparks up my shine.

I had to sternly remind myself that it was all part of the act. Just Jackson selling our fake engagement to the public. But when he gazed at me like I was the only woman in the world, it definitely didn't feel fake.

Maybe he'd be into the friends with benefits thing, that voice piped up.

"When did you realise Ros was the one?"

"I think it was at Finn's wedding," he said, shooting me a subtle wink. "The minute I saw her walk down that aisle, I just knew."

I barely suppressed an eyeroll. What a line.

"It's hard to describe, but it was like everything suddenly clicked into place. One moment, I had Finn McCarthy whining in my ear and a room full of Hollywood's finest staring at me and the next, my vision narrowed and there was just her. Wearing a purple Grecian-inspired dress, strutting down the aisle like it was a runway and she owned it."

I glanced up at him. His gaze dropped to me, and the softest, sweetest smile curved his lips. "I took one look at that fiery sparkle in her eyes, and it felt so right, so meant-to-be."

The audience *aww*'ed, and a blush burned across my cheeks that had nothing to do with acting.

He was simply selling our fake romance — nothing more.

Still, what would be so terrible about basking in the glow of his attention a bit longer? It was nice feeling treasured, even artificially.

Mira looked enraptured by Jackson's story. "That definitely sounds like fate at work. And clearly you agree, Ros!"

I startled, realising I'd been gazing stupidly back at Jackson. Focus!

"Oh yes, absolutely." I smiled at Mira, anything to not look at Jackson again. "When you know, you just know."

The interview continued, questions shifting to wedding plans and hopes for the future. Through it all, Jackson kept up subtle touches — a hand on my knee, casual arm around my shoulders. Sparks hummed just below my skin everywhere we made contact.

Much more and I'd melt into a useless puddle in his arms. How much longer until this torture ended?

It seemed, at some point in the last two weeks, I'd fallen into lust with my fake man. It needed to end, and fast, before I did something foolish. Like ask Hollywood's most notorious playboy and heartbreaker to fuck me six ways to Sunday all over his house.

CHAPTER FIFTEEN

JACKSON

"The Sanderson brothers' scandal couldn't have come at a better time." Jimmy, my agent, rubbed his chin thoughtfully. "The media's eating it up, leaving you and Ros relatively out of the hot seat."

His practised, smiling face split my laptop screen in half. Audra winced on the other half.

"Now, let's not get ahead of ourselves," Audra said, her cautious tone barely masking the smug satisfaction twisting her lips.

"Of course, but we can still appreciate their timing, right?" I couldn't suppress the smirk that tugged at my lips. The Sandersons always had a knack for stealing the limelight and girlfriends, though usually for more flattering reasons.

"Couldn't have planned it better if we tried." I glanced at Ros, sat beside me, her usual stoic facade in place. But I caught the hint of amusement in her eyes.

Two weeks had passed since we outed ourselves on the Mira Jacks Show and things were going well.

"True," Audra begrudgingly conceded. "It has certainly improved your situation, but you didn't need it. All of my hard work is finally paying off."

In our tiny preview of ourselves, the corner of Ros's mouth twitched on the split screen — she was trying hard not to roll her eyes. I bit my cheek, holding in my own laughter.

Your *hard work? Sure, Audra, whatever you say.*

"*That woman,*" Audra wrinkled her nose, "has come clean at last. She admitted to fabricating the whole affair story for a payday."

'That woman' meaning Sammy Miller, who caused all of this chaos to begin with. A few months ago, I might have shared Audra's disdain, but with Ros sitting next to me with zero reservations about our friendship... it was hard to hold a grudge against her. Though that didn't mean I forgave her for nearly destroying my career.

"Not that any of us needed the confirmation," Jimmy said.

"That's great news." I leaned forward, clasping my hands together. "The defamation suit is already in progress I assume?"

"Of course, that's all being handled." He waved his hand, unconcerned. "Your reputation is cleaner than it's been in years."

"So, we're out of the woods?" Ros asked, her voice carrying a note of hope that didn't quite reach her eyes.

"Let's not pop the champagne just yet," Audra snapped. "We're not out of the woods until I say we are."

I ran a hand through my hair, frustrated yet relieved. "What's left to worry about then?" I asked, hoping my irritation didn't bleed through too much.

At least Audra isn't arguing for us splitting up. I still have time.

"Perception, darling." She wagged a manicured finger at us. "One wrong move and the press will spin this faster than you can say 'publicity stunt'."

"Right," I muttered, my mind racing through potential minefields we might still have to navigate. "So, what's the game plan?"

"Nothing changes." Audra smiled, a sparkle of triumph in her eyes. "Keep up the image of a man deeply in love, and we'll handle the rest."

Jimmy nodded. "I've already got multiple projects chomping at the bit to sign you on. It's all coming together, son."

"That's great to hear. Just tell us where you need us and we'll handle it." I threw a smile at Ros. Her expression was unreadable, but her fingers were twisting in the fabric of her skater skirt.

Was she pleased? Annoyed? Did she want to lay low now that the heat was off?

"Good. There's no room for error." Audra nodded. "We've built momentum, and we're going to ride it all the way to the bank."

Jimmy leaned closer to the camera, his gaze serious. "Exactly. This is a crucial time, Jackson. With your next project coming up, we can't afford any missteps."

I nodded, fully aware of the stakes. "I know the drill, guys. Keep the image clean, play the doting fiancé. I'm good, promise."

Ros let out a soft snort, rolling her eyes. Whether at me or my team I couldn't say. Though I had my suspicions.

"Keep us updated on any unexpected outings." Audra leaned back in her chair, not bothering to hide that smug triumph now. "I'll coordinate with the paparazzi. Controlled exposure is key." Her brows knitted together as she shifted gears. "Speaking of being seen, what are your plans for Christmas? It's the perfect time for some cosy, lovey-dovey press."

Ros and I exchanged a look, the awkward silence hanging heavy between us. I cleared my throat. "We, uh, haven't really talked about it yet."

"Maybe we should just — spend it apart?" Ros suggested. "Take a break and reset for the new year."

Audra's face contorted in horror as if we'd just suggested painting the Mona Lisa neon pink. "Apart? What will the press think?"

I could almost hear the screech of brakes in my head. "It's just one holiday—"

Audra cut me off with a swift hand gesture, her blonde hair swaying with the force of her movement.

"Let me paint you a picture, Jackson." Her tone was icy enough to chill the Malibu sun. "Newly engaged couple spends their first Christmas apart? They should be meeting each other's families. Next thing we know, there's a media frenzy, headlines screaming break-up and questioning if you were ever real. Absolutely not. I won't allow it." She jabbed a finger at the screen, punctuating her point.

"That seems a little extreme," Ros said.

Audra's lips pressed into a thin line. "Extreme or not, it's what will happen and doing as I say is what's best for his image. The public needs to see you together, especially during the holidays."

Which I more than understood, but the last thing I wanted to do was introduce Ros to my family when we weren't real. My family would love her, unlike Bree. They would already be devastated when we broke up in October, but if they met her? I'd be reminded of how I'd failed to convince her to be mine for the rest of my life.

"But Christmas is family time." My knee started bouncing. "It's not really fair to drag Ros into my family's madness."

Audra scoffed. "Please, Jackson, this is Hollywood. Fairness has nothing to do with it. It's about perception, and perception is reality."

"I don't know," Ros said, her voice hesitant as she shifted beside me. "Meeting the family is a big step. Especially if it's just for show."

I nodded in agreement, relieved she was on the same page. If our relationship were real, if we were more than recovering friends, I would do it in a heartbeat. I wanted nothing more than to introduce Ros fully into my life, share the cringe moments when my family tested me because they loved me. The idea of dragging her to Scotland for the sake of a publicity stunt made my stomach turn.

My mother would demand we stay in the family home even

though I had my own house less than a ten-minute drive away. For a week.

But that wasn't us.

Not now. Not after I'd pushed her too far.

"I understand your reservations," Audra leaned forward, her eyes narrowing, "but you need to think about the long game here. Your fans, the media, they want to see progression in your relationship. And what better way than a family Christmas in Scotland?"

I studied Ros and her carefully composed mask. She couldn't fool me, not on this. The tense set of her jaw, the slight narrowing of her eyes, it all gave her away. She wasn't thrilled with the idea, and frankly, neither was I.

I raked a hand through my hair, torn. I'd never fought Audra or Jimmy on anything. They always had my best interests in mind, no matter how insane the scheme seemed.

But this?

This involved more than me and my career.

"It's one thing to go on dates and show up at events together, but dragging her to my family's home for Christmas? That's too personal, too real."

"I agree." Ros nodded, her focus never leaving the laptop screen and Audra's scowling face.

Audra's eyes flickered between us, her expression hardening. "Real is exactly what we need. The public has to believe in this relationship, and what better way than spending the holidays with family? It's relatable, it's heartwarming—it's perfect."

I shook my head, my frustration mounting. "It's manipulative, that's what it is. My family isn't some prop for a publicity stunt."

Ros's grip on my hand tightened. "Jackson's right. We've been playing along with this whole thing, but this is too much. We're not actors in a holiday rom-com."

Audra's expression softened slightly, though her determination didn't wane. "I understand your concerns, but you have to trust me on this. I've been managing Jackson's career for years, and I know what works. This will work."

"I appreciate your concern for our... 'progression,' but I have to consider Ros's comfort here. Dragging her into my family dynamics right now isn't fair to her."

It also wasn't fair to my mother.

To give her hope and then take it away in October when our contract ended... it would hurt all of us.

"Don't be foolish, Jackson. This trip is crucial for optics. It'll set up the year perfectly."

"I don't care about optics. Not when it involves my family." I gritted my teeth. "I won't force Ros to pretend with people who mean so much to me."

Audra leaned forward, eyes calculating. "Be reasonable—"

"He said no."

Audra blinked, momentarily stunned.

"He's not ready to face his family with me." Ros shrugged, her gaze steady and unwavering. "And I promised my dad I'd be in New York. So, if being apart is such an issue for you, Audra, then I guess we're spending the holidays in New York."

ROS

"Then it's settled. New York it is," Jackson said in a tone that brooked no argument. I couldn't help but feel a mixture of relief and dread at the same time. "What kind of fiancé would I be to separate Ros from her own Christmas traditions when her dad is much closer than my family?"

I held Audra's gaze, daring her to argue. Inside though, my stomach churned. I hadn't actually made plans with my father yet. We rarely spent more than an obligatory few hours together over the holidays, just enough to assuage my guilt over being an absent daughter.

Not that he didn't deserve my absence.

But what else could I do?

Jackson clearly wasn't ready to face his family with me. Whatever Jackson and I were becoming, it wasn't real. I had to remember that. Once our contract ended, things would go back to normal.

And I wanted that.

My heart could remain safely guarded, as long as I didn't lose sight of the playacting. This Hollywood fantasy would pass. Our contract would end, we'd go back to being friends and grow from this experience.

I wouldn't jeopardise our friendship for anything. Not even to avoid a week of passive-aggressive comments from my step-monster. Jackson was worth handling her disdain. For now, protecting him mattered more than sparing myself the misery.

And if going to Scotland made him that uncomfortable, who was I to argue?

I knew Jackson didn't want to introduce me to his family because our relationship wasn't real. Part of me was grateful. I wasn't sure if I was ready to face the complexities of his world. But another part, a small, silly part, wished things were different.

Audra and Jimmy reluctantly agreed to the New York plan, but not without Audra voicing her concerns. She was already strategising photo ops and possible public appearances. Did the woman never rest?

Jackson nodded along, seeming to agree with everything Audra proposed.

Not that I heard any of it.

I zoned out, only half listening. The thought of spending any significant amount of time with my father and his wife filled me with an overwhelming sense of dread. The hours I spent with them each year were always strained and uncomfortable.

A whole week of pretending we were the perfect family and he hadn't torn out my mother's heart; it sounded suffocating. Like drowning on dry land. I hadn't spent that much time with my father since I'd moved out for college. The second I could get a job, I'd done it and then I'd worked every hour I could without jeopardising my fashion degree to ensure I could keep a roof over my head after freshman year.

The space, and meeting Abi, and then her sister Eva, had saved me in more ways than even I could comprehend. I'd been strong before — who wouldn't be after enduring years of psychological torture from a supposed guardian — but with them I came to realise that there was no shame in being unabashedly myself.

Even better, I learnt that family doesn't have to be blood. You can *choose* and I'd chosen Eva and Abi.

CHAPTER SIXTEEN

"Absolutely not. We are not watching another one of your brooding indie films where everyone just stares at the ocean and sighs," I grumbled, leaning against the kitchen island while Jackson riffled through the cupboards. "Haven't I suffered enough?"

He chuckled at my disgruntled tone. "You picked last time, pixie."

"Months ago! That barely counts now. It's my turn tonight."

"Uh uh." He wagged a finger. "I definitely remember you making me suffer through a sappy romcom."

"It was a romantic dramedy," I huffed.

Chuckling, he abandoned his search for popcorn kernels and invaded my space, leaning in close. "Same difference. Tonight, we watch something with explosions."

The scent of his cologne engulfed me – a mix of saltwater and pine that somehow epitomised everything about him. His presence was like a physical force, drawing my attention to the taut stretch of his plain white t-shirt over broad shoulders.

I opened my mouth to argue but the words evaporated. He was too damn close, his minty breath fanning my face. My gaze lingered on the full curve of his lips, a smirk playing at their edges. Fingers twitched at my sides, itching to reach out, to trace the smile I wanted to taste.

What was happening to me? I shook my head sharply, trying to clear it. This was Jackson, my friend.

"Well?" Amusement glinted in his eyes. "Do we have a deal?"

Sensing weakness, Jackson moved even closer, his hand grazing my hip. "Come on, pixie. Don't you trust me to pick a good one?"

His voice was low, teasing. That Scottish burr curled around my nerve endings deliciously. I shuddered, pulse racing out of control.

Somehow I managed to shuffle along the island and out of the cage of his arms, putting a little distance between us. My thoughts slowly unjumbled.

"You can handle a bit of sci-fi action, can't you?" He followed me and the heat of him wrapped around me like a cocoon.

"Sci-fi... action?" I repeated dumbly, momentarily lost in the moment.

I shook my head again, pulling my gaze from the distracting sight of Jackson's body to focus on his face. His eyes danced with that infuriating, knowing glint that said he'd caught me staring.

"Something wrong?" One corner of his mouth curled upwards.

I gritted my teeth. "You're really going to make me sit through another space battle explosion marathon?"

He placed a hand over his heart dramatically. "Oh come on, the last one wasn't that bad! I promise this franchise steps it up story-wise."

Pressing his palms together, Jackson fixed me with an endearing, pleading expression. "Please, Ros? Consider it an early Christmas present." His eyes widened beseechingly.

Normally I enjoyed our playful banter over movie choices. But right now, being in closed quarters with him sounded dangerous.

Every point of contact where our bodies touched sent sparks dancing across my skin.

Still, refusing might make things awkward. Better to play it cool and act normal. I could resist my traitorous urges for one movie, right?

"Fine, you win." I grumbled, throwing up my hands with a dramatic sigh. "But if I fall asleep, it's on you."

His smirk grew wider as he claimed victory. "You won't fall asleep, trust me. This film's a classic."

I rolled my eyes, secretly relieved to back away from the electric charge between us. "You better have popcorn."

He shot me a droll look before returning to his search. "Of course, I have popcorn."

My eyes narrowed on his toned back. "Great, but keep your salted abomination to yourself."

"You're missing out."

He scooped kernels into the popper. Yes, he was one of those fancy-pants people with a gadget or machine for everything. The only thing I hadn't spotted yet was a candy floss machine.

"Sweet and salty is the perfect balance." He shook his head, amused, as the kernels began to pop like miniature fireworks.

"Sweet and salty is not a balance; it's a culinary crime scene." My nose wrinkled in distaste at the thought. "Only you Brits could think ruining perfectly good popcorn is a snack innovation."

"A million Brits can't be wrong, love," he countered with a wink, pouring the fluffy white clouds into two large bowls.

"Keep your butchered popcorn to yourself." I crossed my arms and watched him flavour the popcorn. "I'll stick with the true classic — butter."

I watched as Jackson poured a generous amount of melted butter over one of the bowls of popcorn, the golden liquid cascading over the puffy kernels, making my mouth water. The rich aroma filled the kitchen, teasing my senses and making my stomach growl. Buttery popcorn was my weakness, and he knew it all too well.

"And don't even think about contaminating mine."

"Wouldn't dream of it." He chuckled, raising his hands in mock surrender, but the mischief dancing in his eyes told a different story.

I narrowed my eyes, pointing an accusing finger at him. "I mean it, Levi. One grain of salt gets anywhere near my popcorn and you're a dead man."

Jackson pressed a hand to his heart. "You wound me, pixie. Have a little faith."

"Not when it comes to snacks." I shook my head adamantly. "Your taste buds are defective."

With one last warning glare, I left him alone in the kitchen and made my way to his study. Unlike the rest of the open, airy home, his study was a cave-like space designed for focus. Heavy blackout curtains blocked the wall of glass overlooking the ocean cliffs, plunging the room into near total darkness when drawn. The only furniture was a massive leather sectional sofa facing an equally huge television that took up most of the far wall and a solid cherry wood desk. No cluttered bookshelves or decorative knick-knacks.

I drew the blackout curtains closed and grabbed soft blankets from the cabinet in the corner, preparing our makeshift cinema.

As much as I hated to admit it, movie nights with him were always cosy and fun. Curled up together in the dark, laughing over popcorn — it felt natural. Easy.

But easy was dangerous. The more time we spent playing couple, the more those boundaries blurred.

A few minutes later, Jackson appeared at the doorway, two bowls in hand. One clearly held the sweet and salty abomination, and the other, thankfully, glistened with the golden buttery sheen. He kneeled before me, presenting the bowls like offerings to royalty, laughter dancing in his eyes.

"Prepare for two hours of edge-of-your-seat action, m'lady."

I scoffed at his dramatics, but deep down, the sight of him on his knees in front of me sent an unfamiliar thrill through me.

If only I'd worn a skirt...

My cheeks burned with the thought.

"Oh, stop it," I grumbled, taking the butter popcorn bowl. My fingers brushed against his, sending a rogue spark up my arm.

"Will this sustain you, your highness? Or shall I fetch chocolate and wine to satisfy your royal cravings?"

I rolled my eyes but couldn't suppress my smile. Spending time with Jackson like this, just the two of us, was dangerous. It blurred lines, made me question things I shouldn't.

"The popcorn will suffice, serf. You may rise and start the film."

Grinning, he popped up and grabbed the remote. As we settled side by side on the plush leather sofa, my nerves returned. Sitting close in the dark felt intimate in a way I wasn't prepared for. I clutched my popcorn bowl tighter, ready to use it as a barrier between us if needed.

But as the opening sequence exploded on screen, he made no move closer. We simply sat together, enjoying the film and trading occasional quips. The companionable mood from earlier returned easily.

Maybe I'd overreacted. We could keep things light, friendly. I didn't have to over analyse his every look and touch. If I stopped projecting complications, it would stay simple.

The film progressed, a blur of sci-fi cliches and over-the-top action. But I couldn't concentrate. Every time Jackson shifted or laughed, my attention snapped back to him. It was maddening.

By the halfway mark, I was fully engrossed in the story, leaning forward to catch every twist. Jackson chuckled at my rapt focus.

"Admit it, you're loving this."

I tossed a piece of popcorn at him without looking away from the screen. "Shh. I'm trying to watch, unlike some people."

He sighed in mock exasperation. "Here I thought you wanted to spend time with me. But clearly you only have eyes for those aliens."

I rolled my eyes and elbowed him. Jackson retaliated by trying to steal my popcorn. We tussled and giggled until collapsing against each other, breathless.

As his eyes locked with mine, still bright with laughter, that earlier attraction simmered once more. Our faces were mere inches apart, lips almost brushing. It would take nothing to close that tiny gap between us...

I froze, my smile slipping. What was wrong with me? I liked our relationship just the way it was, with no risk that he'd leave me in the end like every other man I allowed out of the friend zone.

"Are you alright?" He leaned back, concern etched on his face.

"Fine," I snapped, a little too sharply. "Just don't want your popcorn to invade my personal space."

"Of course not," he said, though his smirk suggested he found my discomfort amusing. "We wouldn't want an international incident over snack territory."

"No, we wouldn't," I grumbled, shifting to put a hair's breadth of distance between us. I focused on steadying my breath, on the coolness of the bowl in my lap. This was just Jackson. The guy who knew all my secrets, who dragged me into this celebrity charade. Nothing more.

But oh, how the reckless part of me wanted to lean in, to close that teasing gap and see what would happen if I let myself indulge in the dangerous thoughts swirling through my head.

I quickly turned my attention back to the movie, hoping it would distract me. But I couldn't focus on the plot or characters, too aware of Jackson's presence beside me.

The sound of his laughter made my pulse jump. When he shifted on the sofa, his arm brushed mine and pleasant tingles danced across my skin. I glanced at him from the corner of my eye, noticing how the flickering glow from the screen illuminated his handsome features.

Stop staring, I commanded myself. But my gaze kept drifting back to him. The way his eyes crinkled at the funny parts, how his mouth quirked in that infuriating, knowing smirk when he caught me looking. Like he could read my riotous thoughts and found it all very amusing.

"See something you like?" he teased.

Heat flooded my face at being caught out. "Just wondering if you're even watching the movie." I crossed my arms. "You seem distracted."

"Maybe I just find the company more interesting."

His voice dropped lower. The sound of it sent delicious shivers down my spine. I swallowed hard, trying to think of a witty comeback. But my brain had turned to mush.

"I, uh…"

Eloquent, Ros. Real smooth.

Chuckling under his breath, Jackson stretched and draped his arm casually behind me on the sofa back. I stiffened as his fingers grazed my shoulder, hyper aware of how close our bodies were.

If I just leaned into him slightly, I'd be tucked against his side, surrounded by his warmth. The thought was far too tempting. My treacherous imagination spun visions of sinking into his heat, resting my head on his chest as his fingers idly played with my hair...

Dangerous territory. Jackson was off limits. Indulging my attraction, even for a moment, could ruin everything between us.

Oblivious to my inner turmoil, Jackson shifted closer until his thigh pressed against mine. I tried refocusing on the movie, but all my senses remained attuned to Jackson beside me. His beachy, masculine scent enveloping me, the heat of him seeping through our clothes, his firm thigh solid against my softer one.

My skin felt hypersensitive, nerve endings alight. It would take nothing to close the scant distance between us and press my lips to his jaw. Feel his stubble scrape deliciously against my skin as I explored the corded muscles of his neck...

Stop! Bad Ros. Down girl.

I had to rein in my runaway thoughts before I did something reckless I'd regret. Jackson was my friend, nothing more. I couldn't lose sight of that, no matter how fiercely my body burned for his.

I tried to focus on the blaring explosions and futuristic landscapes flickering across the screen, but my senses betrayed me. The sheer proximity of his body made each breath feel stolen.

For a second, all I could do was fixate on the warmth radiating around me, the way his presence enveloped me. An urge surged within me, primal and unnerving; I wanted to turn my face into his neck and breathe deep while he held me close. It unsettled me, this longing. I wasn't supposed to want him like that.

"Using your cheesy movie moves on me, Levi?" I teased, trying to defuse the tension. "You think draping your arm like that is going to work? So smooth, Casanova."

He chuckled, a low, resonant sound that sent an inexplicable flutter through my stomach. "What? Can't a man get comfortable without being accused of ulterior motives?"

"Comfortable?" I snorted. "You've got enough space on this sofa to lie down without crowding me. No need to play the 'yawn and stretch' card."

"Ros, love, if I wanted to make a move, you'd know it." His tone dropped, teasing and taunting. "I've got moves you haven't even seen yet."

Even as my cheeks heated, I scoffed. "Please. That move was straight from Acting 101."

"Was not." He pretended to take offence. "Maybe I just... like being near you."

Jackson held my gaze, his voice softening. I tried to ignore the flutter in my stomach. His words were playful, but they tugged at something deeper.

My lips parted but no words came out. That unfamiliar vulnerability in his eyes left me speechless.

The moment stretched, weighted with possibility. I wet my dry lips. Jackson's gaze dipped down, tracking the movement. Heat coiled low in my core.

No, no, no. Abort mission. I tore my eyes away, heart pounding.

"Nice try, but you can't distract me from this quality cinema with your cheesy lines." My teasing tone came out strained. I cringed internally but barrelled on. "I'm analysing the artistry of these explosions."

A beat of awkward silence passed between us and I started to wonder if I could have handled it better.

"Oh really?" Jackson said, quirking a brow. "Then I'd better take notes for my next action film."

I rolled my eyes while relief coursed through me. I chose to ignore the flicker of disappointment mixed in. "Please. Like you need tips."

"Maybe I'm studying your facial expressions for inspiration." He leaned in with mock solemnity. "Such nuance and emotional depth."

"My expressions? I've been stoic as a stone over here."

"Au contraire." Jackson pointed at my face emphatically. "When that alien's head exploded, I detected at least... two distinct emotions."

I swatted his hand away, laughing. "You're so full of it."

He clutched his chest. "I bare my artistic soul and this is the thanks I get?"

For a blissful moment, the simmering attraction faded into the background. I could almost imagine nothing had changed between us, that we were simply two friends enjoying a night in.

But when our chuckles faded, that intense awareness of him returned in full force. I fidgeted with my necklace, hyper-conscious of each point where our bodies still touched.

The silence between us shifted from easy to charged. My mind spun trying to think of a neutral topic, some way to get us back to safer ground.

I cleared my throat awkwardly. "So, uh, some action sequence, huh?"

"Riveting," Jackson deadpanned.

We both glanced at the screen. Jackson scrubbed a hand over his jaw. "Want me to rewind a bit? Could've missed some key explosions."

"Tempting, but…" I worried my lip between my teeth. Act casual, I reminded myself. "It's kind of nice, just talking like this."

Jackson's face softened. "I've missed it too." He nudged my shoulder playfully. "When you're not yelling at me over popcorn, that is."

I snorted. "Next time, make two batches, and we'll avoid the international incident."

"Deal." His eyes crinkled at the corners when he smiled. My chest did that weird fluttery thing again.

Stop it.

I focused intently on the screen, hoping Jackson didn't notice my flustered state. Maybe if we just watched the movie in silence, I could get my inconvenient yearnings under control.

But the silence quickly grew awkward. I could feel Jackson's gaze burning against my skin as the minutes dragged on.

"It's too bad we can't just make out and get it out of our systems."

CHAPTER SEVENTEEN

ROS

*D*id I just say that out loud?

"I mean, uh..."

So much for keeping things light and firmly in the friend zone.

To my surprise, Jackson didn't seem offended. If anything, he appeared intrigued.

"That… could be an option, you know." He kept his voice low and his tone careful. "If we wanted things to seem more… believable."

Now it was my turn to gape at him. "What are you saying?"

Jackson raked a hand through his hair. "Just that we clearly have… chemistry." He shrugged, aiming for casual. "Maybe letting it play out naturally, no strings attached, would make this whole fake relationship thing easier."

I stared at him, waiting for my disgust to kick in. It didn't. Instead, reckless curiosity unfurled inside me.

"Like… friends with benefits?" I asked slowly.

He searched my face. "Only if you were comfortable with it.

Could just be a casual, physical thing between us. We wouldn't even tell Audra or our friends if we didn't want."

Never in a million years had I imagined Jackson would suggest such an arrangement. But even more shocking was my temptation to say yes.

Still, doubt held me back. "Wouldn't that make things messy? Complicated?"

"Doesn't have to." He regarded me evenly. "We're both adults. If we set clear boundaries..."

He trailed off, letting me fill in the blanks.

Madness.

Blurring the lines between friendship and more was a recipe for disaster. I should shut this down immediately.

But the reckless part of me was intensely intrigued. We were undeniably attracted to each other. Having a physical outlet could ease all this unresolved tension and give us space to get back to being friends. And he had a point — it would make our interactions as a couple more believable.

"What about emotions? No strings attached is harder in practice."

"We'd have to be honest with each other. If feelings started developing beyond friendship..." He shrugged, a confident smile tugging at his lips. "We'd put an end to it before one of us got hurt or our friendship took a hit."

"And if things ended badly? What would that do to our arrangement?"

"Doesn't have to be permanent," Jackson reasoned. "We try it out, set a timeline. If it's not working, we go back to normal, no harm done."

I nodded slowly. Put like that, it seemed manageable. We could turn the attraction between us into an advantage instead of trying to resist it. Take the edge off so we could focus on rebuilding our friendship.

I eyed him, my heart pounding like it was trying to break free. The idea should've sent me running, yet I considered his proposal as if it were as simple as choosing which socks to wear.

A little over a month ago, all he'd wanted was to date me. Maybe this wasn't such a good idea. But then hadn't we put that awkwardness behind us? Nothing said he still felt that way. Plus, he would be getting sex now. What more could he possibly want?

"Complicated," I managed to say, though the word felt too tame for the storm he'd triggered inside me. My stomach flipped and my mouth went dry.

"Less complicated than you think." His eyes glittered with something that wasn't just mischief—it was a dare.

"It could crash and burn," I said, grasping for straws and barely holding myself back. "What then? We'll have paparazzi documenting our spectacular downfall. Headlines screaming about our breakup. Audra would be pissed."

"Sounds dramatic." There was humour in his tone, but I wasn't ready to laugh it off.

"Emotions, Jackson. They complicate everything." The words were heavy, a confession and a warning all rolled into one. "They're messy and unpredictable."

"Like salted caramel." He brushed his fingertips across my cheek, staring into my eyes with a serious expression that made my pulse flutter in my throat.

"More like vinegar on ice cream."

"It would be worth it."

The silence between us was a living thing, heavy and expectant. That damned popcorn bowl sat abandoned, a casualty of the tension that buzzed through the air. The agreement sat on the tip of my tongue, desperate to get out.

I exhaled, nerves and excitement mingling unexpectedly. "Screw it. What's the harm in trying?" My words felt like a challenge to the universe.

Jackson's eyes widened. "Really?" His voice was cautious, but I could hear the undercurrent of hope that he couldn't quite hide.

I bit back a smile at having caught him off guard for once. "If it all blows up, we'll forget it ever happened. We'll just go back to being friends." It sounded so simple, so easy when said out loud. "I'm willing if you are."

"Oh, I am absolutely willing." He grinned and his attention dropped to my lips again. He leaned towards me like he intended to kiss me.

I pressed my hand against his chest holding him off. "Ground rules first," I said, my voice breathless and tinged with excitement.

He sat back, smirking. "Rule one: This doesn't change our friendship."

"That's a given," I nodded. "Rule two: No sleepovers. We keep our spaces separate."

He nodded in agreement. "Rule three: we tell no one. Not our friends, not my team. This is between us and stays under lock and key."

"That's fair." I paused, considering my next words. "And rule four: If either of us starts feeling more than just... physical, we call it off. Immediately."

"Deal." Jackson extended his hand, and I shook it, sealing our unconventional agreement.

For a moment, we sat in silence, the weight of our decision hanging between us as we stared into the other's eyes. Now what?

"I guess this makes us friends with benefits," I whispered, a thrill of excitement coursing through me.

"Friends with benefits," he echoed, his voice husky.

My fingers found the warmth of his neck, and I yanked him towards me with a boldness that surprised even myself. His lips crashed onto mine, and oh, how they burned. Jackson responded with a ferocity that matched my own, hands finding purchase on my body, tugging me closer.

I shifted into his lap, every part of me suddenly desperate to erase the space between us. Our kiss was hard and hungry, the kind that left no room for doubt or second-guessing. He ground against me, his erection pressing urgently, and I gasped into his mouth, every sense alive with the scent of him, the taste of him, the undeniable rightness of this moment.

"Ros," he groaned, and God, the way my name sounded on his lips was better than any sound I'd ever heard.

Next thing I knew, we were a tangled mess of limbs on the couch, our clothes discarded as if they were nothing more than a pesky obstacle to our newly discovered passion. Jackson's hands roamed my body, leaving a trail of goosebumps in their wake. He worshipped me with his lips and his touch, as though exploring every inch was a privilege rather than a right.

When he tugged my lacy underwear down my legs, his eyes darkened with desire. "You're so damn hot," he said, his voice rough. His fingers traced the curve of my hip, and I squirmed under his touch.

He brushed his hands over my thighs, then traced the sides of my waist, and finally, his fingers found their way to the apex of my hips, teasing my clit.

I moaned, my body arching into his touch. His lips found my neck, trailing open-mouth kisses down until he reached my breast. As his fingers circled my clit, he traced his tongue around a taut nipple, teasing it to an even tighter peak.

He sucked the nipple into his hot mouth as he thrust two fingers inside of me, pulsing them in and out, stretching me in the most incredible way.

It might have been a while since I'd last...

Not that I'd ever tell Jackson. Didn't need it to go to his head.

My fingers dove into his hair, needing to hold onto something, anything as he stoked the need inside of me higher and higher.

When I couldn't take it anymore, I tugged on his hair, silently begging him to give me his mouth again.

He released my nipple with an audible pop, smiling lazily while I continued to tug at him. "What do you need, pixie?"

More. I wanted him so badly. I wanted him to fill me, to take me in every way possible. I didn't want to wait anymore, I wanted him now.

"Quit stalling, and fuck me already." My breath was ragged, and my skin felt like it was on fire.

He smirked, the look in his eyes promising slow torture. "I'm not rushing you," he said in a deep, sultry voice. "I'm going to make you come so hard, you'll be begging for my cock every moment you can."

His fingers left my clit, and I whimpered in disappointment. Jackson just chuckled, sliding off the sofa and repositioning me into a reclining position, my legs spread wide. He wedged his shoulders between them, forcing me to stretch wider.

My breath rushed out of my lungs at the first swipe of his tongue through my folds. I moaned as his fingers found my clit again, teasing me just enough to keep me on the edge of pleasure.

His eyes remained fixed on me, dark with desire. He guided me to the brink, and then pulled back, laughing softly as I whimpered in protest.

"You're so wet," he breathed, his hot breath teasing me just as much as tongue and fingers. He licked his lips as if he savoured the taste of me. "I can't wait to feel you around me, to feel you squeezing me."

He continued to tease me, his fingers and tongue working in concert to drive me to the edge of insanity. I writhed on the sofa, my nails digging into the couch cushions as I begged for release.

"Stop teasing me and let me come," I gasped, my body trembling with need.

"Just a little longer." Suck. "You look so beautiful, flushed and desperate for my cock." Nip. "And you taste incredible. I never want to stop."

I whimpered at the thought of that, agreeing and disagreeing all in one sound.

I could feel my body tightening, the tension building to the point of bursting. My fingers found their way back into his hair and held him to me so he'd stop teasing me.

He hummed, the sound vibrating against my clit and making my eyes flutter.

"Now be a good girl and come on my tongue."

My core clenched at his words, but sweet relief hit as Jackson thrust two fingers inside me, curling them in just the right way to send me over the edge. I cried out, my body shaking with pleasure as his lips sealed around my clit. He sucked harder, eliciting a soft moan from me as his fingers continued to pulse inside me, milking my orgasm for all it was worth.

When my body sagged, nothing but the tiny flickers of after-shocks left, he sat back, smirking up at me with pure satisfaction in his hazel eyes.

"That was just the start." He stood up, his erection rock hard and standing at attention. "I have condoms in the bedroom if you want..."

"No." I shook my head as my stomach jumped into my throat. "I have an IUD and I'm clean."

He swallowed. "It's been a long time for me, pixie."

"Then we're good," I said, my tone pleased.

He chuckled as he reached for my hand. He tugged me to my feet and sat down in my place. I turned and stared down at him, confused. Then he pulled me forward until I sank onto his lap, straddling him.

Our lips met in a passionate kiss as our hands roamed over each other's bodies. The tip of his cock grazed my sex, making my core clench with need.

"Ride me, Ros." His fingers gripped my hips. "Show me how much you've craved me."

I nodded, my heart racing as I positioned myself over him. His eyes followed every move, need and desire burning in them.

"You're so beautiful." His hands stroked up my torso to cup my breasts. His fingers plucked and rolled my nipples, sending a shock to my clit.

I nodded, not trusting my voice. I wanted to say how much I needed him too, but I couldn't find the words.

Slowly, I sank down onto him, exhaling a shaky breath as his thick, hard cock filled me.

"Fuck," he groaned, his head falling back and his fingers stilling as we both adjusted. "You feel even more incredible than I imagined."

His words sent a flush of arousal through me, and I started to move, sliding up and down on his shaft with slow, controlled strokes.

"More." My voice shook with need. "I need to feel you deep inside me."

"Then take me," he said, his voice low and husky. "Take all of me."

I increased the pace, my hips rolling and grinding, as our bodies moved together in a rhythm that was intoxicating. His eyes never left mine, his gaze filled with both arousal and vulnerability.

"You're right," I whispered, my voice barely more than a whisper. "I've craved you for so long."

His fingers slid into my hair, pulling me close. His lips met mine in a fierce, passionate kiss.

I circled my hips and he lost control, his hips bucking up to meet my movements.

There was something empowering about this position. I held all the cards, I could make it as fast or slow as I wanted. I could tease him or fulfil his every wish.

"Yes," I moaned, my body arching, my core clenching around him.

I rode him harder, faster, chasing the first flicker of an orgasm like nothing else existed.

"If you keep going like that, I'm not going to last." He gripped my hips, trying and failing to make me slow down.

"I don't care," I panted, my eyes locked with his. "I want to feel you come inside me."

I couldn't resist the temptation any longer. As if possessed, I slammed down onto him, my hips pulsing wildly, our bodies locked in a frenzy of ecstasy.

"Fuck!" he growled, his voice strained and filled with pure

need. "Next time, I'm in control," he ground out through a clenched jaw.

Jackson's words hung in the air, and I couldn't help but smirk. "Should have thought of that before you set us up like this."

My orgasm blindsided me, dragging me over the edge and locking down my body. He groaned, his hands taking control of our movements, forcing my body to keep moving up and down his length while I collapsed against him, burying my face in his neck.

His cock jerked inside of me as I clamped down on him. With a hoarse cry, he came.

"That was more than worth the wait." He pulled my head back and his lips met mine in a greedy kiss, our bodies still locked together. Jackson's strong arms wrapped around me, pulling me close.

Floating in orgasmic bliss, I decided that this was the best idea I'd ever had. Why hadn't I suggested friends with benefits sooner?

CHAPTER EIGHTEEN

JACKSON

Outwardly, nothing changed in our relationship. We pretended to be nothing more than friends during the day — or at least I pretended. And at night, when the sun dipped below the horizon, I made it my mission to make Ros scream my name as many times as possible in one night.

Then I'd leave her warm, soft body, crawl into my cold bed, and pretend I hadn't left a piece of myself in the other room.

"Okay, remember, it's all about balance and timing."

I was shirtless, my wetsuit hanging loosely around my waist, the cool breeze brushing against my bare skin.

Her eyes kept wandering over my chest with this dazed quality that made me want to drive my hands into her hair and kiss her senseless.

"You know, you might actually stand up on the board if you stop ogling me."

Her cheeks flushed a delightful shade of red. "I am not ogling." Her eyes betrayed her.

"Sure, pixie. Just keep your eyes on the horizon, not my abs," I said, winking at her.

She huffed, trying to hide her smile, and positioned herself on the board I'd set up on the beach. We hadn't made it into the water yet. I'd promised her months ago that I would teach her to surf, when she'd learned it was my preferred method of working out the stresses of my life. I just hadn't had an opportunity until now.

She did one more exercise, executing it flawlessly.

"Okay, let's get into the water."

I helped her pick up the surfboard and we waded into the cool waves. Concern and excitement shone in her eyes as I pushed the floating board towards her.

I gave her a reassuring nod. "Wait here a sec, I'll grab my board and be right back."

As I ran back across the beach to get my own board, it struck me how far we'd come in such a short period of time.

I returned with my board under my arm and stopped next to her. "Ready to conquer the waves?"

Her answering nod was sharp and jerky, her eyes fixed on the horizon ahead. Together, we paddled out. I guided her on catching the right wave, explaining the subtle cues and timings. She was a quick learner, her focus unwavering, even as the cool water splashed around us.

"Okay, see that wave coming? Start paddling now," I instructed, my voice carrying over the sound of the waves.

She paddled vigorously, and I matched her pace, ready to cheer her on. As the wave caught her board, she pushed herself up with an impressive burst of strength.

"Yes, that's it!" I shouted, watching her balance and ride the wave. The sight of her standing triumphantly on the board, her hair wild in the sea breeze, filled me with an indescribable sense of pride.

As the wave ebbed, she lost her balance and tumbled into the water, surfacing with a bright, exhilarating laugh. I paddled over quickly.

"How did that feel?" I asked as she clambered back onto her board.

"I can't believe I did that." She shook her head in disbelief.

I grinned, thrilled to see the exhilaration on her face. "You're a natural."

"I doubt that."

"You know, on my first try, I only stood up for like two seconds before face-planting into the water," I said with a chuckle. "Took me weeks of practice before I could ride a wave as far as you did today."

Her eyes widened with surprise. "Really? I thought you were born with a surfboard under your feet!"

"Far from it. It was a lot of falling, getting back up, and trying again. But you..." I smiled, admiration clear in my voice, "you're a quick learner."

She beamed at the praise, a satisfied glow emanating from her. "Maybe I missed my calling as a professional surfer."

I laughed, shaking my head. "Ready to catch a few more waves?"

At her eager nod, we spent the next hour practising — paddling out, waiting for the perfect swell, popping up to ride it in. Each time Ros stood and coasted smoothly to shore, my chest swelled with pride.

Eventually, I called a stop, not wanting her to overexert herself on the first day. We trekked back up the beach together.

"I can't believe I just learned to surf! Me, a New Yorker." She laughed, eyes bright. "Not that I'll get to practise much back home. No way am I paddling out into the freezing Atlantic."

I smiled, tamping down the pang in my chest at the mention of her leaving. Silently, I hoped she'd choose to stay here with me instead. But I didn't want to pressure her.

At the car, I peeled off my wetsuit, catching her openly

admiring my shirtless torso. I bit back a grin, enjoying the desire in her eyes.

"What, am I distracting you again?" I asked innocently.

Ros blushed but held my gaze. "Maybe. Can you blame me? You should wear wetsuits more often. Especially half off like that."

Smirking, I tossed the suit in the trunk before stepping closer to her. "Well, anytime you want a private surf lesson, just say the word." I let my tone dip suggestively.

Her cheeks flushed even darker, but she didn't break eye contact. "I'll... keep that in mind," she whispered, her voice husky.

Heart pounding, I moved closer, backing her against the ledge of the Jeep's open boot. I cupped her face in my hands and tilted her chin upwards. "You know, practice makes perfect."

Our lips met, hungry and insatiable. Her hands slid up my chest, caressing over damp skin, jumpstarting every nerve in my body. My need for her was overwhelming, an ache I couldn't deny any longer.

While we devoured each other's mouths, I picked her up and set her down on the edge of the boot. With her now at the perfect level, I crowded closer, grinding our hips together until she moaned at the pressure.

Ros wrapped her legs around my waist, crushing us together as we kissed as if our lives depended on it. My brain short-circuited; all I could think about was having her right then and there.

A loud bark sounded nearby, arrowing through the fog of need.

I froze at the unexpected sound, my mind struggling to process it through the haze of desire. She pulled back, blinking in confusion, her lips swollen from our frantic kissing. The sharp bark came again, followed by the pounding of paws on sand.

"Saved by the bark," I joked, taking a step back to catch my breath. "Let's get you home," I said, offering her a hand to help her down from the Jeep. "I believe we have some unfinished business to take care of."

She took my hand, smirking. "Too right."

ROS

The second he got the front door open, Jackson tore the towel away from my body and tugged me into his chest.

I laughed at the desperate lust darkening his hazel eyes. He kissed me, hard, but then he pulled away too soon and I reached for him.

He used my grip to spin me around and press my front against the hallway wall. I gasped, my heart pounding while his hot mouth trailed down my neck.

"You have no idea how hard it was to keep my hands off you out there," Jackson growled in my ear.

I grinned, remembering the sight of him shirtless after surfing. "Trust me, I was struggling too."

He nipped at my collarbone, making me shiver. "Mm, so you liked the view?"

"Oh, yeah," I breathed, arching my spine and grinding my ass against the bulge in his swimming trunks.

"If I'd known that's what it took, I would've worn this wetsuit more often." His hands roamed over my damp, bikini-clad body, making me moan into the cold wall. "Tell me, pixie. If I'd taken you on the sand in front of everyone, how would you have reacted?"

A moan escaped my lips at the thought of him wanting me that much. Damn, if that didn't turn me on even more. I clenched my thighs together trying to quell the ache.

"I'd probably have begged you for more," I whispered, heat creeping up my neck.

"Is that so?" he purred, his hand sliding under my bikini bottoms, inching closer to my core. "Maybe I should've given them a show." His fingers slipped inside my pussy, and I bit my lip to muffle my moan. "Mhmm, you really do like that idea, don't you? You're soaking."

"We're in the hallway!" My hips pushed against his hand.

He chuckled against my neck. "Is this too private for you?" He raked his teeth against my pulse, making me shiver. "I could take you out on the patio and see if there are any helicopters hanging around. Give the paps their own show?"

He didn't mean it, I knew he didn't, but that didn't stop the rush of liquid need.

"I can't... I need..."

"Need what, Ros?" he growled, his fingers playing with my clit.

"You," I panted. "Now."

That was all the invitation he needed. He scooped me up in his arms and carried me upstairs in a rush. The bedroom door slammed shut behind us as he tossed me onto the bed. My bikini was gone in seconds, and I watched him shuck off his trunks before joining me.

Then he made me come harder than I ever had before.

CHAPTER NINETEEN

JACKSON

"Two and a half months with this eejit. That's impressive, Ros." Finn grinned pointedly at Nathan. "I didn't think you'd last a week."

"Who're you calling an eejit, McCartney?"

"Oooh, someone's getting tetchy." Nathan ducked, dodging the bread roll I threw at him. "What's wrong, afraid she'll ditch you?"

"Now, boys, no throwing food in my house," Mona said, slipping into a stern Mam voice I'd never heard before.

"Sorry, Mona."

She nodded at me and I pressed my lips together struggling not to laugh. Shaun would murder me if I did.

"It's been pretty easy honestly." Ros shrugged and picked up her wine glass to hide her grin when Finn's expression fell.

"Sure, sure. Any plans to leave him we should know about?" Nathan glanced between us with a sympathetic smile.

"Nathan!" Cat, his girlfriend, shook her head and he placed

his hand on hers, patting it as he threw an understanding smile her way.

Then he turned back to Ros and continued, "Just in case we need to make plans to meet him in the pub?" He hissed as Cat dug her nails in his hand. "What? It's the holiday season. We're all going to be on the other side of the Atlantic. It's best to know these things in advance."

"Stop stalling, Nate, and pay up." Finn held his hand out, his expression expectant. "That car is mine."

My eyes narrowed on the blond-haired asshole Englishman sat opposite me. "You bet against me?"

"Don't take it personally," Nathan said, scowling as he dug through his pockets.

"Don't take it personally? I lent you my pissing house and this is how you return the favour." I held my hand to my chest, really settling into the affronted role. "I can't believe you."

I could.

"Cut the shit, Levi." Nathan threw his keys to Finn, spearing me with a dark look. "You'd do the same and you know it."

I chuckled, though irritation did prickle through me that my supposed friends actually bet on my relationship. Even if it was fake.

Sure we were just friends with benefits but that was a step in the right direction. I just needed to give Ros time to realise that we were incredible together and I'd never be able to let her go.

Cat laughed at Nathan, flicking her long blonde hair over her shoulder. "Oh, come on, Nathan. You'll survive without it. Maybe this will teach you not to bet on your friends' lives in the future."

"Harsh, love." Nathan crossed his arms. "That 1962 Ferrari is my baby."

"I'll be sure to take extra special care of her." Finn winked as he helped Shaun top up wine glasses.

Ros met my gaze, amusement dancing in hers. "Should we be offended by their lack of faith?"

"Please, they've always been a pair of cynics."

She laughed, light and easy. The sound warmed me better than the mulled wine or full Christmas spread laid out before us.

We sat around Shaun and Mona's dining table, surrounded by our closest friends. The sun had set an hour ago, leaving us cocooned in the best way possible. Food littered the table. Mona had gone overboard, as she usually did. This was the one time of year she got to cater her own party. With their baby, Cerys's arrival, it was surprising Shaun hadn't forced her to accept the help of a catering team this year.

Even so, our glasses were filled with champagne and the air smelled of cinnamon and cloves. Every inch of the house had been decorated for Christmas. The sunken living room was aglow with the twinkling lights of the towering Christmas tree, its branches heavy with crystal ornaments and cascading ribbons. Candles flickered on every available surface, casting a warm, inviting glow throughout the open-plan kitchen and living area.

It was a couple of days before Christmas Eve, and per tradition, we had all come together to share a meal before each of us went our separate ways for the holidays. Before we found our better halves, this meeting had been nothing more than a video call or a meet up in the pub if we were in the same country. That had all changed when Mona became Shaun's assistant and he'd fallen head over heels for her.

These moments, when we could get together and forget the pressures of our careers and public lives, were precious. If not for my asshole friends that was.

I couldn't deny that Finn had a point, however.

I almost even wished that the last two and a half months had been hard in some way. At least then I would have been freed of my need to somehow convince Ros to give me more. Of course, had I figured that out in the last few months, none of it would have been an issue.

It felt like a lifetime ago since I struck the deal for our arrangement, but also not.

Some days, I imagined time slipping through my fingers,

scared that I'd wake up one day to find the year had sped by, forcing me to rely on nothing but memory to relive her happy sighs when she had her first cup of coffee in the morning. Or her frustrated huffs when her hair grew too long and annoyed her. Or her unrelenting need to rely on superstition each time she set foot on a red carpet, with no less than six safety pins tucked into her dress — one less for the one I'd stolen as she claimed at our first premiere. I might have tucked that sucker into my own jacket.

She had become a pro at handling the attention her new life brought. I was confident that there was more between us than just incredible sexual chemistry, but still, I wasn't sure if the connection I felt during our quiet moments alone was real or imagined.

"Where is everyone off to over the holidays?" Ros asked as we finished up our main course.

"Shaun and I are heading to Cornwall with Isla to visit our parents and brother," Mona said, her tone excited. She smiled at her sister who sat next to her, an almost picture perfect copy of her now that Mona had allowed her pink hair to grow out. "Mam hasn't seen Cerys since she was a few weeks old. I can't wait to see her reaction when she giggles at her."

Isla grinned. "She's going to cry and I'm going to be ready and waiting with a camera to catch every second."

Ros smiled, but it lasted a fraction of a second before a wistful, sad look took over her face. While everyone laughed, their attention focused on Mona and Isla, I caught Ros's hand in mine beneath the table and squeezed, offering some comfort even though I couldn't fathom why their family plans would make her sad.

She glanced at me, a small smile curling her lips. "I'm okay," she mouthed, squeezing my hand back.

My chest ached at the easy way she accepted the comfort. A few weeks ago, she would have shrugged me off and put on a brave face.

"Cat and I are going to Devon, so she can finally meet my parents," Nathan said, pulling my attention away from Ros. He wrapped an arm around Cat's shoulders. "My mother's been making demands ever since the news broke about us."

"And she's still holding grudges that we didn't go to her when we needed to escape the media attention in Scotland last year." Cat shook her head, amused but seemingly nervous.

"Mothers," Nathan and I groaned at the same time.

Our friends laughed while Nathan shook his head. "She's still in a right strop over it. She forgets I know her. All she wanted was to rub it in reporters' faces that we picked her house to hide in."

Shaun laughed loudly. "I can just hear your Mam now. 'See here you vultures! My famous son isn't here. That's not his car, definitely not his face peering around the curtain upstairs and no, you can't hear his Canadian girlfriend laughing in the kitchen!'" His shrill impersonation made us all crack up again.

"Janet never was a fan of busybodies. Maybe she wanted to punish the press for poking around your business," Finn said.

"I wouldn't put it past her." Nathan bit into his final piece of pig in blanket, amusement crinkling his eyes now. "She loves putting nosy sods in their place."

"It could be worse." Abi leaned back in her chair, grinning.

"Jesus, don't." Finn groaned, dragging a hand across his face.

"Way to bait a hook, Finn." Nathan sat up, his gaze drifting between the two of them. "Spill it, Abs. How is Finn going to suffer in Ireland?"

She bit her lip for all of a second and Finn's expression shifted to one of hope. Then she opened her mouth and smothered it.

"Saoirse already has his baby photo album waiting for me and his mother's promised to finally finish a story she started at the wedding."

"It's not an interesting story," Finn grumbled.

"I beg to differ." Abi crossed her arms, and stared at Finn like he'd lost his mind, which was always possible. "I want to know how the battle ended, Finn."

A grin tugged my lips, memories of their vow renewal in New York washing over me. After one too many whiskeys, Finn's mother decided to spin a tale about his childhood battles against the fairies in her garden.

Naturally, Nathan, Shaun and I were hooked. If we came across something we could hold over each other's head until the end of days, we went after it with desperate grabby hands. We had begged Fiona for the rest of the story, but she'd refused, no matter how much of her favourite top-shelf whiskey we handed out. The woman knew how to hold on to her secrets and use them to her advantage.

Abi glared at her husband. "I'm getting the rest of that story, Finn."

"And here was me worrying she wasn't going to be ready for a full week with the McCarthys." Shaun shook his head, his eyes shimmering with tears of laughter.

Ros glanced around the table as we all nodded our agreements. A snort of laughter fell from her lips, catching us all off guard.

"You're all a bunch of idiots." She shared a smirk with Abi's sister, Eva. "Care to share how you've convinced them, after all this time, that you're some wilting wallflower that needs protecting from the in-laws?"

Abi shrugged. "It was pretty effortless really."

We all swapped confused looks. Ros and Abi shared sneaky smiles that sent warning bells blaring in my brain.

"Abi's a boss at wooing parents," Ros said. Eva nodded her agreement. "She won't be trapped with no escape, she'll be ruling the chaos and directing the inquisition into Finn's childhood within five minutes of arriving in Ireland, I guarantee it."

"Thank you. These idiots couldn't understand it." A soft chuckle slipped past her lips and my heart skipped a beat.

Our lives were so close to perfect. If our arrangement were real, if we could just push beyond friends with benefits, if she would just trust me...

Half the battle was done. We didn't have to worry about

whether our friends got along. My friends were her friends and vice versa.

The guys glanced between the two of us before Nathan cleared his throat. "Is that why you're not going home for Christmas? Scared Ros will win your parents over and they'll be forced to follow through on your fake engagement?"

Her eyes sparkled with amusement, but my cheeks burned. Though that would have been one benefit of going home. Why hadn't I thought of that?

I forced out a laugh, keeping it light. "You caught me. I'm terrified Mam would lock me in the basement until we set a date and paid a hefty deposit on a venue in St Andrews."

Truth was, the thought of going home and fielding more scrutiny made my gut twist with want. How ridiculous was that?

The one girlfriend I'd ever been serious enough about — we'd grown up together.

Finn raised a brow. "So it's not to avoid a certain la—?"

"No. I promised we'd spend Christmas with Ros' father in New York, and that's what I'm going to do."

I narrowed my eyes in warning. We'd agreed my history with Bree was permanently off limits. A few months after I got my big break, she split my heart in two, threw the engagement ring at me and sold my secrets to the gossip rags.

"I've uprooted your life enough, right Ros?" I threw a glance at her, waiting long enough for her nod of agreement. Then I focused back on my friends. "Besides, I'll be home in a few weeks after the BAFTAs so there's nothing for her to get her knickers in a twist over."

Ros chuckled. "They know you're lying, jackass."

Shaun, Finn and Nathan grunted in agreement.

"Aye, but you didn't need to confirm it." I shook my head. "Now they'll ask a million questions and blow up our group chat for the week with awkward bloody questions. Is a peaceful Christmas too much to ask?"

She eyed me a moment before shrugging, seeming to agree.

Until Finn opened his bloody mouth and shoved his foot in it yet again.

"Face it, you've decided that the risk of Ros's father realising you're faking it with his daughter is less traumatising than going home." Finn leaned back in his chair and placed his hands on his head. "I get it. Really I do. I wouldn't want to run into B—"

"Yes, my brother can be an asshole when I have a new woman in my life. You don't need to remind me." My eyes narrowed on him, hopefully conveying how fast I'd end his life if he said her name in front of Ros even once.

While everyone laughed, my gaze settled on Isla. I was one jab away from squirming in my seat like a schoolboy with a secret that I had no interest in Ros discovering. I didn't need to know how she would react learning I'd been engaged before. The longer I could keep her in the dark about my emotional baggage the better.

Once she admitted she loved me and I was sure she wouldn't turn tail and run from the first whiff of emotion, then I'd share it all.

"Isla, didn't I hear something about you reconnecting with Bryce Reid?" I asked, hoping to divert everyone's attention.

Isla blushed and looked down at her plate before responding. "Well, I wouldn't say we're connecting. We had coffee a few days ago, that's all." She glanced up sheepishly. "We've known each other for years. I was actually his agent when he first started his career."

"You ran into Bryce?" Mona asked excitedly, leaning towards her sister. "Why didn't you tell me? Do you want a second chance with him?"

"Of course not," Isla scoffed, but her cheeks flushed even redder. "My life in Glasgow is perfectly fine as it is, thank you very much. Besides, I don't need the chaos of dating a celebrity." She shot a pointed look at Mona. "Though, I do wish you lived closer."

Mona winced. "I'll give you the last part. I miss being close to you too." She reached for her hand across the table before her expression shifted. "But you can't expect us to believe you're truly content without a hint of romance in your life. When you first told me about him, you sounded wistful, sis."

"Exactly." Cat nodded, giving Isla an encouraging smile. "We've all been in your shoes before, thinking we were happy just focusing on our careers. Until something—or someone—changed that."

"Or someone," Eva echoed softly, her tone heavy. "When I was diagnosed with cancer, my entire world turned upside down. My job, which had been my sole focus for so long, suddenly felt so insignificant." She twirled her wine glass, momentarily unable to meet our eyes. "At some point, I realised life's too short to live just for someone else's expectations. I promised myself that I would never do that again after my all-clear. We all need more than work to feel fulfilled."

Nods and murmurs of agreement circled the table, and I found my gaze drifting back to Ros. If she were faced with such a terrifying reality, would she come running to me? Not that I wished illness on either of us, but I knew with certainty that she'd be the first person I would want to turn to.

Eva took a deep breath, sneaking a quick glance at Abi. "I quit my job last week and booked a one-way ticket to Bangkok for the first of January."

Abi's eyes widened in surprise, her hand gripping her fork tightly. "Eva, that's... wow."

"I want to backpack and experience the world the way I always intended to." She bit her lip, staring at Abi with a pleading expression. "I need this, Abs."

Tears welled up in Abi's eyes, and she blinked them back unsuccessfully. Finn and Eva rushed to her side, taking her hands as they tried to comfort her.

"But... what about all the important moments?" Abi mumbled between choked sobs. "What if you aren't back when the baby comes?"

The word 'baby' hung in the air like the scent of pine needles and cinnamon, and all conversation halted. Our eyes darted from Abi to each other, disbelief etched on every face.

"Baby?" I echoed, hardly daring to believe it. Ros shifted in uncomfortably in her seat, her expression carefully controlled. My eyes narrowed. "What do you know, pixie?"

"Don't look at me." She crossed her arms. "I'm a steel trap. Nothing's getting past these lips."

"Abi, are you…" Cat trailed off, unable to finish her question amidst the sudden flurry of emotions.

"Surprise?" Abi managed a weak chuckle, wiping tears from her cheeks. "Finn and I are going to be parents."

"Now? Seriously?" Finn sat back on his heels, grinning as the festive atmosphere filled the room. "You wanted to make a thing of it and you just blurt it out now?" He laughed, shaking his head at Abi's unexpected announcement.

"Shit! I didn't think…" Tears shone in Eva's eyes. "I'm a terrible auntie."

"Hey! Co-auntie!" Ros pushed back her chair and joined the group gathering around Abi. "And you're not terrible. You've held yourself back long enough, Eva."

"I know, but maybe I should cancel the trip. I want to be here for you and the baby," Eva said.

"Absolutely not." Abi shook her head vehemently. "You moved to LA for me; you can't put your life on hold forever because of me."

"Why not?" Eva asked. "You did it for me, didn't you?"

"That was different and you know it." Abi's voice and expression softened. "I'm the older sister. It was my job to look after you, and I'd do it again in a heartbeat. But now's your time to be selfish. You deserve it."

A tense silence stretched between the sisters for a moment, each of them studying the other as though looking for weaknesses and planning their next move.

"Just don't go for longer than six months," Abi said, her voice softening until I had to strain my ears to hear her. "I need you in the room with me."

Eva instantly softened. "Fine, but I want a million photos a day for the next six months."

Abi and Ros laughed.

"I mean it. I want to know every detail. I want to be the obnoxious sister on a video call during your ob/gyn appointments. Clear?"

"Deal," Abi said, sealing it with a hug.

"Congratulations, you two," I said, clapping Finn on the back. "You'll be amazing parents."

"Thank you, Jackson," Abi replied, her smile wobbly but sincere.

Cat studied Ros as she hugged Abi. "You knew. How did you know?"

"I found out a few days before the Beautiful Lies premiere." Abi smiled, her cheeks flushed with excitement as she took Finn's hand in hers. "I slipped up when I called to warn her about Jackson's disappearance from the party." Abi took Ros's hand with a smile. "Thanks for keeping my secret."

"Any time." She grinned before shooting me an amused look. "Told you, no secret's getting past my lips."

I couldn't be happier for our friends, growing in their lives and relationships together, but it put an ache in my chest that I couldn't escape no matter how I tried. It made me wish for impossible things. Particularly, that one day, this fake relationship could become something real. And as I glanced over at Ros, her eyes meeting mine across the table, I wondered if maybe, just maybe, she was starting to feel the same way.

CHAPTER TWENTY

JACKSON

I'd never considered video calls torturous before. They saved me from a hefty commute to the studios time and time again and helped me stay in contact with my family on the other side of the world when I wanted to.

Watching ourselves on the screen, waiting for the moment all five of my immediate family came online raring for an inquisition so intense it would put the press to shame? Yeah, that was torture.

Beside me, Ros fidgeted, her foot tapping against the rug. I set my hand on her knee, stilling her. She shot me a tense smile. "They already hate me for stealing you this holiday, right?"

"Definitely not. It'll be fine," I assured her with more confidence than I felt. "They'll love you straight away."

The screen beeped, and in a blink, the faces of my family filled the screen. My father beamed at me. Iona, my older sister, waved, her eyes bright. Jennifer grinned. She was currently my parents' favourite because she'd made the journey home to Scotland for Christmas. Fraser gave a nod of acknowledgement. And then there was Mam, with her wild curls and a look that could melt steel.

"Jackson, lad. Good to see you!" my dad said, his voice booming through the laptop speakers. "And this must be the lovely lass we've heard so little about!"

My mother squinted at the screen, her bright eyes scanning Ros.

"Jackson Robert Douglas, how could you wait so long to introduce us?" My mother asked, her tone hard and disappointed. "And to get engaged without even a visit." She tutted, shaking her head. "I raised you better, boy."

Heat crept up the back of my neck. December had almost flown by. It was already Christmas Eve, and I'd successfully avoided inflicting this conversation on Ros. But there was no point delaying any longer.

Fraser shook with laughter. "Ooh, someone's in trouble!"

I forced a smile. So much for my family making a good first impression and not scaring Ros off straight out of the gate.

"Everyone, meet Roseline Butler." I gestured to the woman I wanted to love me. "Pixie, welcome to the madhouse."

Iona mouthed "pixie" back at me, her smile growing with delight.

Ros waved. "Nice to meet you all!"

"D'you reckon she's ready for this lot, Jackie?" Fraser teased, a playful glint in his eyes. "Nice to see you again, Ros."

She grinned, leaning closer to the camera. "I'm tougher than I look, I promise."

Fraser chuckled. "Oh, you'll fit right in."

"That's what I've been saying for months, but did any of you listen to me?" Jen shook her head.

"If your brother had used his fancy private plane to introduce us in person, we might have." My mother's tone was cutting.

Guilt ate at me for all of a second before I remembered I'd done it on purpose. I still wanted the first time my parents met Ros in person to be for real. I wanted to be able to answer all of my mother's awkward, hyper-personal questions truthfully.

We'd made progress in the last few weeks, sure, and maybe my hopes of that day coming had risen. But no matter how many times we slept together or how much closer we grew, she still clung to the 'friends' title.

Fraser sighed. "Don't take it personally, Mam, but you're scary. I wouldn't want to inflict that on a woman until I was certain she wouldn't duck and run when the first question came out of your mouth."

I shot Fraser a grateful look for the excuse to cling to. "What can I say, I'm kind of attached to her. Didn't want to scare her off." I nudged Ros. Relief rolled through me when she laughed.

My mother rolled her eyes but let it go with surprising ease. I eyed the screen, searching for signs of mulled wine. It was midday on Christmas Eve in LA but with Scotland being eight hours ahead, it would be the perfect time for my mother's famed Christmas drinks to make an appearance.

"How did you two meet?" My dad asked from his armchair by the fireplace. "Jackson's been rather tight-lipped about the details."

I glanced at Ros and waited, content to let her decide how much she wanted to give. After a second, she met my gaze with a teasing smirk.

"I was a co-maid of honour at Finn and Abi's wedding," she said, her eyes twinkling with mischief. "And when I walked into this beautiful venue, I saw Jackson across the room in his tux, and I thought, 'there's a man I need to get to know.'"

Fraser let out a whistle. "A woman who knows what she wants. I like it."

"We locked eyes, and I swear I got chills." Her eyes glazed over as if she was remembering the day and she smiled. The sight of it made me harden. "I mean, who wouldn't? Look at him."

Iona laughed. "She's got a point, Jackie. You do clean up nicely."

I chuckled, nudging her shoulder. "As I remember it, you

barely glanced my way after that. Not until after the ceremony when you came charging over to give me a piece of your mind about Finn not messing with Abi."

"Hey, someone had to defend Abi's heart from possible TV playboys."

"Then she cornered me, hissing threats like a riled-up mama bear. Told me straight out she'd make me suffer if Finn messed with Abi." I shook my head, memories washing over me sharp and clear. "Pretty sure I started falling for you right then and there, pixie."

She stared into my eyes, her gaze searching. I hoped she could see beyond the words, beyond the façade of our arrangements. Fake relationship, friends with benefits, none of it mattered.

I meant every word.

ROS

"What are your intentions towards my son?"

I blinked at the question. There was a gigantic, garish diamond on my finger. What more did she want?

"Oh, you know, planning to break his heart and run off with all his Hollywood millions." I shrugged, letting my smile soften the words. "The usual."

Fraser sniggered and Jackson covered his mouth, hiding a smile. His mother, however, looked less than impressed.

My amusement melted away and I adopted a more serious tone. "I'm not sure what you want to hear. I agreed to marry him. What else is there?"

In one box, Jen rolled her eyes.

"Don't mind Mam, she flipped into hardcore wedding planning mode in her head the second any of us turned eighteen," Jen said. "Every girl Jackson blinks at gets the full interrogation."

Jackson's mother waved her hand, scowling. "I need to be sure this one will stick! Jackson's got a talent for mucking up anything good in his life."

Ouch.

Without thinking, I grabbed his hand and squeezed, threading our fingers in solidarity. Just like that, his shoulders relaxed. He released my hand and tugged me back into his chest, wrapping an arm around me.

He pressed a chaste kiss to the top of my head, squeezing me against his warmth. I should have been stronger, but my heart gave up the fight. It rolled over for him.

Time to show Morag I had some backbone… while a six-foot-four Scottish hunk used me as his teddy bear.

I smiled sweetly. "Well lucky for you, I have zero plans of letting your son escape me any time soon."

Jackson's warmth cocooned me, his breath tickling my ear and sending delicious shivers down my spine.

I tuned back into the video call to catch the tail end of Jackson smoothly steering the conversation towards our Christmas plans, or more to the point, the lack of our presence on Scottish soil.

Jackson's mother sighed, feigning disappointment. "Are you sure you won't be able to join us for Christmas at all?"

"I'm sorry, Mam." He shook his head, grimacing. "We're heading to New York for Christmas."

A pang of guilt hit me in the gut. I bit my cheek before I let slip that I'd rather be getting on a plane to Scotland tonight than condemning myself to a week with my dad.

My father wasn't the easiest person to be around, especially considering his history. He had cheated on my mother, causing a messy divorce when I was eight. Then, my mother passed away when I was twelve, leaving me with no choice but to live with my dad and my stepmother.

"Ah, I see." His mother tried to mask her disappointment with a smile. "A New York Christmas. It sounds... lovely. It'll be an interesting change I'm sure."

Lovely and interesting my ass. The woman looked ready to reach through the screen and drag us both to Scotland by our ears.

"Oh, I'd love to spend Christmas in New York." Absolute delight filled Iona's expression. Her mother scowled at the excitement in her voice. "Is it like the scenes we see in films, with people ice-skating in Central Park and the skyscrapers lit up in twinkling lights?"

I pulled a face. "It's not as glamorous as the movies make it out to be. My dad lives in a quiet area. I try to avoid New York City during Christmas."

Still, the sudden urge to see the Rockefeller Christmas tree, taking in all the lights with Jackson's hand in mine filled me. Crowds and all.

"Oh, I didn't think of that." Iona's happy expression fell. "I'd hate to visit Edinburgh this week too."

"I never spend Christmas away from my father and the city's not the point of it really. It's the only time of year we get to spend time together since my mother passed."

It was a half-truth. I always went to my dad for the holidays, but it wasn't exactly by choice. The complexities of our relationship and the unresolved emotions from my childhood made these visits more of a duty than a joy.

She softened at the explanation.

"Besides, it's not like you have to wait long to meet Ros," Jackson said, and his mother perked right up.

"Oh?"

"We'll be in London for the BAFTA ceremony in a few weeks, and we're planning to spend a week in St Andrews after it's done."

Say what now?

Nowhere in our shared calendar did it say we'd be spending a week in a foreign country. I shot him a sidelong glance, and he gave me a sheepish smile.

"Did I forget to mention that?" he asked.

My brows climbed. "Maybe."

"So, you're planning on sticking around until the end of January, then?" his dad asked, a glint of hope in his eyes.

Jackson held up my hand flashing the engagement ring. "What the bloody hell do you think this means? Of course, she's sticking around."

His father grunted. "A sparkly piece of jewellery means nothing and you well know it." He leaned forward and dropped his voice as if no one else on the call would be able to hear him. "Time's ticking, and your mother is eager for some grandbairns."

I blinked, my mind struggling to catch up with the sudden shift in conversation. Bairns? What the hell was a bairn?

Jackson choked. "One step at a time. Let us marry before we start thinking about kids."

Kids? Seriously? We hadn't decided on a fake wedding date, and now we were talking about spawning little Douglases?

Absolute delight blanketed his mother's expression and she started talking a mile a minute, her Scottish accent getting so deep, I couldn't pick up a word.

The laughter erupted from the screen, hearty and full of amusement. Jackson's siblings found it all too entertaining.

Jackson's neck turned a lovely shade of red, and he mumbled something about needing to check the oven. Smooth, real smooth. He stood up, leaving me alone with his family, who were still chuckling like a bunch of hyenas.

I shifted uncomfortably in my seat, glancing around the room for inspiration. Steering conversations away from awkward topics was not my strong suit. Usually, I'd be the girl brazenly blazing ahead while everyone else squirmed.

It also didn't help that my mind had latched onto the image of a little Jackson with blond hair running around the house, up to mischief like a child of mine would be.

Ridiculous longing filled me. I didn't know if he felt the same way or wanted real commitment and a family. We'd never talked about any of it. We had a contract. One year of my time. Nowhere in that contract did it mention kids. Or marriage for that matter, but that hadn't stopped Audra tacking an engagement onto our plans.

And yet... that mental picture of a child with his eyes and smile wouldn't fade. It scared me how easily I envisioned our life together. Made me wonder if I'd fallen for this fantasy relationship harder than I realised.

One thing was certain though... it was getting harder and harder to remember this thing between me and Jackson was strictly make-believe. And that terrified me more than any disapproving future in-laws.

CHAPTER TWENTY-ONE

ROS

Our journey to New York ended faster than I would have liked. When the plane touched down, Jackson had to pry me out of my seat with the promise of a black and white cookie. How he'd known I could be bribed with food, I couldn't say, but I enjoyed the benefits while the cookie lasted.

Then his fancy hired SUV pulled up outside my father's old semi-detached triplex house. Nothing fancy compared to Jackson's cliffside mansion back in LA. Just a narrow three-storey row house packed tightly between others on the street. The happy baked goods-induced buzz evaporated.

"You know, we could do another lap of the block? He's not expecting us yet," I said, an annoying edge of desperation leaking into my voice.

Jackson shook his head, smiling like he thought I was joking. The man should have known me better by now.

"Or maybe even find a hotel."

I slapped my forehead, instantly furious at myself. Why had I thought we needed to stay with my father when I was 'engaged' to a millionaire? Dammit.

"It's going to be okay." Jackson shuffled towards me with a determined glint in his eyes.

He rested his elbow on the top to the seat and leaned forward, effectively caging me in. A shiver raced through me as his sea breeze scent filled my lungs. Fuck.

My gaze dipped to his plump, kissable lips. The urge to close the gap between us and taste him without a camera pointed at us was overwhelming.

But would it really be so wrong to take what I wanted?

We'd already spent countless hours in bed. He knew my body better than any man at this point. I regularly started my day kissing him.

But this was different.

If I kissed him now, it would be more personal than I'd allowed us to get. It would be an emotional support kiss. I would be asking him to distract me while supporting me through something I really didn't want to do.

That wasn't something friends with benefits did.

Jackson must have seen something in my gaze because it darkened with desire a second before he ran a thumb over one cheek.

"I'm sure your father will love me," he whispered. "Just give me a chance."

The wrongness of his words snapped me out of my lust-filled haze.

"What? No!" I leaned back, my gaze roaming his face with confusion. "It's not you I'm worried about, Jackson." I winced as the lie sat thick on my tongue. "Okay, so part of it's about you. I... don't expect too much, okay? My family is nothing like yours."

"Okay?" he said, his tone confused. Then a slight frown creased his forehead. "I'm not judging anyone. I'm here because I want to be with you. It doesn't matter where you come from."

I'm here because I want to be with you.

Those words struck me hard. Did I dare take them at face

value? My heart desperately wanted me to, but my sensible brain wouldn't let go of the past. It held far too many memories of the men in my life lulling me into a false sense of safety before leaving me once they got what they wanted.

We've only got a year. After that, he wouldn't need me anymore. I'm not sure I'd survive the heartbreak if Jackson turned out to be the same as every man before him.

Jackson cupped my face, forcing me to meet his eyes. "I mean it. I'm not here to judge. I'm here for you."

I pushed away from him, a familiar wall snapping back into place. "We'll see."

He sighed, but didn't push the issue.

With a soft click, the driver opened Jackson's door. I took a deep breath and followed him out onto the sidewalk. The street looked the same as always, a line of semi-detached houses with varying shades of mismatched bricks, each trying to outdo the other in a game of architectural one-upmanship.

Ours was one with a garage terrace and a collection of plants that were supposed to be decorative but really were trying too hard. The old building showed signs of wear and neglect. Unsurprising, considering my family had never had a lot of money to spare. Had my dad not bought the house at the right time, he would have been priced out of Queens by now.

I headed towards the trunk to retrieve our bags. However, Jackson was quick to catch up, his hand gently circling my wrist to stop me.

"I've got this," he said, his voice low and reassuring.

He reached past me, effortlessly grabbing my duffle bag. It was a simple gesture, but the unexpected warmth it sent through me caught me off guard. This was Jackson Levi, the Hollywood heartthrob, voluntarily carrying my bag as if it weighed nothing.

"Thanks," I muttered, trying to shake off the strange flutter in my chest.

He smiled, his eyes soft with understanding. It was a small

thing, but it felt like he was shouldering more than my bag — as if he was silently saying, "I've got you."

We climbed the steps to the house, dread consuming me. Why hadn't I insisted on spending Christmas in Scotland or even LA? Anything would have been better than bringing Jackson home to my dad and step-monster.

"Ready?" Jackson asked, sensing my hesitation.

I swallowed hard and nodded, fighting to keep my voice steady. "As ready as I'll ever be."

Reaching out, I knocked on the door. The sound echoed through my chest, amplifying my nervousness. For a moment, time stood still and a speck of hope bloomed in my chest. Maybe they weren't in. Maybe they'd gone on vacation and forgotten to tell me.

The door swung open, snuffing out the hope.

"Hey, sweetheart!" Dad pulled me into a bear hug, squeezing me tight and confusing the shit out of me all at once.

We didn't hug. Ever.

As he released me, he shot Jackson an approving look. "Jackson Levi." Dad shook his head, absolute wonder shining in his eyes. "I'd seen all the press, of course, and Ros told me you'd be coming, but seeing it is a whole other level." He blew out a shaky breath and held his hand out. "Nice to meet you."

"Likewise, sir." Jackson shook his hand, chuckling at his wide-eyed starstruck expression.

"Please, call me Hank." He took my bag from Jackson before he could protest. "Come on in. Warm up. It's bone-chilling out there."

Surprise rushed through me at how easy it had been. Maybe this could work.

We followed Dad into the living room, past the first of many walls lined with embarrassing photos of me. The scent of cinnamon and vanilla hit me along with a wave of heat from the fireplace. Cheryl must have been baking something, a stark contrast to the cold exterior of the house. And the woman herself.

Stepping inside this house always left me with a horrible sense of stepping back in time. Nothing had changed—not the furniture and certainly not the faded floral wallpaper that looked like it had come straight out of an 80s catalogue.

And definitely not the lingering tension from my dysfunctional youth. It permeated everything, despite the tempting scents of Cheryl's holiday baking.

"I thought you were getting rid of that old recliner."

He chuckled. "You know it's the most comfortable seat in the house."

"Yeah, if you're into time travel."

Jackson laughed as he glanced around. "I like it. Adds a unique touch."

I smirked at him. "Unique or a health hazard?"

Dad's laughter grew heartier. He leaned against the doorframe, eyes crinkling at the corners. "Careful, Ros. That 'health hazard' once rocked you to sleep."

I raised an eyebrow. "Rocked is an overstatement. More like threatened to collapse under my weight."

"So, it's a vintage rocking recliner?" Jackson asked.

Dad nodded, still grinning. "Exactly! Ros just fails to appreciate its unique ergonomic design."

For a fleeting second, I relaxed, a warmth settling in my chest. It was a welcome reprieve, a departure from the strained conversations we'd had since Dad cheated and tore our family apart.

He seemed different, more like the father I used to know. I didn't know what was worse, remembering it or experiencing it with the weight of nostalgia colouring something that was once pure.

Cheryl's arrival shattered the peace. She walked in with a too-bright smile plastered on her face, her eyes zeroing in on Jackson.

"Oh my, it's really you! Cheryl Thompson, Ros's stepmom." She raced towards him, holding out her hand to shake and instead pulled him into a hug when he wasn't expecting it. "I'm such a huge fan. I've seen all your movies," she gushed, like an unhinged fangirl.

The urge to gag burned through me at her fawning tone. It was a look, just not one I'd ever expected to see on her. With a polite smile, Jackson shrugged her off and stepped away.

"Thank you so much for having us." He flashed that 10,000-watt smile guaranteed to weaken knees and quicken heart rates. "I can't tell you how grateful I am to spend Christmas with Ros. I couldn't bear the thought of being separated from her during the holidays." He shot me an affectionate look, smoothly playing up the doting fiancé role.

He shrugged off Cheryl's grip on his hand and pulled me close, pressing a lingering kiss to my temple while I struggled not to melt under the attention. The man deserved an Oscar for this performance — Dad gazed at him starry-eyed.

Cheryl, on the other hand, had a different agenda.

"Well, isn't that lovely. Why don't you come sit next to me and we can chat?" She reached for his hand again and tried to pull Jackson away from me, towards the couch, a little too eager for my liking. "I want to hear all about your life in Hollywood. Do you know any other celebrities?"

"There'll be plenty of time for all that later." Dad, bless him, stepped into her path and forced her to let go of Jackson. "Let them get settled, love. You can interrogate the man while we eat."

She released him and Dad turned back to us, gesturing to the stairs.

We followed him up the narrow stairs, the worn carpet doing nothing to silence the creaking wood. The walls were lined with family photos documenting every embarrassing phase of my life. As we passed a particularly cringe-worthy photo of a preteen me in braces and an ill-fitting haircut, Dad chuckled.

"Ah, the braces phase." He paused to helpfully point at the picture. He grinned at me over his shoulder. "Ros insisted on getting neon green bands. Said it was a fashion statement."

I groaned, my cheeks heating. "Thanks for sharing that with

the world, Dad."

Jackson laughed. "Neon green? That must have taken guts. I'm impressed."

"Ros was always so... unique growing up," Cheryl said in a sweet tone that barely masked her disdain. "Never quite fitting in with the other girls, right, dear?"

I clenched my jaw, trying to hold myself back. Normally, I'd shut down her shitty comments without a moment's thought, but with Jackson here... for the first time in my life, I was worried about tainting someone's view of me.

"That's what makes her special, though," Jackson said, his voice pitched louder than hers. "She's never been afraid to be herself."

"And here's the infamous prom photo. Ros insisted on going with blue hair, much to the horror of the entire school."

My eyes narrowed, but before I snapped at her, Jackson glanced over his shoulder and smirked at me. "I love it. Maybe we should both dye our hair for the BAFTA ceremony. Can you imagine Audra's reaction?"

The man was a pro at deflecting bullshit. How had I not realised that?

When we got to the landing, Dad clapped Jackson on the back, a proud glint in his eye. "See, Jackson appreciates your uniqueness, just like I do."

With a warning glance at Cheryl, Dad swung my bedroom door open. "Here we are — Ros's room, exactly as she left it."

With her attempts to shame me backfiring, she snuck back down the stairs, but not before I spotted the flush of red on her neck.

I stepped into my room, riding on cloud nine. Nothing could touch me.

Nothing but the sight of my teenage haven in all its cringe-worthy glory.

The pink walls assaulted my eyes, plastered with posters of boy bands from the early 2000s as if they stood a chance at shielding the room from the pink invasion. Stuffed toys huddled in a corner. My white vanity table bore the battle scars of my black nail polish rebellion.

"You really had a thing against pink, huh?" Jackson's amused voice broke through my silent horror.

I shot him a wry smile. "More like pink had a thing against me."

He strolled further into the room, eyes scanning the peculiar mix of rebellion and remnants of adolescence. His fingers traced the chipped edges of the black-stained table. "The black nail polish is a nice touch."

I shrugged, feigning nonchalance. "Had to add a bit of edge to combat the overwhelming girly vibe."

My dad, standing at the doorway, chuckled. "Ros always had a flair for the dramatic."

"Still does," Jackson said, smiling at me. My stomach somersaulted at the sight of it.

The room shrunk, closing in on us, and my insides turned mushy.

"Alright you two, dinner will be ready in about an hour," Dad said, his tone chipper and totally oblivious to the tension in the room. "Why don't you get settled and meet us downstairs when you're ready? We can have some drinks and catch up."

I tore my gaze away from Jackson's and let it wander across the room. It settled on the bed. The small double bed built for a teenager.

We hadn't broken a single rule since starting our new arrangement. No sleepovers. Jackson had half-heartedly tried to talk me into staying in his bed multiple times in the last few weeks, but I had always resisted.

The thought of lying next to him, feeling his warmth and knowing how much I craved his touch, didn't send my mind spiralling into a whirlwind of conflicting emotions.

Definitely not.

That itchy, buzzing feeling in my chest was just…

Oh hell. Maybe, just maybe, breaking this one little rule wouldn't be the end of the world. It was just one week, right?

I grimaced at how I was trying to justify it to myself.

"Well, good." Dad stepped into my room long enough to grab the door handle. "Dinner's in an hour. Get settled then come down for drinks — I want to know all about the wedding plans!" Oblivious as ever, he closed the door and left us, staring at the bed.

The room felt smaller, the pink walls almost closing in on us. I glanced at the double bed again, mentally measuring the distance between Jackson and me. There wouldn't even be an inch of space between us.

The air in the room shifted, charged with an unexpected tension. I glanced at Jackson, who appeared unsure about our predicament. My pulse quickened, a strange mix of anxiety and excitement bubbling within me.

He cleared his throat. "I can always sleep on the floor," Jackson said, his tone polite, and I could sense the faintest trace of awkwardness in his eyes. "It's not a problem."

I waved off his suggestion with a casual shrug, my best attempt at maintaining an air of nonchalance. "Nah, it's cool. We're adults. We can share a bed all night without catching feelings."

The words sounded casual, but my heart was playing a drumbeat of its own. What did it mean if we shared a bed all night, outside the bounds of our friends with benefits agreement? Did it mean something more? And why did the idea of it send a surprising wave of excitement through me?

He looked at me, eyebrows slightly raised, as if he were gauging my reaction. "If you're sure. I honestly don't mind the floor."

"Yeah, no big deal," I said, my voice a little too high-pitched, even to my own ears.

"Besides," he added, grinning at me with a glint of heat in his eyes. "I'm sure we can find creative ways to fit on that bed."

"Jackson!" My face burned. "Not in my father's house."

His laughter filled the room, dissipating some of the tension.

CHAPTER TWENTY-TWO

JACKSON

*I*f I were a believer in godly entities, I'd have to sacrifice a pig at the next full moon. I needed to thank someone for my stroke of good luck at least and I didn't think Ros's father would be amused if I clapped him on the back in gratitude.

One bed.

The thought played on a loop in my mind, drowning out Cheryl's prying questions. It made dealing with my mother's annoyance and swapping balmy Los Angeles for frigid New York more than worth it.

One bed meant a whole blissful week falling asleep beside my prickly pixie instead of alone. It was all I'd wanted for weeks.

Through most of the meal, her stepmother's eyes were fixed on me like I was the main course. The Christmas decorations cast a festive glow over the dining room, but Cheryl's relentless interrogation threatened to dampen the holiday spirit. The questions started innocently enough, but after her disgusting treatment of Ros when we arrived, I should have known it wouldn't stay that way.

"You know, I heard a rumour about your friend Shaun Martin," she said. "But of course, I didn't believe it."

I wiped my mouth with the napkin, stalling. "That's good because most of the things the tabloids print are absolute fiction."

"Absolutely," Cheryl agreed, nodding as if we were sharing some profound secret. Her eyes, however, bore into me like she was trying to crack a code. "So he's not an alcoholic?"

I stifled a sigh, resisting the urge to roll my eyes. "Not at all. Just tabloid nonsense."

Of course, he had been once. He hadn't touched a drop in three years. Maybe that still made him an alcoholic, but I refused to hand this vile woman details about my friends' personal lives.

"But surely it's not all nonsense?" She leaned in, her eyes sparkling with curiosity. "You did get into a fight with Chris Sanderson last week on the Jimmy Michaels Show, didn't you?"

"That show is based out of New York." My brow furrowed. "We were in LA last week."

"Really?" She straightened up, almost affronted by the truth. "I could have sworn... never mind." She smiled, the edges brittle and cold. "But that woman, what was her name?" Her eyes fell shut as she massaged her temples, searching her clearly wonky memories. Then they popped open, excitement skittering across her face. "Oh, that's right. Sammy Miller. That was it."

My fingers twitched at the mention of the woman who had tried to destroy my career based on a lie. Ros's hand found mind beneath the table, but I didn't dare look away from her pathetic excuse of a stepmother.

"How can you be engaged to my stepdaughter if you had an affair with a married woman three months ago?" Cheryl lowered her voice conspiratorially but her eyes glinted with relish. "I heard her husband's divorcing her because of it, poor man!"

Hank paused with a forkful of food almost to his mouth. His eyes narrowed while he waited for my response. Ros gritted her teeth, ready to jump in on my behalf, but I squeezed her hand, warning her not to.

"If you're wasting your time with the gossip rags, then you already know she admitted to making it all up for a payday." My jaw clenched. "It was well-publicised. But I guess some prefer the dramatic version."

Ros's grip tightened on my hand. I glanced at her, offering a reassuring smile that only grew when I clocked the annoyance burning in her eyes. Her dad nodded to himself at my answer, visibly relaxing.

"Jackson, you don't have to—" she started, but I cut her off.

"It's fine, pixie. Some people have nothing better to do than buy into the scandals." I turned back to Cheryl, carefully neutralising my expression. "I'm betting she has the headlines memorised. Care to share your favourite? I always get a kick out of seeing their latest work of fiction."

Ros tutted. "Maybe something about how aliens are secretly running Hollywood?"

Cheryl's eyes narrowed, the gears in her head audibly whirring. The room settled into an awkward silence, tension mingling with the aroma of Christmas ham.

"Well, I—"

"Enough, Cheryl." Hank picked up his glass, fixing her with a hard look. "It's Christmas. Let's not ruin it with rumours and tabloid nonsense."

Cheryl mustered a tight-lipped smile, her eyes gleaming with an underlying determination. She shifted her attention, attempting to present an image of the perfect hostess.

The fact Ros had ever chosen to spend a week in this house with so much hostility shocked me.

Had I known I would have forced Audra to find a different plan. A week in some Caribbean resort maybe.

Ros leaned in until her mouth hovered near my ear, her voice a soft murmur meant only for me. "Sorry about that. She can't resist stirring the pot, especially when it comes to me."

I chuckled, a low rumble escaping me. "No need to apologise." I pressed my forehead against hers, smiling at the concern in her eyes, but loving that I got to do this, that she let me get this close with other people around. "I've faced worse than a nosy step-mother. Besides, it's not like I don't have a few tricks up my sleeve."

She smirked. "Oh, do tell."

I shifted to whisper in her ear, my lips grazing the shell on purpose. She shivered and I pretended not to notice. "Let's just say, if Cheryl wants drama, we can give her a show worth watching."

A hint of a blush coloured her cheeks, and the corners of her lips quirked. Before I got distracted imagining ways to prolong the glow, she leaned away from me and changed the subject.

"Do you know what happened to Mom's veil, Dad?" she asked. "I'd love to use it for the wedding if possible."

Hank's expression softened. "Of course. I think it's in the attic somewhere."

"I think that old thing went to Goodwill years ago," Cheryl said, barely hiding her smirk.

Hank's gaze darted to her, shock momentarily blanketing his features. "It had better not." His voice shook, gruff and loud. "Why would you have even touched it? Meredith left all her things to Ros."

She froze, panic flickering across her face before she got it under control and forced a plastic smile to her lips. "You're abso-lutely right, darling. I must be thinking of something else."

He stared at her, uncertainty deepening the lines around his eyes. For a couple of seconds, the creaking of the pipes and the crackle of the wood in the fireplace filled the tense void in conversation.

Ros cleared her throat. "It's okay if you can't find it."

Her hesitant voice snapped Hank from his staring contest with Cheryl.

"Nonsense, love." He smiled, but it didn't reach his eyes. "I'll dig it out before you leave." He reached for his glass again, only this time he lifted it up, his expectant gaze fixed on us. "But speaking of wedding plans… to Jackson and Ros, congratulations on your engagement."

We raised our glasses, clinking them together. Cheryl managed a tight smile.

"Though, I have to admit," Hank continued after taking a sip, "I always thought you were against relationships entirely," he said, his brow furrowed. "Imagine my surprise hearing about your engagement."

Ros nodded, her gaze wavering between me and her dad. "It surprised me too."

I bit my cheek.

Cheryl left the room, making excuses about preparing dessert.

"I suppose I didn't expect my rebellious daughter to dive head-first into matrimony. But if you're happy, that's what matters." He leaned back in his chair, his expression shifting from surprise to something more sad. "I've made my fair share of mistakes. Cheated on your mom, leading a double life for years. Acting like a complete idiot, yo-yoing between Cheryl and her."

Ros's jaw clenched as her gaze dropped to her lap, her fingers tracing patterns on the table, anything not to look at her father.

"I blamed your mom for things I shouldn't have," Hank said regretfully.

She snorted. "Understatement."

"Looking back now," he continued, his voice firm, "I see how much damage I did by acting the way I did."

There was something about watching a grown man slowly fall apart… like a car crash but with emotions.

He scrubbed a hand down his face, shame darkening his eyes. "No matter how I tried, I couldn't let Cheryl go despite all the wreckage. I was a right fool, too caught up in my own selfish needs to realise what I was losing."

The more he talked, the more my eyes widened and the pieces fell into place. Ros scowled at him with something close to fury twisting her expression, but me? A misplaced jolt of excitement coursed through me.

It wasn't because of me.

Hank sighed heavily, the sound punctuating the awkward tension now swirling around the dinner table. "So when you got older and never dated anyone seriously, I worried I'd broken your trust in men forever."

She hadn't rejected *me*. She'd rejected the idea, the concept of a relationship and all the emotional attachments that would come. When this family visit ended, I'd lay myself bare and prove once and for all that I was all in if she'd have me.

Hank stared at Ros, waiting for her to speak, to say anything. Instead, she clung to my hand, her lips set in a hard line while a tremor worked through her body. Her neck burned red and I didn't need to know much about body language to figure this one out. We were moments away from an eruption and there was nothing I could do about it.

"Over the years, I've learnt a thing or two—"

She snorted. "If only you could have learnt those things *before* you destroyed your family."

"I'm trying, Ros." Hank stared at her, his expression plainly begging for her forgiveness or at least patience. Her lips firmed, refusing to give it. "As I was saying, none of it will ever mean more than this: Life is short. We have to grab every moment, every happy second, and hold on tight." Panic flitted across his face when Ros's stony expression darkened. "You never know what'll happen tomorrow or next week or next year. But right now, in this moment, you know you have someone who loves you for who you are."

How would he react if he knew all the sordid details that had brought us here?

"I know I let you down when it came to being a role model for what a man should be," her dad said, his voice full of regret. "But Jackson's different. I can see that."

She laughed, the sound bitter and disbelieving. "How the hell would you know? You just met him. For all you know he could be getting ready to fleece me like every other man I've ever been involved with."

Never mind the fact the only thing I was interested in stealing was her heart.

Hank reared back like she'd slapped him. "Then I have more faith in you than you do." His eyes turned glassy. "I'm sorry, sweetheart, I wish I could go back and change it all."

She snorted. "No, you wouldn't."

His mouth dropped open for a second before his brain caught up with his mouth. "Of course I would."

Her brows arched. "You married her!" She nodded at Cheryl. "You made a choice that rewarded you for being a shitty husband and father. Why would I believe a word you said?"

I wanted to step in and say something, anything to make the situation less tense, but the last thing I wanted to do was make Ros think I didn't support her.

"And how the hell can you say any of that with a straight face?" Ros scowled at her half-eaten plate, shaking her head. "You had someone who loved you for who you were, and you cheated on her and lied about it for years." The look of absolute devastation on her face near enough ripped my heart out. I'd do anything to never see it again. "You're hardly the person to tell me what I should and shouldn't do or believe."

"Now wait," her father spluttered as she pushed back her chair and stood, dropping my hand. "Sit back down, Roseline. We can fix this. I know we can."

"I'm not that optimistic," she said, her tone heavy with sadness.

Her gaze landed on me, pleading and desperate. I would do anything for her if she just kept looking at me like that. I stood too, my gaze roaming her face as I waited for her next move.

"Don't do anything rash. We can talk about this," Hank said, panic claiming his voice.

"Maybe in the morning. I'm too tired right now."

She stared up at me with a question in her eyes I couldn't read.

Was she trying to tell me she wanted to leave, go to a hotel, back to LA? Or did she want to stay and face them in the morning? I couldn't ask her any of that right now, so I settled for wrapping my arm around her and leading her out of the room. What else didn't I know about Roseline Butler?

CHAPTER TWENTY-THREE

ROS

I raced up the stairs with an intense pressure building behind my eyes while anger pulsed inside of me. If I'd stuck it out and finished dinner, I would have broken down crying and made Cheryl's day. That witch loved to rub it in when she thought she'd gotten to me.

Why did I have to be an angry crier? Of all the things I could have inherited from my mother, why did it have to be that?

The argument had been a long time coming, but fuck, I wished I could go on avoiding it. My dad couldn't see reality, only what Cheryl manipulated him into believing. At first, I'd tried to correct it, but the more I tried, the worse life at home got for me. The insults, the constant nitpicking about my food choices, my fashion sense, my friends — *Why can't you be like normal girls, Roseline? If you were prettier, you'd be popular. Maybe if you stopped listening to depressing emo music, you'd be invited to prom.*

So I stopped trying.

I moved out. I dodged phone calls and texts, sent vague thank you notes to my dad if a random package turned up at my apartment. I'm ashamed to say I became the person who ducked into businesses, crossed the road or hid in a crowd to avoid the smallest interaction that might evolve into an invite to a torture session.

The only one I couldn't escape had always been Christmas.

Except when I lived in New York, I had an excuse to go home after dinner. I guess we could have gone back to my apartment. Jackson had paid the rent for the year. But I really didn't want to deal with Audra when we didn't follow her plans to the letter.

Besides, call me cheesy if you like, but the only thing that had made this time bearable was Jackson. With him here, I'd discovered this crazy belief that I could face anything and anyone — not just face, but best.

We entered my old room and Jackson shut the door behind me. I stared at the pile of stuffed animals, my mind turning to ways I could rid myself of the pulsing anger without taking it out on my father. *Would it be immature of me to throw toys around?*

"Are you okay?" he asked, his voice pitched low.

"Define okay."

I turned towards him, my face scrunched up as I tried to figure out how to answer him without making him think I'd devolved into a teenager having a temper tantrum.

"Do you want to leave?"

I stared at him for a second, shock working its way through my system, calming me. "You would do that?"

He nodded. "If you don't want to be here, we'll leave."

My mouth went dry at the sincerity in his eyes. He meant every word and I couldn't fathom it. My eyes started burning again but this time with overwhelming joy.

Shit. I'd always had such good control of my emotions. Why did it have to slip now?

I focused hard on his chest, fighting the pressure back before I legit lost control and buried my face in his lovely chest to blubbered all over him.

"Just say the word."

My focus jumped back to his face. "Where would we go?" I asked, my voice weak.

"A hotel in New York? Back to Los Angeles? Bora Bora." He shrugged. "I don't care as long as you're happy."

"I—"

Words failed me. Other than Abi and Eva, no one — especially no man — had ever had my back like that. I thought men only said things like that in cheesy rom-coms. They certainly never directed it towards me.

Until now.

Not that I needed saving. But it felt... nice, I guess. Having someone in my corner, not wanting a damn thing in return.

Except maybe I wanted him to want things in return. Maybe I wanted to give the tiny ball of fragile emotion in my chest room to grow more attached to him.

I'd underestimated Jackson Levi. As we stood there, surrounded by the relics of my rebellious era, memories flashed through my mind. Not just the trips to thrift stores or the super exclusive dinner reservations, but the times he showed real support and tried to bring genuine happiness into my life — things I never expected when we started this fake relationship.

And I'd wasted how long protecting myself from this Carebear of a man?

I wanted to kick myself.

Instead, I rose up on my toes and reached for him, locking my hands behind the nape of his neck and pulling his lips down to meet mine. I channelled every regret into it, gliding my lips slowly over his, waiting, hoping he'd reciprocate and I hadn't imagined it all.

For a moment, he froze. His hands rested on my hips, supporting me, but he didn't kiss me back. My heart ached with the sting of rejection and I started to pull away, my mind rushing to come up with some excuse that wouldn't make the rest of our time together awkward.

"Ros," he groaned.

His hand threaded into my hair while his other arm wrapped around my waist, crushing me against his chest with an air of desperation. His lips reclaimed mine, instantly deepening the contact and stealing my breath.

I melted against him, content to let him take the lead. His tongue teased mine, coaxing me into a slow dance that rid me of all worries, all annoyances — nothing existed beyond the press of his body.

He groaned as I shifted against him, rubbing myself shamelessly against the growing bulge in his jeans. I moaned as he tugged at my hair in response.

The small noises he made against my mouth drove me wild. With every flick of his tongue, my heart raced faster and faster. His hold around me tightened, one hand still cradling the back of my head while the other explored every inch of me the way he loved to do.

When he finally broke away, leaving us both gasping for air, he whispered against my lips, "Well, that was pleasantly unexpected."

I chuckled. "I'm just keeping you on your toes, Levi. Can't have you getting too comfortable."

He leaned his forehead against mine and for a moment we stood there in blissful silence. His warmth wrapped around me, and the steady rise and fall of his chest matched the calming circles his hands traced on my back. It was a moment of reprieve, a break from the whirlwind of family drama.

But, like an annoying song stuck in my head, thoughts of Dad and Cheryl's behaviour at dinner snuck back in. The bitterness and irritation returned, ruining the moment.

I thought about Dad, lying to Mom while he cheated on her. Fooling himself, thinking Cheryl could ever be someone other than the vile human she was, that he could fix the damage his actions had done to me. It was the same old story.

Then it hit me hard. Pretending not to be interested in Jackson beyond friendship and scratching an itch? That was a lie too.

"I'm not like them," I whispered.

He smiled and squeezed me. "I know."

"No," I said, my tone overly harsh. "I mean I am *not* and will *never* be like them." I stared into his gorgeous eyes and willed him to forgive me. "I want to live my life as open and honestly as humanly possible and I've been lying to you."

"How so?" His brows rose.

He released me, taking a cautious step back.

"I want you," I rushed to say, my turn to feel the pull of desperation. "Really want you. Not just as some side perk. I've wanted you since forever, since the wedding." He smirked at my confession but remained silent so I continued, "I thought I knew better so I suppressed it and lied to you, but if I keep doing that I'm no better than him."

"You're nothing like them, pixie."

"Yes, I am." I nodded hard. "I lied to you. He lied to my mother for years. I will not do that to you."

He closed the distance he'd created, that smile still firmly in place.

"Why are you smiling? This is serious." I backed up a step.

"I'm smiling because I've waited months for those words and you just gave them to me." His hands rested on my shoulders, stopping my slow creep backwards. He ducked his head until we were almost eye to eye. "Listen to me carefully, Roseline Butler. You're maddening sometimes, but I love you, too."

His words hung in the air, and for a moment, my heart did a funny dance. Love. It was a word I'd never expected to hear, especially from Jackson. Warmth spread through me, but fear tugged at the edges.

I searched his eyes, desperately trying to find any sign that this was another act, another layer of our fake relationship.

"Are you serious?" I asked, cursing myself for sounding so vulnerable. But I needed to know, needed him to confirm that this wasn't just another line in our script.

He nodded, his gaze steady. "Dead serious, Ros."

A mixture of emotions tangled inside of me — warmth, fear,

uncertainty. Love was a heavy word, a commitment, and I wasn't sure I was ready for that. But as I looked into his eyes, something softened in me.

Without saying a word, I launched myself at him. He chuckled, falling back a step towards the bed before I fused our lips together and wrapped my legs around him. It was a promise, a silent agreement that maybe, just maybe, I could let my guard down. For Jackson, I was willing to try.

We'd had sex before, but this time it felt different. This time, it wasn't just a casual hookup or part of our fake relationship. This was real. His eyes darkened, and I felt myself blush under his scrutinising stare.

His hands found their way under my t-shirt, his calloused fingers skimming my skin. A moan escaped me, and I deepened the kiss. His hardness pressed against my centre, and desire unfurled low in my belly, making me desperate and needy. Our tongues danced together, exploring each other as if it were the first time.

I couldn't get enough of him, the way he made me feel alive and a little scared.

Jackson pulled back, slowly peeling the t-shirt over my head, leaving me clad in just my bra and jeans. His hands roamed over my naked flesh, taking their time to caress every dip and divot.

Not one to be left behind, I made quick work of his buttons and his shirt joined mine on the floor. I raked my nails across his chest, pressing myself ever closer to his body.

With the pinch of his fingers, my bra fell to the ground between us, my naked breasts spilled free and into his waiting hands. I groaned as he massaged them, flicking his thumb across my sensitive nipples.

There was a benefit to spending a month fucking like it didn't matter. We knew each other's bodies, what made us squirm, what made us ticklish and what we hated. Jackson used every lesson to his advantage, working me into a frazzled, needy mess within minutes.

I pulled back from the kiss and his attention shifted to my neck. He traced a line down to that hyper-sensitive spot between my neck and shoulder that never failed to make me beg.

"I need you not to be a tease tonight."

He hummed in a non-committal response. Another thing he knew drove me wild.

"I'm serious. You want to make love to me but I need you to fuck me, Jackson." With a hand in his hair, I forced his head back until he met my gaze. "I need to do something with the anger. Help me work it off."

"Happily," he whispered, smirking.

I fumbled with the button of his trousers, and he helped me, discarding them along with his boxers. My jeans and panties followed.

I wanted him, all of him. I drew in a sharp breath at the sight of him: toned abs, defined muscles, and a hard cock that begged for attention.

He was perfect, and he was mine.

My hands roamed across the hard planes of his chest, tracing each defined muscle. He shuddered under my touch, his erection twitching against my belly. I wanted him inside me, wanted to feel him filling me up and claiming me as his.

"I want you so bad," I moaned, grinding against him.

He chuckled. "Tell me what you want."

"I want you inside me, fucking me hard. Make me come so I can forget everything except how good you feel."

His arms banded around me as he lifted me into his arms. Holding me tightly, he walked us to the bed I'd spent my childhood in.

Once he'd laid me down, he stepped back.

"You're so fucking beautiful." Lust and something else I couldn't decipher swirled in his eyes.

"Jackson, stop staring at me like that." I squirmed under his heated look.

"Never." He canted his head to the side, his gaze dipping to the apex of my thigh. "Open your legs for me, show me how wet you are."

I blushed, but did as he asked.

He growled low in his throat, the sound sending a shiver down my spine. "So fucking wet for me, pixie."

He climbed onto the bed and knelt between my knees, spreading my legs further.

His fingers swiped across my folds, spreading my arousal up and around my clit. "You're so fucking wet for me."

He sucked the digit into his mouth, groaning in appreciation.

"I need you." I didn't care if it sounded like I was begging. Anything to feel the addictive stretch of him inside of me sooner.

"Soon."

He lowered his head between my thighs. His tongue lapped at the sensitive bundle of nerves, making me arch my back in ecstasy.

"Jackson!" I moaned as he continued to torment me with his tongue.

"Never going to get tired of hearing you say my name like that," he purred against my core.

"You better not," I panted, gripping the sheets. "Fuck, do that again."

I threaded my fingers through his hair, gripping it tightly as he traced a path from my pussy to my clit, tongue flicking and sucking until pleasure spiralled outward from my core. My back arched off the bed as I screamed out his name again. My body trembled in the aftermath of my release while my mind floated somewhere else.

We'd done that hundreds of times. Yet this time it felt... more. More serious. More feeling. Just more in every way.

I barely noticed as he pressed a final kiss to my clit and crawled up my body. Then his hot, wet mouth sucked my nipple into his mouth, shocking me out of the post-orgasm daze.

I moaned as my nails scraped across his scalp, holding him to me. He increased suction while his fingers teased the other one and the desperate need to be filled, to be pounded into until I couldn't catch my breath, couldn't think about my screwed up family, unfurled inside of me again.

I tugged at him, trying to force him to move up my body.

He chuckled against my skin before he pulled away, smirking down at me like he'd just won the lotto. He hovered over me, a soft look in his eyes that clashed with the hard press of his cock against my stomach.

"I'm going to fuck you until you can't see straight, let alone think." He lowered his head, his lips ghosting across my cheek to my ear. "And then I'm going to make love to you until I'm so deep inside that hesitant heart of yours, you'll never get me out."

My stomach flipped at his hoarse words, while my mouth went dry in a mixture of excitement and fear. But I wanted this, I wanted more of him than I'd ever had before.

Heat pooled low in my stomach as he flipped me onto my front, pulling me to my knees. His hard cock pressed against my entrance, teasingly.

"Beg me, Ros."

I shook my head, despite the answer on the tip of my tongue.

He growled in frustration, but didn't remove himself. "Beg me, or prepare to be edged all night."

"Fine!" I surrendered, gritting out between clenched teeth. I rocked back against him, desperate for any pressure. "Please Jackson, fuck me like you mean it."

He slid in slowly, filling me to the hilt, and I gasped. The familiar burn was there, but this time it was different. It felt... right.

A throaty moan escaped my lips as he bottomed out, his hips pressed flush against my ass.

I gripped the sheets tightly as he started to move, pounding into me with ruthless thrusts that stole my breath and made it difficult to stay on my hands and knees.

The headboard banged against the wall and I experienced a moment of concern that my dad would hear us. Then he drew back slowly before slamming into me, hard. I cried out, pleasure singing through every nerve.

"That's it, pixie. Let me hear how good I make you feel."

He set a relentless pace, pounding into me over and over. His fingers dug into my hips as he held me in place for his rough thrusts.

It was exactly what I needed.

He leaned over me, his hot breath tickling my ear. "You feel so fucking good. I'm never letting you go."

"I don't want you to let me go," I whispered.

With a hand in my hair, he turned my head and claimed my lips, kissing me hard and sloppy while his hips kept pulsing in and out, in and out.

At some point, my brain turned to mush as an orgasm ripped through me and my muscles forgot how to support me. My arms gave out and I collapsed onto the mattress.

His cock slipped out of me and I almost complained about the loss. Then he turned me over, gathered one of my legs in the crook of his arm and plunged back into me.

"Now we go at my pace," he said, his tone softer, but still hoarse with desire.

His hazel eyes bore into mine as he moved. Slow, deep thrusts that made my toes curl and my eyes roll back in my head. He was everywhere, caging me against the bed with his hard, slick body.

"Feel that?" His voice was ragged as he lowered his mouth and captured a nipple between his teeth, while he pumped his hips into me. "That's me, claiming you as mine."

He teased my nipple until it was sensitive and I was a shaking, whimpering mess, on the verge of another climax. He moved his lips to my other nipple, repeating the process.

"I-I can't," I panted, my eyes fluttering closed. "I can't take much more."

"Say it," he panted against my ear.

"What?" I blinked up at him, my brow furrowing in confusion.

"Tell me you're mine."

I hesitated. Old habits die hard.

"I'm yours," I whispered, hips bucking up to meet his every forward push.

"That's my pixie," he praised, his voice thick with desire. "Say it louder."

"I'm yours!" I moaned as a third orgasm crashed over me, stealing my breath.

He growled my name, his hips stuttering as he finally found his release inside me. He collapsed on top of me, breathing hard.

Jackson and I lay there, panting for air and basking in the afterglow.

"I love you," he mumbled against my neck.

I opened my mouth to respond, but the words got stuck in my throat. "Thank you," I whispered instead.

As soon as the words were out, I wanted to smack myself. Thank you? Really? That was the best I could come up with when this amazing man had just bared his heart to me?

My face burned as Jackson pulled out slowly and sat back on his heels.

"I... I'm sorry, I just..." I cursed myself for being such a coward.

"It's okay, Ros. You'll tell me when you're ready."

CHAPTER TWENTY-FOUR

JACKSON

I thought winning my first Academy Award was the best high I'd ever experienced.

I was wrong.

I grinned up at the ceiling, unable to believe my luck. After wanting her for so long, wishing and hoping she'd someday see me as more than a friend she occasionally fucked. Now she was here with me, not because of any contract but because she wanted to be. Curled up beside me on this tiny bed that was definitely not made for two grown adults, her leg hooked over mine while she snored into my chest.

What if she woke up and realised she'd made a mistake?

Last night was intense. I hadn't been prepared for the shit-show I'd walked in on. She'd been rightfully upset.

What if she'd only chosen to take a step forward because she wanted to prove a point to her dad? Not that he would know anything had changed, of course. My stomach turned at the thought of it.

All too soon, she shifted against me, groaning at the morning light seeping through beneath her blinds. I glanced down at her as she nuzzled impossibly closer. Even mostly dead to the world, she managed to make my heart do somersaults.

"Morning, beautiful." I brushed a stray hair back from her cheek, unable to resist touching her.

She wrinkled her nose. "Too early for talking."

I bit back a laugh. "Message received, your highness." I brushed my lips over her rumpled hair. "I'll keep quiet and let you get your beauty sleep."

"Better," she mumbled before pressing her face against my chest again.

I settled for running my fingers through her hair, reassuring myself this was real.

We lay like that a while longer as her breathing deepened again. Part of me still couldn't believe it. Eventually she gave up trying to force sleep, sighing as she blinked up at me.

"I can practically hear you thinking, Jackson. Out with it."

I chuckled as she sat up, taking the duvet with her to pointlessly cover up her nakedness. She stared at me, her brow furrowed while she tried needlessly to intimidate me into speaking.

"Just thinking about us." I sat up and leaned back against the headboard. "I want to make sure you meant it."

She canted her head, considering me. "Getting cold feet already?"

"No, never." I reached for her, almost out of habit now. My thumb found her bottom lip before caressing her jaw. "I've wanted us to be a real thing for months, you know that. I just don't want you rushing into this for the wrong reasons when a few days ago you were adamant we stick to the rules and protect our friendship."

Understanding lit her eyes. She leaned forward and brushed her lips softly against mine.

"I want you, Jackson. Only you." She held my gaze, willing me to believe her.

"And I'm glad to hear that but I can't help but worry that you decided last night while emotions were already running high."

"I'm an idiot, I'm aware of that." She sighed, rolling her eyes at herself. "I know, my timing is shit. I should've been an adult and recognised how I felt about you much sooner, instead of trying to resist this." She reached for my hand, threading our fingers together on top of the duvet. "I was scared. Kept telling myself your world was too chaotic and unstable for me to handle. That I'd just end up being another notch on your bedpost once the novelty wore off."

My brow furrowed. "I would never have —"

She pressed her fingers to my lips, silencing me, smiling. "I know that now, but I don't know if you've noticed this… I'm not exactly a rational person." We both laughed at her dig. She traced my jaw softly. "But I was only hurting us both by pushing you away. The truth is, I want to trust you. I'm tired of letting fear hold me back when this feels so right."

I turned my head to brush a kiss over her palm. "I'll earn that trust, I promise. One day at a time."

She smiled softly. "I know you will. You already are." She bumped her forehead against mine. "No more running or second guessing this. I'm all in, Jackson. The career stuff, the fame — we'll figure it out together."

A short while later, Ros and I made our way downstairs. As we turned into the cramped entryway, her father stepped out of the living room. His smile quickly faded as he caught sight of the bags in my hands.

"You're not leaving?" he asked, surprise colouring his tone.

Ros glanced up at me, her teeth worrying her lower lip. My heart ached at the indecision in her eyes. We'd discussed this, weighing the pros and cons, and come to the conclusion that leaving was the best thing for her mental health. With her father, she could pretend, mostly, that everything was fine. Play the happy family and give her dad what he wanted. But Cheryl refused to pretend.

I nodded at her, silently encouraging her to be honest. She took a deep breath, her eyes meeting her father's.

"I figured it would be for the best," she said, her voice steady but tinged with regret.

He flinched, lines etching deeper across his forehead. His mouth opened and closed twice before he got words out.

"For the best?" He scrubbed both hands down his unshaven face, looking every one of his fifty-something years. "How can leaving your family on Christmas possibly be for the best?"

Her brow rose, unimpressed. "My family?" She glanced pointedly upstairs to where her antagonistic stepmom no doubt waited.

"Ros, please. I'm trying here." Hank winced, shoving his hands into his jeans pockets. "Can't we have a nice holiday together just this once? I thought we were finally making some progress here…"

My fingers tightened around the smooth leather handles of Ros's bag. The urge to step between them warred with the certainty that she could handle this herself. She squared her shoulders, all five foot three inches sparkling with defiance.

"We did try that, last night, remember?" Each word shot out clipped and sharp as bullets. She sucked in an unsteady breath, clenching her fists. "I keep playing nice, keep coming back hoping things will be different. But every time, I leave with more emotional bruises, while you make excuses for that toxic woman."

Shame and denial fought for control of Hank's expression. He shook his head like he could somehow shake off her words through sheer force of will.

"I know Cheryl can be difficult." Hank winced, knowing even as he said it how pathetic that sounded. "But she's still my wife when all's said and done."

"Really?" She gaped at him incredulously. "That's your big justification?"

Hank wilted slightly under her blistering stare. But he wasn't giving up yet.

"Deep down, you know she means well."

Ros snorted. "The only thing that woman means is every vile word that falls from her lips." She took my hand, intertwining her fingers with mine, a silent declaration of our unity. "I understand you know you messed up now, and I appreciate that. I've tried to forgive, but it's too late. There's just too much damage. I don't want to be the person your example made me." She glanced up at me and smiled. "I want to be the woman he sees."

She tugged on my hand as she started walking again, turning sideways to slip past her father with a sad smile.

"How about we start fresh?" The desperate note crept back into Hank's placating tone. "I'll make your favourite Christmas cookies, the sugar ones with the sprinkles. We'll get a fire crackling, open some gifts…"

She crossed her arms, mouth flattened into a resolute line. "That's not going to cut it anymore, Dad. I'm done plastering on a smile, biting my tongue 'til it bleeds while your wife takes her bitterness out on me."

Hank flinched at each biting word. But for once, Ros didn't cave in the face of his crestfallen expression. I fell a little more in love with her at that moment.

He rubbed the back of his neck, still scrambling for the magic words to undo decades of damage. "People make mistakes, Roseline. I should know that better than anyone." His eyes turned glassy with shame. "Doesn't mean they can't change…"

She shook her head bitterly. "The only thing that woman regrets is not being able to ship me off to boarding school the second you brought her wretched ass into this house."

Hank sagged against the wall like all the strings holding him upright had been sliced.

"You deserve so much better, sweetpea." He grimaced. "Your mom would be so disappointed in me now…"

Ros avoided talking about her mother. I knew she lost her

when she was only twelve and she'd loved her right until the end. Anyone would be scared after going through that and then being forced to live with her cheating father and the stepmother who clearly hated her.

"Well she's not here. Is she?" Bitterness dripped from each word. "So I have to look out for myself."

I ached to pull her into my arms, to somehow erase all this heartache. But she wasn't made of glass and she would hate me for coddling her.

"I get that now. Whatever I need to do to fix this, I'm ready." He took a half step closer, arms half extended, like he really wanted to close the gap between them. But he stopped before he forced Ros to back away. "I'll talk to Cheryl, make her see reason. I swear on your mother's memory."

She rocked back on her heel, her defensive stance easing just for a moment. A glimmer of hope flickered across her face, probably wishing that her father, who she once trusted, could somehow regain that trust.

Just as quick, the walls slammed back up. Her mouth pressed into a thin line. "That's not your promise to make."

His expression crumpled and his shoulders sagged. He rubbed at his worn face, emotion cracking through the genial mask. "I never meant to hurt you. I just want my family together for the holidays."

"I know," she said quietly. "But maybe there's a reason we haven't spent more than a day together since Mom died." She shrugged. "I can't do it any more."

Stepping forward, she briefly hugged him. "I get that you're trying to fix things between us. But this relationship can't be one-sided anymore."

Confusion clouded his eyes as she kissed his cheek. Pulling back, she shook her head at the sight of it.

"I won't keep showing up hoping for apologies or efforts that never stick. Not if you're going to keep making excuses for that woman." Disgust twisted her lips. "I matter enough to demand better."

"Of course you do." He held onto her, trying but failing to stop her retreat. "That's not what I…"

"Maybe we need space for a while." She worried her bottom lip again. "If you get serious about making amends… well, my number isn't going to change."

The unspoken ultimatum hung in the air between them as she took another step towards the front door.

"But it's Christmas…"

Like the holiday should magically erase all issues.

"I know the timing's shit." Regret softened her expression. "Maybe that'll help motivate you…" She shrugged half-heartedly, but it didn't stop her from opening the front door. "Merry Christmas, Dad," she said before she tugged me out the door.

The frigid morning air hit me like a slap, but I didn't care. We hurried down the front steps towards the SUV and driver waiting at the kerb. The driver's side door opened before we cleared the steps and a man in a suit rounded the car with a smile.

"Mr Levi." He nodded as he reached for the bags in my hand.

"Thank you," I said before I focused only on Ros. I cupped her cold pink cheek in my gloved hand. "How're you holding up, pixie?"

She leaned into my touch, offering a small but genuine smile. "I'll be alright. I need to get out of here though." She stepped back, breaking my hold as she glanced up at the tired house. "Take me somewhere happy, Jackson."

"You've got it."

I guided her to the open door and waited patiently as she got settled before I followed her in. The driver closed the door. She slumped down in her seat, releasing a deep breath as the tension drained from her.

"Better?"

She glanced up at me, a small smile toying at the edges of her lips. "More than you know. Thank you."

I smiled back at her, relieved to see some of the tension leaving her face. After all the heavy confrontation with her dad, she deserved a break.

"So what do you want to do now?" I asked. "Name it, and I'll make it happen."

Ros tilted her head, eyes sparking with mischief now. "What I want might require a disguise. Or your own private bodyguard detail."

"Somehow that doesn't surprise me. But no need to go incognito on my account." I wrapped an arm around her shoulders, giving a gentle squeeze. "The hat and glasses cliche is so overdone anyway."

She chuckled. "Oh no, I insist. Can't have you mobbed by fans if we're going to fully embrace the true New York Christmas experience."

I quirked an eyebrow. "Care to enlighten me about this mysterious Christmas experience? Preferably before I agree to anything too outrageous."

"And spoil the surprise?" She tutted.

ROS

I bit my lip, trying not to laugh out loud and draw even more attention to us. But Jackson's disguise was just too ridiculous. The huge fuzzy hat and round glasses paired with a bushy fake beard made him look like an overeager tourist. Or possibly a street-artist, ready to jump into a flash mob. It was impossible not to notice him, especially with his Academy Award-winning smile.

Yet even with the silly getup and two undercover bodyguards hovering nearby, Jackson's whole face still lit up. His eyes shone as he gazed around Rockefeller Center, utterly entranced by the Christmas decorations. The iconic tree towered above us, its twinkling lights casting a warm glow on the ice-skaters below. The air was filled with the scent of roasted nuts and the sound of Christmas carols.

Even better? There wasn't a paparazzo in sight.

We hadn't told Audra we were coming. She would be furious and I couldn't wait to watch her head explode over video call when she found out we visited Rockefeller Square without giving her the PR heads up.

I leaned close so only he could hear me snicker. "You know that beard makes you look crazy, not incognito right?"

Jackson rubbed his scruffy chin, grinning sheepishly beneath the mess of fake facial hair. "Does it? I was rather proud of this disguise."

I rolled my eyes. "I hate to break it to you, but you look one hundred percent certifiable right now."

"But at least no one will recognise me, aye?" He nudged me playfully. "Admit it, I make a dashing eccentric gentleman."

"If by dashing, you mean a dash to the lost and found perhaps." I wrinkled my nose, still chuckling. "Pretty sure that's where you stole that hat from."

Jackson clapped the oversized wool hat to his head in mock offence. "I'll have you know this is the height of New York winter fashion."

I burst out laughing, unable to keep a straight face. Jackson Levi worrying about fashion trends? That had to be a first.

But I'd play along for now. Taking his arm, I guided us towards the iconic Christmas tree and ice skating rink in Rockefeller Center. "Well, you definitely blend right in. All the stylish New Yorkers wear exactly that."

Jackson leaned down to murmur in my ear. "Laugh all you want, Butler. But I'd rather look ridiculous than have fans mobbing me before you've had your fill of the Christmas spirit." He nudged me gently. "And don't pretend you aren't enjoying this rare taste of normalcy too."

I bit my lip, holding back another grin as we stopped before the magnificent towering tree. This was all so surreal. Jackson Levi was my boyfriend. My boyfriend! It felt like a dream I didn't want to wake up from, but it was real. He loved me.

And he wasn't wrong — having him all to myself without a hundred cameras in our faces did feel special. And getting to show him my city made my heart happy.

He gazed up at the glittering Christmas tree, awestruck. The bright twinkling lights reflected in his eyes behind those silly glasses. Seeing his simple childlike wonder made me wish moments like this came more often for him.

"Not too shabby, huh, Oleg?" I asked, using a silly made-up name to keep with his quirky tourist persona.

Jackson chuckled at the name, patting my hand that rested on his arm.

"What do you think?" I said, bumping his arm with mine. "Reckon it measures up to Scottish trees?"

"It's impressive, I'll admit. But our ancient forests produce true giants, lass." He stroked his fuzzy beard, grinning.

I cocked a brow. "Oh really? Sure you aren't exaggerating a wee bit?" I mimicked his accent on the last words.

Jackson placed his hand on his chest in mock offence. "Me? I would never." He shook his head sadly. "Clearly you need educating on the mystical woods of my homeland."

I bit my lip, holding back a grin. "Forgive my ignorance. Do enlighten me." I waved a hand in invitation. "Does Santa have trouble navigating the enormous trunks?"

"He does alright. His sleigh practically glides between our proud giants." His lips twitched, barely able to keep a straight face.

"Sure, he does."

I shook my head and slid my hand back into the crook of his elbow as we turned to take in the crowds filling Rockefeller Center. So many smiling families and tourists flooded the plaza. Snippets of countless languages and accents reached my ears beneath the piped Christmas carols.

"You know, this is nothing like a Scottish Christmas," Jackson murmured. "Much flashier show than my town puts on."

I nudged him. "But does St Andrews have an iconic landmark dripping in ten thousand lights?"

"We've got a tree in Market Square in town... mind you, it's probably only a hundred strings of lights total." He chuckled. "But that glow means the world when you're bundled beneath the snow as a kid."

I shook my head, smiling. "I should've known everything comes back to snow with you Scots."

He grinned. "Well, it does set a festive mood, doesn't it?"

"And here I was, thinking it was all about kilts and bagpipes," I said, feigning innocence.

A pang of guilt needled me. "I'm sorry I made you miss Christmas with your family."

He glanced down at me in surprise. "You have nothing to apologise for. I chose to be here with you, remember?"

"I know, but..." I bit my lip, unsure if I should voice my thoughts. Oh what the hell, I might as well say it. "I still feel guilty. Like I ruined your holiday."

Jackson stopped and turned to face me fully. He tipped my chin up gently with one finger until our eyes met.

"You could never ruin anything for me, pixie," he said sincerely. "All I wanted was to spend Christmas with you." His thumb stroked my cheek. "Besides, there's always next year."

"So you do miss it? Being back home this time of year?"

Jackson considered the question, eyes drifting over the crowd of people surrounding us. "I do miss some things..." He smiled wistfully. "Mam scolding my siblings while my wee nieces and nephews dash about hyped on sweets. Da testing his new power tools by the fireside..."

He trailed off, lost in some memory that left his eyes glazed for a long moment. I swallowed hard, fighting a pang of envy at what sounded like a warm, lively holiday celebration compared to mine.

I tried to laugh, I really did, but it came out a weak whistle of pathetic. "That sounds wonderful. Lively."

"It is," he agreed. "And then there's Boxing Day. Ever heard of that?"

"Of course. The day you all nurse your hangovers and eat leftovers."

Jackson nodded, an amused glint in his eyes. "Exactly. If we were home now, we'd be walking the dogs along the beach, and enjoying a fry-up with all the Christmas dinner leftovers."

I chuckled. "Sounds like a food coma waiting to happen."

He grinned. "It definitely is. And I wouldn't have it any other way." He squeezed my gloved hand tucked in his elbow, drawing me closer to his body. "But home doesn't necessarily mean a place, right?" He smiled down at me. "It's a feeling. That's why I wanted us to start some traditions of our own this season."

I grinned at him. He was so full of shit.

"You mean avoiding an inquisition by hiding out in New York?"

Jackson winced. "I swear that wasn't the original plan..."

"I'm teasing, don't worry." I waved off his apology. "But honestly? I'm happier here with you than I would've been with Dad and Cheryl for round two."

Jackson studied my face, judging if I meant that. "No regrets about skipping the family chaos then?"

"None." I shook my head firmly, threaded my fingers through his. "I'm right where I want to be."

For the first time in my life, my heart felt open to all the possibilities that lay ahead.

"You know, if it weren't for you, I would have spent this week alone."

He looked down at me, those blue eyes softening. "Alone? On Christmas?"

I nodded, a small smile tugging at my lips. "Yeah. After last night's drama, I would've gone through the motions with my family, smiled through the awkwardness, and then headed back home. But home isn't really home anymore. Not since Abi and Eva moved to LA."

His brows knitted together in concern. "And then what?"

"Then nothing." I shrugged, feeling a lump forming in my throat. "Abi and Eva used to be my Christmas partners-in-crime, you know? We'd veg out on the sofa, watch cheesy holiday movies, and drink mulled wine until we couldn't tell the difference between bad acting and the festive spirit."

His grip on my hand tightened, a reassuring warmth. "Well, that sounds like a crap way to spend the day."

"It does," I admitted. "This is much better."

I glanced around, taking it all in: the chatter, the carols and bells, the lights, the scents. This was what I thought of when I imagined New York Christmas.

"Then it's a good thing I froze up on the red carpet and dropped us both in the shit," he said, a playful glint in his eyes. "You'll never be alone for Christmas again."

His words warmed me and I smiled. A few months ago, I would have said it was the worst thing he could have done to me. Now, I couldn't help but feel grateful that he'd panicked and forgotten his media training. Stupid as it might sound, I wouldn't change any of it for the world.

CHAPTER TWENTY-FIVE

ROS

"*E*xplain it to me again."

"Ros, there's no secret handshake." Jackson chuckled at my sceptical expression. "Jen is just very good at pulling strings."

"You can keep repeating that all you like. It won't make me believe that itty-bitty Jen could scare a restaurant into setting up a private dining experience on their rooftop for us." I glared at Jackson, folding my arms across my chest. He grinned back at me, totally unaffected.

The nerve of the guy.

Didn't he know that when you entered a committed relationship, you had to give up all your secrets? That was a thing, right? If it wasn't, it needed to be.

I shook my head as I took in the stunning panoramic views of the Los Angeles city lights twinkling below us. I couldn't help myself. It was incredible. Magical even.

We were tucked away in a corner of the rooftop restaurant, shielded from other diners by a thick screen, decorated in vines.

And when I say corner, I mean a corner view. Flickering candles sat in the centre of the table, their scent barely reaching me before the breeze swept the smoke away. Fine china plates lay on top of a crisp white tablecloth that billowed lightly in the breeze. Above us, a full moon shone, the only light in the inky blue-black sky aside from the aeroplanes passing thousands of miles overhead.

It felt straight out of a romantic movie, and I wasn't quite sure how to handle it. Me, the sceptical New Yorker who avoided heart-fluttering romance. Yet here I was, on a real first date with Jackson.

"You're staring again, pixie," he said, pulling my attention back to him. An amused glint had settled in his eyes the second we walked into the building and probably wouldn't fade before we left. "I promise, the view won't disappear if you blink."

I rolled my eyes. "I can't help it. This view is…" I trailed off, searching for the right word.

"Mesmerising?" he suggested with a knowing smile.

"Yeah, that. Mesmerising." I nodded, a half-smile playing on my lips. "Now if only you'd tell me how you pulled off this trick…"

"Trick? Ros, this is a genuine, A-list date. No tricks involved."

"Sure, as genuine as a Hollywood headline." I chuckled, but then my attention snagged on that view again and I sighed. "But I'll admit, this is impressive."

Jackson smiled. "Only the best for you."

I rolled my eyes, deflecting the sincerity I didn't know how to handle. "Enough with the charm, Casanova. You already impressed me with the private jet."

He laughed, seeing through me. I was still figuring out how to balance dating Jackson for real while staying true to myself. But somehow, he made it all easy and less scary.

It had been two days since we left my dad's place in New York. After an amazing night enjoying all the Christmassy things I wanted in the city, we'd just gotten back to LA.

Nothing had changed publicly. Probably wouldn't.

As far as the press was concerned, we were still a loved up, engaged couple and we needed it to stay that way. But for me, every moment felt more special, more important, now that we'd decided to really give this relationship a try.

A smile tugged at my lips as I turned back to him. "Alright, enough stalling. Spill, Levi. How did you pull this off."

Jackson laughed. "I told you, it was all Jen's doing. She knows the owner here and called in a favour."

I narrowed my eyes, not quite believing it was so simple. There had to be more to it. "There's no way Jen has that kind of pull," I said. "You paid, you must have."

"Ye of little faith! Jen's got connections here I swear."

I shook my head, grinning. "Uh huh. And my grandma was Beyonce."

"She was?" he asked, somehow keeping a straight face. "Well that explains your sass and style."

I tossed my napkin at him with a laugh. "You're ridiculous."

He dodged the linen missile easily. "Maybe, but I'm serious too."

"Alright, keep your secrets about Jen's magical restaurant powers," I conceded. "I'll get it out of you eventually."

He just winked, infuriatingly smug. "Good luck with that, pixie."

"Do you bring all your dates up here?" I asked, trying to sound nonchalant.

He tilted his head, considering me. "Now who's fishing for info?"

I bit my lip, cursing myself for prying into his romantic past. It's not like I wanted him digging into mine.

"You're the first person I've brought up here," he said after a moment. "I was saving this place for someone special."

My cheeks flushed, a giddy feeling bubbling up inside me. I quickly glanced away, overwhelmed while age old doubts whispered in the back of my mind.

What if the novelty of dating an ordinary girl wore off? What happened when our agreement ended? Sure he wanted me now, but would he then? What if the chaos of his celebrity life eventually became too much? I knew Jackson craved authenticity, but was I really enough? Or would he leave, just like all the others had?

Jesus, listen to me. Three months with the man and I'd let myself devolve into a neurotic mess.

You're better than that.

I pushed the doubts aside, determined not to ruin our first real date with my insecurities. For now, I'd enjoy getting to know the real Jackson beneath the fame. The man who made me feel special, who looked at me like I was the only person in the world.

Our meals arrived and we fell into a comfortable silence while we ate.

"It really is breathtaking up here," he said some time later, his voice soft and dreamy. "But not as beautiful as my dining companion."

I rolled my eyes, but couldn't hide a small smile. "Any more lines like that and I'm tossing you off this rooftop."

He grinned, satisfied he'd gotten under my skin.

The man always cleaned up well. Constantly having to be prepared for a camera to appear at any moment demanded that. Tonight, there was something more natural about him. He wore a white dress shirt, unbuttoned to his chest — all the better to tease me with — and slacks. Pretty normal stuff.

But his dirty blond hair fluttered around him in the wind, unusually unbound for a public outing. My eyes were drawn to the braided leather bracelet circling his wrist, something I had never seen him wear outside the house.

It was made up of knotted and woven strands in different earthy shades of brown, accented with beads and shells. It suited his personality perfectly — a little bit rugged, a little bit polished.

Beyond that though, he just seemed more relaxed. His smiles came easier. He laughed more. Emotions flitted across his face, so clear I could almost read them. Oh, wouldn't he hate that.

"What's that smile for?" Jackson asked, dragging me from my thoughts.

"Hmm? Oh, nothing," I said, shaking my head. "Just thinking how lucky I am."

His eyes softened. He reached across the table and took my hand, his thumb gently stroking my knuckles.

"I'm the lucky one," he said sincerely.

My heart did a little flip, the way it always did when Jackson looked at me like I hung the moon. I still wasn't used to being like this with him, open and vulnerable beneath. Call me a masochist, but I was starting to enjoy the bite of discomfort that came with it. One day, it would get easier, I knew that.

We chatted idly after that about easy things — the food, wondering what our friends were up to tonight, debating what cheesy rom com to watch when we got home. Easy, comfortable conversation flowed between us like it used to before Jackson had asked me out. The awkwardness of our early fake relationship days seemed so far away now.

I couldn't stop watching him, studying him as he talked, taking in the crinkle of his eyes when he laughed, the smooth timbre of his voice, the way his thumb kept stroking my skin absently. Heat pulsed beneath the surface everywhere we touched.

"What about you?" he asked, snapping me from my drooling. "Any big dreams you're ready to tackle next?"

I did have an idea, but wasn't sure if I was ready to share it or to follow through. But if not now, then when?

"I was thinking…"

Jackson perked up. "Yes?"

"Well, since I have all this free time now, maybe I could finally try launching my own label."

His eyes lit up like I'd suggested all-you-can-eat wings night. "That sounds like a great idea."

"I have so many ideas. It would be really bold and alternative, you know? Mixing punk rock edge with high fashion glam."

As I described my dream aesthetic — up-cycled fabrics, unique silhouettes, nods to music subculture — Jackson listened intently, asking thoughtful questions. He didn't seem to care that I gushed endlessly about palette ideas and sourcing special materials. Jackson made me feel like my hopes and ambitions mattered.

"I'd need an investor to get it off the ground. Though with all that money you're paying me maybe I don't need one," I said eventually, thinking out loud. "Rent a studio space, purchase equipment and fabrics…"

Jackson reached across the table and took my hands in his. "Say no more. I'm in."

My eyes widened. "What? Really?"

He nodded. "Whatever you need to make this happen, I'll take care of it."

"That's… I… I don't know what to say."

"Say *yes, Jackson*."

Emotion choked me for a second while he waited patiently for me to get it together. I'd expected moral support from Jackson, but not this level of encouragement. With his help, my vision didn't seem so far-fetched anymore.

I took a sip of wine, letting the crisp flavour roll over my tongue before swallowing, giving myself time to get the overwhelming rush of emotions under control.

"Thank you," I whispered when I could form words. "You have no idea what this means to me."

"You were there for me even when I didn't deserve it." He lifted my hand and pressed a gentle kiss to my knuckles, sending butterflies swirling wildly in my core. "It's the least I can do to repay the favour."

His gaze lingered on mine, a warmth in his eyes that made me feel like I was the most important person in the room.

"I still can't believe someone as amazing as you was single," I blurted out before I could stop myself.

He chuckled, the sound amused, but he glanced away as he said, "Fame isn't exactly a friend to relationships. It comes with its own set of challenges."

"Oh come on, you must've had people lined up from coast to coast, like you're the last hot dog at a Fourth of July barbecue."

He smirked. "Maybe, but none of them understood me like you do."

"Flattery will get you everywhere," I said, trying and failing to lighten the mood.

Jackson set his drink down, his eyes serious. "Honestly? That was the truth. The celebrity changes people. Makes them get all twisted and obsessed about fame, money, hotness rankings in the tabloids." He shook his head, his brow creased.

A thread of sadness stabbed at my heart. He'd always seemed so confident, the king of suave and charm. Now there was a vulnerability to him I had never seen before.

"Hey, it's their loss and my gain." I scooted my chair closer and nudged him with my shoulder. "If they were too stupid to see past the flashbulbs and appreciate the smart, thoughtful guy underneath, then buh-bye to them."

The corner of Jackson's mouth quirked. "I never expected to find someone who sees me." His gaze met mine, a serious edge that made my breath still and every fibre of my being perk up and take notice.

"What can I say, I have a soft spot for broody actors with a heart of gold."

He barked out a laugh at that. He nudged me, mirth dancing in his eyes. "Is that what I am? A walking cliché?"

My laughter joined his, echoing across the rooftop and out into the night sky.

"Cliché or not, you're my cliché." I squeezed his hand.

"I wish I'd known all it took was broody actors to turn your head months ago. I would have played it up."

My brows rose. "Would you now?"

"Absolutely. I could have brought you dramatic monologues and moody stares, the whole package."

I snorted. "I'm sad that I missed out on those gems." It would have been glorious and I would have laughed for weeks.

"But in all seriousness." The amusement drained from his eyes as he studied me with a coy smile. "You see the real me — not the actor, not the tabloid headlines. I've been waiting to find someone I can truly be myself with. And I have that with you."

"I get it," I said, my voice choked. I swallowed the lump in my throat, "Fame comes with a lot of crap — no privacy, ridiculous rumours, paparazzi constantly breathing down your neck. It's draining."

His grip on my hand tightened, and I could see the worry lingering in his eyes.

"But you know what? Gossip and nosy reporters don't scare me off. As long as we're real with each other, I can handle the rest."

A small smile tugged at the corner of Jackson's lips, but uncertainty still lingered in his gaze.

I nudged him, half teasing. "Come on, where's that Levi confidence? Together, we can handle anything – like Yves Saint Laurent and Pierre Bergé."

His forehead creased. "How did we get to Yves Saint Laurent and Pierre Bergé?"

I grinned. "They were partners, in business and life, supporting each other through thick and thin."

"And what does that have to do with us?"

"We've got each other's backs." I leaned back in my chair, holding his gaze. "You know, playing to our strengths. You're the smooth-talking actor/businessman who knows this industry inside out and can charm the pants off anyone. And me? Well, I'm the creative force, the brains behind the beauty."

"Brains behind the beauty? Are we running a fashion empire now?"

I chuckled. "Not exactly, but you get my point. We support each other."

CHAPTER TWENTY-SIX

JACKSON

The day had dragged on far too long. The afternoon board meeting with my friends seemed endless, but that was just one of the downsides of running our own production company. It had to be done if we wanted to keep producing films we were passionate about without middlemen who didn't understand our visions.

All I wanted now was to curl up on the sofa with Ros and watch some cheesy eighties film she'd insist was a hidden gem.

"Ros, I'm home!" I called out when I got back, dropping my car keys on the table in the entryway.

Silence answered. Huh, that's odd.

I checked the open-plan living room and kitchen. Normally, when I went out, she commandeered the dining room table for her latest dress cut. Not that I'd stop her doing it when I was here, mind you.

There were no swashes of fabric leaning haphazardly against my walls, no wisps of cut linen on the floor. The table looked pristine.

Where was that woman?

A smile teased my lips. Knowing her, she'd gotten caught up in a new design or thrifting online for vintage finds.

I trudged upstairs, ready to tease her for losing track of time again.

A buzzing noise reached my ears as I cleared the landing. It was insistent yet rhythmic, and I couldn't quite place what it could be. My mind raced through potential sources as I followed the sound, until I found myself standing outside her bedroom.

The door was slightly ajar, but I couldn't hear her voice—only that strange buzz.

Maybe she went out and forgot her phone? Her friends could be trying to find it.

I pushed the door open wider and froze in the doorway, my entire body tensing up.

Ros lay on her bed, her unfocused eyes fixed on the ceiling and her mouth slightly open, gasping with pleasure. Her pale skin was bare, every inch of her naked and on display. She teased her nipple between her fingers, causing a rush of heat to surge through my veins. Her back arched into the mattress.

Looks like she didn't want to wait for me to get home.

I grinned as need slammed into me. My cock hardened instantly, straining against the confines of my jeans.

My eyes dipped lower, drawn to the purple object fixed between her legs. It looked like a vibrator but not like any I'd ever seen before. It almost seemed to suction to her so she didn't need to touch it. From what I could see, part of it lay against her clit while another pressed into her vagina. The sight of it only fuelled my arousal, making my cock throb and my fists clench with the urge to touch myself or go to her.

I did neither.

I stood there, aroused and toeing this line of it being wrong, even though we were officially in a relationship. But I didn't care so much right then. That odd conflicted feeling made me feel like a voyeur and I didn't hate it.

She gasped and her body shook. Her fingers clenched around the vibrator, pressing it harder against her. Her cheeks flushed red as she bit down on her lip. Her hips buckled upward, seeking more contact from the device and all I wanted, all I could think about was replacing it.

The sound of it humming against her skin was almost deafening, but also oddly arousing. My own breathing became ragged as I watched her close her eyes and throw her head back.

My feet started moving, taking me to the bed, the need to make her come again and again winning over the thrill of watching.

As she neared her peak, she threw her head back and let out a low moan that echoed through the room. It vibrated through my chest and made my cock twitch in my jeans as she bucked against the mattress once more. She arched her back and cried out softly before collapsing onto the bed, panting heavily.

Her gaze latched onto me as I reached the bed. She didn't try to cover herself or hide what she had been doing.

"How long were you standing there?" she asked, stretching her arms above her head in a languid, cat-like motion that showcased every inch of her gorgeous body.

"Long enough," I said, my voice gravelly with desire.

I crawled onto the bed, hovering over her. She gazed up at me, her green eyes dark with lust. Without breaking our stare, I reached down and gently removed the buzzing vibrator from between her legs. She let out a soft gasp at the loss of contact.

"What are you doing?"

I turned the device around so the suction part couldn't block my access and lay down between her legs.

"Helping," I whispered, lowering my head between her thighs.

Her lips parted and she let out a soft moan as I ran my tongue along her slick folds.

I wrapped my lips around her sensitive clit, flicking it with my tongue as I slid two fingers inside her warmth. She was so wet and ready, her inner muscles clenching around my fingers.

Ros moaned, her hips bucking upwards as she clutched at the sheets. Her eyes fell shut, aftershocks teasing her as hard as I did.

Then I slid the vibrator back into her. Her eyes flew open as I pumped it in and out, the movement easy with her release, and flicked the vibrate back on.

"It's too much," she panted.

"You can take it."

She shifted restlessly on the bed, one moment trying to get closer and the next trying to get away. I held her down with a firm hand on her stomach while I suckled, nipped, circled that little bundle of nerves.

"Jackson!"

"Tell me what you want, baby," I growled against her.

"You," she moaned, her hips jerking upward. "Now."

I hummed in agreement around her clit.

Soon.

She needed to come first.

I upped the vibration, pushing it to the max. A choked cry fell from her lips as she came again, her body tensing and twitching beneath me.

Smirking, I pulled the vibrator out and tossed it aside.

"How's your fashion label coming along? Any new designs or ideas today?" I asked as I pressed a kiss to her inner thigh.

Silence followed my question and I lifted my head, meeting her confused stare.

"Ros?"

"I added a couple more designs, but they're not good enough yet."

"I bet they're great."

I kissed my way up her body, listening to her laboured breathing and soft moans as she struggled to keep her thoughts straight and answer my questions.

She pulled a face. "They will be."

"When do you think you'll be able to launch?" I flicked my tongue across her nipple, eliciting a gasp. "Focus, pixie."

She glared at my smirking face. "Easy for you to say. You don't have a six foot four god using you as a chew toy."

"You think I'm a god?"

I chuckled before clamping my lips around her nipple and sucking hard, just the way she liked it. She moaned, her fingers threaded through my hair and her hips shifted restlessly against my stomach, grinding into me.

"Of course..." Pant, "that's all…" Gasp, "you'd hear."

I released her nipple with a pop. "Just trying to get the facts straight." I moved up her body and hid my smirk against her collarbone.

She sighed as I teased the area with my teeth and tongue. "I don't know yet. There's just so much I need to learn."

"You'll figure it out." I nipped her earlobe, her moans driving me wild. "And I'll help in any way I can. Just ask."

"Thanks for the vote of confidence, but it's a big step."

"You've got this." I kissed my way down her jawline and then stopped at her lips. "I have complete faith in you." I nipped at her bottom lip playfully before sliding my tongue inside her mouth.

She kissed me back with equal fervour, sucking on my lower lip and gripping handfuls of my shirt. I cupped her breasts, squeezing them as she moaned.

Breaking the kiss, I sat up on the bed and pulled my shirt over my head. "Pep talk over. Now, where were we?"

"You were about to fuck me?" she asked, voice sultry and needy, her eyes glued to the bulge in my jeans.

I smirked and unbuckled my jeans, freeing myself. "Oh, I definitely was."

Naked, I kneeled between her open thighs, hooked my elbows under her knees and lifted her. She sighed happily as I positioned myself at her entrance.

I lined myself up with her dripping core before pushing inch by excruciating inch inside her. Her walls clamped down around me, hot and tight, like a vice around my cock.

"Fuck," she whimpered as I bottomed out.

"Better than your vibrator?"

"Yes!"

Her hips pulsed against me, silently begging me to move, to fuck her into the mattress. I smiled, enjoying how worked up she was, but I held firm, hovering over her while she adjusted.

"Slow or fast?"

"Both," she gasped, circling her hips in a way that made me grit my teeth, "oh god, I don't care. Anything as long as you're inside of me."

I chuckled, my cock throbbing inside her. "Greedy, aren't we?"

"You know it," she moaned, arching her back.

Slowly, I pulled out until only the head of my cock rested against her entrance before sliding back in with a groan. Her nails dug into my biceps as she clung to me for dear life.

"How... how was your meeting?"

"Boring as fuck." I pumped in and out of her, my balls slapping against her ass. "I would have much preferred to spend it with you."

"Really?" she panted, "What would we have done?"

"Fucked all day long," I growled, picking up the pace. "I can't seem to get enough of you."

"Mmm, me neither," she moaned, her hips meeting mine with an eagerness that made me groan. "I missed you."

I slid a hand between us, finding her clit.

"I changed my mind," she said, desperation dripping from her words and painted across her face. "Faster. I need you to go faster."

I obliged, thrusting in and out of her tight heat, harder and faster.

"Yes!" she hissed.

I leaned down and sucked on her aching nipple, pounding into her like a man possessed, desperate to feel her come around me. I would never get tired of watching my strong, independent Ros fall apart for me.

"Jackson!" she screamed, her body tensing and walls clamping around me. Her eyes closed and her body shook as her climax tore through her.

"That's it," I moaned, pinching her nipple as she rode out her orgasm.

I plunged into her one last time, my balls drawing tight as the familiar tingling sensation started in my spine and worked its way down. My cock jolted as I came deep inside her. My balls ached, every muscle tensing as wave after wave of pleasure washed over me.

I collapsed on top of her, mindful not to crush her as we both panted for air.

"Holy fuck," I gasped, still buried inside her. "That just gets better and better."

"That was... amazing," she gasped beneath me.

"Tell me about it," Ros muttered, her tone tired.

*L*aying there, panting and covered in a sheen of sweat, I couldn't help but smile.

"What're you grinning about?" She swatted my chest.

"Nothing, just..." I chuckled, trailing off as I kissed her forehead. "I never thought this would be my life. You... us."

"What do you mean?"

I brushed a strand of hair from her face, marvelling that I could be this open and unguarded with someone.

"I mean I never expected to find this. A real partner who knows the real me, fame and baggage included." I shook my head. "Someone I can just be myself with, without pretence."

Understanding dawned in her eyes. She cuddled against my chest, hand splayed over my heart.

"Before you, my life was... complicated. It was always about managing perceptions, about the next big scandal or headline. But with you, it's different. It's real."

"I get that," she said softly. "It's not easy letting your guard down when you never know who might sell you out."

"Aye, fame makes it hard to know people's true motives sometimes." My thumb idly stroked her shoulder as I gathered my thoughts. "I've had women get close to me for the exposure or potential payout down the road. Had strangers convinced we were secretly together."

She tensed against me, probably thinking of Sammy Miller, the woman who caused all of this. I guess in a way I had to be grateful to her. Without her ridiculous claims, I wouldn't be holding Ros right now.

Her hand traced idle patterns on my chest as she listened intently.

"Sometimes, it's just strangers on the street," I continued. "They smile at me, create entire fictional lives in their heads where we're in a relationship. Those can be the dangerous ones. Then there was Sammy Miller..."

Her hand froze and she tilted her head back, taking a cautious peek at my expression. I wasn't angry about it anymore. Couldn't be now.

"No one can ever predict which rumours will take hold. My agent wishes he could." I smirked, remembering every rant he'd made about wishing the Greek gods were real because he'd make a deal with Apollo for second sight without a moment's pause. "We just deal with the fallout and hope for the best. But it damages you after a while."

I frowned at her ceiling, momentarily annoyed at myself for setting us onto such a depressing topic.

"And it's left me cautious, like you. Worried no one would want the real me, baggage and all." I pressed a kiss to her hair. "But with you, I don't have to second guess. I don't feel like I'm constantly on guard. You understand me in ways others don't. That means everything, pixie."

She lifted her head to meet my gaze, eyes shining with empathy.

I pulled her closer, relishing the feel of her in my arms. "That's all I've ever wanted, Ros. To be with someone who wants me for me, not for the fame or the headlines."

"Of course I do." She grimaced. "Though I wish I hadn't wasted so much time, avoiding us."

I smiled, emotion sitting heavy on my chest.

"I'm not worried. We have the rest of our lives to make up for it," I murmured before capturing her lips.

We traded lazy, contented kisses, lost in the simple joy of being wrapped up together. But Ros pulled back, gnawing her lip.

"What's wrong?"

She bit her lip, looking unsure. "There's something I should probably tell you. I haven't been completely honest."

I frowned, sitting up against the headboard and drawing her with me. "Okay. You can tell me anything, you know that."

Taking a deep breath, she explained about losing her fashion house job and Dakota trying to exploit her connection to me, even though we weren't really together then.

Guilt gnawed at me as she described getting fired over those photos. "Christ, I'm so sorry. I never wanted my mess to hurt your career."

But she shook her head. "Don't apologise. Honestly... I'm kind of glad for how things turned out." My brows climbed in shock and she rushed to explain. "Not for losing my job. But it forced me to take control of my path again. To take a chance on you, on us."

Relief loosened the knot in my chest. "Well in that case, I suppose I owe Dakota a thank you." We both laughed at the absurdity.

Sobering, I cupped her cheek. "I'm just happy you felt able to open up and take that leap with me. And I swear I meant it when I said I'd do whatever I can to support your dreams."

Ros smiled, leaning into my touch. "You already do. I feel so much freer now — in my love life, my trust, my creativity. Even my career prospects." She kissed me softly. "You make me braver, Jackson."

My throat tightened with emotion. Knowing I made her feel that way was the greatest gift.

"Right back at you. We make each other better."

And we had our whole lives ahead of us to keep growing together. Though, staring at the guest room, I couldn't stop myself from frowning.

"You know it would be so much easier to do this, if you were sleeping in my bed full time, right?" I squeezed her tighter against my chest.

She peered up at me, a glint of amusement in her narrowed eyes. "What would be easier?"

"Oh, you know," I shrugged, playing it casual, "sustaining your appetite for my body." I could barely finish the sentence with a straight face and Ros laughed.

"Be serious."

"I am. You've got quite the appetite."

"Jackson!"

"Okay, fine. It doesn't make much sense for you to sleep in the guest room now we're officially a thing. I want you closer. I need to wake up with you in my arms." I rolled us until she lay flat on her back under me. I rubbed the back of my neck, a tad nervous but determined. "It's stupid but I want to fight with you over the covers, hear you moan at me in the morning if I snore and yes, it's a vivid dream of mine to wake you with my mouth on your pretty pussy."

Her cheeks flushed but she didn't look away, didn't show an ounce of distaste for the idea. If anything it seemed to turn her on.

"Why don't you move your stuff into my room? Sleep in my bed, with me?"

She smiled, wide and radiant. "I'd love that."

CHAPTER TWENTY-SEVEN

ROS

"I'm pleased to say our press campaign for 'Beautiful Lies' is paying off." Audra smiled. "The Golden Globe win last week certainly set the tone for the rest of the award season."

I nodded, like I didn't already know all this and hadn't been sitting in the audience with Jackson, millions of cameras pointed at me while they broadcast my face across the entire country.

We sat in Jackson's living room, strategising his schedule for the rest of the year. Well, they strategised. I sat quietly and absorbed it all with a strange sort of calm.

It was a lot to take in and honestly, I was shocked by how calm I felt. A few months ago, having my life dictated like this would've made me bolt for the door. But somewhere along the way, between the staged kisses and pretending to be Jackson's fiancée, things had changed.

"Next up, we have the BAFTAs in London," she said, her fingers tapping on the tablet. "Then, Jackson, you'll return to LA and start training for Rogue Squad 6. Aidan Parker will meet you here for your first session two days after you get back."

"That's fine, but we're spending a week with my parents, so make sure there's space in the calendar."

Audra's eyes narrowed. "Really, Jackson? A whole week? You know how tight everything is, especially with the awards season and the upcoming projects. Every day counts."

"I do, but we've discussed this before." His jaw tightened, but he kept his tone neutral. "My family time is non-negotiable. You were aware of this when you drafted my schedule."

"Absolutely." She directed a tight smile at him. It didn't reach her eyes. "But I suppose family comes first." The subtle emphasis she put on the word "family" made it clear she considered it an unnecessary distraction.

"I'm sure you can shift things around to accommodate it."

"Of course." Her nostrils flared slightly. She made a show of scrolling through the calendar and rearranging items with sharp jabs of her stylus.

I hid a smirk, enjoying seeing Jackson stand firm against her passive-aggressive pushback for once. Having him throw a wrench in her perfectly arranged plans was messing with her dictatorship, and I loved to see it.

"There," she huffed, dropping the tablet in her lap. "I've cleared a full seven days before you return to train for Romania. Will that suffice?"

I opened my mouth to tell her exactly where she could shove her opinion about Jackson's family time, but he gave an almost imperceptible shake of his head.

With effort, I snapped my mouth shut and offered Audra a sweetly sarcastic smile instead.

"Of course, there will be various film festival appearances, premieres, charity galas, and the Met Gala in May," Audra continued, her voice steady as if we hadn't interrupted at all. "Scots Bank wants to endorse you, so there will be photoshoots and interviews to come."

The list seemed endless, a constant whirlwind of events and appearances. I couldn't help but feel like a supporting character in Jackson's life, always there but not quite the main focus.

I snuck a glance at Jackson beside me on the couch. His attention was perfectly fixed on Audra, his brow furrowed slightly as he listened to her drone on about the next year.

He always got that serious, contemplative look when discussing work. I had to resist the urge to reach over and smooth the little crease from his forehead.

Things had definitely changed between us. Enough that I didn't freak out about Audra dictating my life alongside his.

Don't get me wrong, I still thought Audra was an arrogant bitch who cared more about Jackson's image than his actual happiness. But somewhere along the way, I'd gone and done the unthinkable.

I'd fallen for the guy. Hard.

When Abi had left New York for Finn, I'd thought she was insane. Uprooting her life for a man, who does that? Not me, I'd said.

I'd practically set them up and I couldn't understand why she would give up her existence in the best city on the planet.

Now I understood.

Because let me tell you, it took a lot of love to force me to stay seated on the couch while bitchface went on and on as if half this shit wasn't common sense.

Yes, we dress nice, you arrange photos. Got it.

"Of course, Ros will join you in Romania," Audra said, tapping something on her tablet screen. "We can't have anyone speculating about relationship problems, not when the big breakup is planned for October."

Audra might as well have dropped a nuclear bomb in the middle of the living room. I shot Jackson a wide-eyed look, waiting for him to set her straight. To clarify that he and I were genuinely together now, not just keeping up some publicity sham.

What the fuck?

Irritation and hurt stabbed through me. Why wasn't he saying something? I shifted away from him on the couch, no longer able to appreciate the warm press of his thigh against mine. The sunny room suddenly felt cold.

"Well, we'll see how things look in October."

My breath left me in a pained exhale. That was it? I dug my fingernails into the couch cushion, biting my tongue hard enough to taste blood.

I'll say it again: what the ever-loving fuck?

Audra arched a sharp brow. "Jackson, darling, you know we need to plan this out carefully. Your adoring fans will be distraught."

The smugness in her tone grated on my nerves.

"We need to have everything laid out well in advance," Audra continued, her fingers tapping on the tablet screen as if she were already drafting the script for our supposed breakup. "We can't afford any slip-ups. Not after last time."

The words seemed to hang in the air. I glanced at Jackson, getting as close to begging as I would ever allow myself, wishing for him to say something, anything, that would fix this. But he remained silent, staring back at me with a perplexed look.

What the hell did he have to be perplexed about?

"You'll leave Romania a few weeks before Jackson," Audra said, her tone brisk and business-like. "It'll give the impression of a slow drift apart. Then we can start leaking rumours from 'trusted sources' about a rift."

Numbly, I let the rest of Audra's words wash over me without fully registering them. Lowered public appearances, controlled leaks about relationship troubles, scripted distant body language.

She described it all in detail, her tone as detached as if she were scheduling a dental cleaning and not orchestrating the meticulous dissolution of something real and precious. Of my entire heart.

And all the while, Jackson stared at me, his brow furrowed but saying *nothing*.

"One possibility I'm keen on developing is a narrative where Bree returns to claim her childhood sweetheart."

Jackson's attention snapped back to Audra, his face white.

Who the hell is Bree?

"We could orchestrate something public." Audra pursed her lips, her gaze falling on the ring I twisted around my finger. "Of course, it's handy that you gave Ros Bree's ring."

Her ring? He'd given me *a reject ring?* I wanted to demand answers, to tell him to go fuck himself, to demand he set Audra straight and buy me a new ring.

I shifted away from him. He was just like all the others. Stringing me along until he got what he wanted and then cutting me loose.

Just like she wanted.

"I'm sure Bree would be amenable." Audra rolled her eyes. "She's sent you enough emails over the years to be interested in making it up to you."

Jackson looked at me, really looked at me for the first time since she'd started deconstructing our relationship brick by brick, concern etched on his face. "I'll explain after, I promise."

I wanted to laugh, to cry, to scream.

Why had I foolishly thought he would ever fight for me?

No, Jackson would jump off a high-speed train if Audra told him to.

"…have to set a date for the wedding, of course," Audra was saying briskly, tapping something on her tablet. "I can pull some strings and get you an easily cancelable reservation so we can mitigate any speculation that this relationship was manufactured."

This couldn't be happening.

I refused to sit through a second more of it.

I stood, my movements stiff and sharp. "Email me my part of the schedule once it's finalised," I bit out, my voice devoid of emotion. "I have errands to run."

Audra nodded, looking pleased. "Of course. I'll send it over once we're done here."

I thanked Audra and left the room without looking at him. If I peeked, if I saw so much as a flicker of confusion on his face, I'd lose my shit, and I really didn't want to do that in front of him right now.

❄

By the time the taxi pulled up outside Finn and Abi's house, my eyes were raw and puffy. I knocked on their door, taking deep breaths to control the tears. The door opened and Abi took one look at my devastated expression and pulled me into a fierce hug.

"Oh honey... what happened?"

I choked on the words, some sense of shame silencing me.

Instead, I asked, "Somebody tell me who Bree is?"

"Christ," Finn muttered, dragging a hand across his face. "What did the fucker do?"

"Doesn't matter. Give me details."

Finn and Abi exchanged a loaded glance before guiding me to the living room sofa. Abi draped a soft blanket around my shoulders while Finn pressed a glass of wine into my hands.

"Talk to us, Ros," Abi said, her voice gentle once we were settled. "What's going on?"

I stared into my wine glass, anger and hurt churning inside me. "I just found out Jackson gave me his ex's engagement ring to wear. Some woman named Bree."

Finn winced. "Bree was Jackson's first love. They were childhood sweethearts. He proposed to her right before he moved to LA, and she was supposed to follow him. She decided it would be perfectly reasonable to wait two years before she did." He rolled his eyes, his tone cutting. "Then, when Jackson's career started taking off, suddenly she couldn't get to LA fast enough."

I sipped the wine, the bitterness on my tongue mirroring my thoughts. "What happened then?"

"She changed. Started partying non-stop, using Jackson's name to get into clubs, get free stuff. She'd promise his attendance at events without even asking him, not caring if it was something he'd want to be associated with."

I leaned back, trying to process the information. It sounded so unlike the Jackson I knew, yet so painfully familiar.

"Then the rumours started." Sadness tinged his voice. "Small things at first. Then they got bigger, nastier. He nearly got kicked off the Rogue Squad franchise because of it. It drove him mad, trying to figure out who was behind it."

"And?" Even as I asked, I knew and dreaded the answer.

Regret flickered in Finn's eyes. "He hadn't thought to look in his own house. He only realised it when something he'd only told Bree leaked."

The thought of him sitting there, silently taking all of Audra's suggestions, effectively agreeing to reintroduce someone who had more than hurt him personally, but also his career, it made my anger flare back to life.

"I'm done," I said, my tone so hard it could bend nails. I stood up and started pacing. "I'll fulfil the contract, I'll smile for the cameras and pretend to be madly in love, but I am done with Jackson Levi."

"Maybe you should take a minute," Abi said, her voice cautious.

I ignored her. I loved her, but Abi had developed a tendency to be the voice of reason and I did not need reasoning right now.

CHAPTER TWENTY-EIGHT

JACKSON

A week passed by, and it felt like I was trapped in a different universe. A universe where Ros had become a ghost in my life, always hovering at the fringes of my thoughts but remaining stubbornly out of reach.

I barely saw her. When I did, it was only during the carefully orchestrated public appearances Audra had planned.

By the time Friday rolled around, I'd come to expect that if it wasn't on our shared schedule, I wouldn't be seeing her at all. And even when we did cross paths, she stonewalled me with a determination that left me completely bamboozled.

I stood in the walk-in wardrobe, staring at the empty space on the shelf where her clothes used to be. It was as if she'd vanished into thin air overnight, wiping out every trace of herself from my bedroom and my life. She'd stopped sleeping in my bed and replying to my texts on day one, but this? This was a slow creep I hadn't picked up on until it was too late.

And I was still at a loss as to what I'd done to upset her.

Confused, I roamed through the house, hunting for any sign of her and finding zilch. No more half-done sketches covering the kitchen island, no Doc Martens willy-nilly by the door, no lingering scent of her floral shampoo in the bathroom.

Even her cherished sewing machine had vanished from its usual spot in the corner of the living room.

Ros was sending a message loud and clear: she was done with me.

But why?

Hadn't I made my feelings clear? I had told her I loved her, so why hadn't she stood up to Audra?

The one possibility I didn't want to consider was that maybe, to Ros, this whole relationship was as much a charade as Audra believed. One with a clear end date. The idea of it was a knife to my gut.

I sank onto the sofa, dropping my head in my hands with a frustrated groan.

How had we gone from sleepy morning kisses over coffee to this distance in a matter of days?

Maybe the only reason she had let it go this far was because it had an end date. A way to pass the time and enjoy certain... fringe benefits.

But she didn't see it as something meaningful or built to last.

Not the way I did.

If anyone should be upset, it should be me.

All she'd had to do was admit our new reality to Audra, to tell somebody how she felt about me. Instead, she'd clammed up tight like the stubborn lass she was.

She'd moved out without a word, she was avoiding me again and she'd probably moved on with her plans to launch her label without me — maybe she was using my name to open doors. Just like Bree.

And she hadn't broken the terms of our agreement so I was still funding her: label, lifestyle, and fashion addiction.

One moment I was spitting mad and the next desperately sad.

So desperate that I couldn't trust myself to make a rational decision on anything.

She cared for me, I knew she did. I hadn't imagined the tenderness in her eyes, her touch… had I?

She never told you she loved you.

Not verbally sure, but she said it in other ways. Didn't she?

Or at least, I had thought she did. Her laughter at my jokes, those late-night conversations we had shared, the way she looked at me when she thought I wasn't looking — they had to mean something, didn't they?

Maybe I was a fool, grasping at straws. Seeing devotion in gestures that were only casual affection in her eyes.

Was the fact we'd agreed to an end date the only reason she'd felt safe enough to let me close? I hated to admit it but — probably.

I thought we'd grown beyond this in the last few weeks, that her words and actions in New York meant she'd fully committed to me.

But clear as day, I was wrong.

She couldn't tell a single soul that she loved me.

I'd expected us to talk things through after the planning meeting with Audra. But she didn't come home that night, nor the one after.

I glanced at my phone, debating whether to call her. She hadn't responded to me all week except in curt, impersonal messages about upcoming publicity events. Nothing about us or where we stood.

My thumbs hovered over her name, hesitation gnawing at me. What if she rejected my call? Or worse, told me it was over between us? The uncertainty was pure agony, but it was a sight better than confirmation that I'd lost her for good.

I had to try.

JACKSON

Hey pixie, just checking in. We need to talk.

Nothing good ever came from those words but what else was I meant to say when my girlfriend made it her mission to avoid me?

I stared at the screen, watching those three pulsating dots taunt me. Why wasn't she responding? Didn't she realise how worried I was? How much I needed to understand what had gone wrong so I could make things right between us and get back to the normal of waking up next to her?

After two endless minutes with no reply, dejection washed over me, but just as I tossed the phone aside, it pinged.

ROS

I'm fine. Just need some space to think right now.

Space to think?

I glowered at the screen. I wouldn't let her go without a fight, no matter how much she tried to avoid me.

Grabbing my keys, I stormed out the door before I could second guess myself. I had to set this right between us, whatever it took. I refused to lose the best thing that ever happened to me without understanding why.

Luckily, I had a solid guess where she'd hidden herself.

"**W**ell, don't you look like shite," Finn said, eyebrows lifting as he took in my scruffy appearance.

I grimaced, ruffling a hand through my hair. "Nice to see you too, mate."

Finn's mouth twitched. "Get in here before the neighbours start thinkin' we're harbouring a fugitive."

I snorted as I stepped inside and followed him into the open plan living area, a near mirror image to mine: stark white walls, huge picture window with a view across LA and a top of the line kitchen. Only his space felt more lived in. Abi had added her stamp to the place with colourful throws, pillows and photos of all of us.

"So, what'd you do to muck things up?" He pulled a couple of beers out of the fridge and tossed one to me.

I caught the beer with a sigh. "Honestly, I have no idea. She's completely shut me out."

He leaned against the counter, cracking open his beer. "Jesus. We should write a manual on how to navigate relationships. Might save us a lot of trouble."

I chuckled dryly. "Aye, 'How to Screw Up Your Love Life: A Guide by Hollywood's Finest.'"

Taking a long drink, I tried to unwind, but the tension in my shoulders wouldn't let up. "She's been avoiding me for a week. I don't even know where she's staying." I added the last bit with a pointed look at him.

He crossed and uncrossed his legs as he leaned against the counter, suddenly interested in studying the marbling on his breakfast bar rather than looking at me.

Finn's hesitation didn't go unnoticed. He was usually more straight to the point, but this time, he looked like he was dancing around a landmine.

"Out with it. You know where Ros is, don't you?" I pushed, unable to keep the edge out of my voice.

He pulled a face. "I really don't want to be caught in the crossfire."

"Which is code for she's staying with you." I crossed my arms. "Help your best mate out, Finn. If I can't talk to her, I can't figure out what I've done and fix it."

"And I get that." He rubbed a hand across his jaw, a sheepish glint in his eyes. "But my wife's the one calling the shots in this house, and I'm not about to get on the wrong side of Abi, especially while she's carrying our kid."

I slumped back against the counter, the fight going out of me.

"I also promised Ros I'd respect her privacy. Surely you can get your head around that."

"You're right, I'm sorry," I said, my voice cracking. I squeezed my eyes shut, willing myself to think clearly through the ache in my chest. "I'm just so bloody frustrated. I don't know how to reach her."

"I get it. It's rough." He gripped my shoulder and I stared into his understanding eyes. "But sometimes, giving space is the best thing you can do."

I frowned at the half-empty beer bottle in my hand. "I thought we were past all these games."

Finn nodded. "Relationships aren't easy, especially with all the pressure. It's like walking a tightrope sometimes."

I laughed bitterly. "More like a minefield."

He chuckled, then became serious again. "Listen, I can't be telling you what to do, but maybe think about what's happened recently. Reflect a bit."

"She hasn't told you?"

Finn shook his head. "Just that you two were done and she didn't want to lay eyes on you outside the bounds of your agreement."

The words hit me like a punch in the gut. "I just... I don't understand. I thought we were good. I thought she..." My voice trailed off, unable to complete the thought.

Finn sighed, leaning back against the counter. "Look, I don't know all the ins and outs of your relationship, but maybe you need to be seeing it from her point of view."

"I thought I was," I muttered, rubbing a hand over my face. "But maybe I missed something."

"Maybe you did. And maybe you need to figure that out before you try to talk to her again. Especially if you haven't set the record straight with Audra and binned any plans to involve Bree in your life." He gave me a hard look. "What the fuck were thinking with that one?"

"That was Audra's ridiculous idea." I brushed it off with a wave of my hand. "It's not going to happen."

"Did you think to tell Ros that? Or even Audra?"

My brow furrowed, confusion and frustration rippled through me. "No, of course not. Why would I want my ex back?"

Finn laughed, the sound not kind. "You're an eejit, Jackson. An utter fucking eejit."

I frowned, pondering his words. "I thought she understood how much I care about her. What else was I supposed to do?"

"Oh, I don't know, maybe told your publicist to take her shite ideas and shove them where the sun don't shine?" His brow arched.

"I…"

"I thought not." He sighed, shaking his head as he stared at me. "I don't know how to help you. This is complicated and you're making it even worse with your bleeding assumptions."

How much more obvious could I have been?

I nodded slowly. "I guess I just assumed we were on the same page." I rubbed my forehead, feeling the weight of his words. "I'd ask for advice, but you're still useless even though you're married," I said with a wry smile, trying to lighten the mood.

Finn cracked a small smile. "Marriage is… complex. Especially when you add pregnancy hormones to the mix." He shuddered. "I won't wish it on even those feckin' eejit Sanderson brothers."

I smirked at that, but the image of one of them struggling with an unexpected newborn could only lift my mood for so long.

"Aye, but at least you and Abi talk things out. Ros won't even give me a second of the day." I leaned back against the counter, my mind a whirl. "I keep going over our last conversation, trying to suss out what I said or did. But it doesn't add up. We were right as rain before that meeting."

"Were you really fine, or were you just avoiding the tough conversations?"

His words echoed in my head.

Were we really fine before that meeting? I thought back carefully, re-examining our interactions over the previous weeks.

On the surface, things had seemed solid. We spent most evenings together, talking or cooking or watching films curled up on the sofa. Nights were even better, falling asleep tangled together in bed.

But now that I looked closer, there had been signs something was off.

Tense silences after calls with Audra discussing upcoming events for us as a couple. Ros deflecting questions about her free-lance design work. Me cancelling dinner plans because of a work commitment.

Individually, they were small things. But together they painted a picture of two people avoiding harder conversations and making assumptions.

I'd told myself we were on the same page without really being sure it was true.

"Shit," I muttered, swiping a hand down my face.

Finn was right — I'd ignored little cracks developing instead of addressing them. Let myself believe everything was fine because it was easier.

And Ros had done the same, keeping doubts to herself rather than calling me out. We'd both fallen into the trap of making assumptions instead of communicating.

Christ, I really had cocked this up. But beating myself up wouldn't fix things now. I had to find a way to show Ros she did come first, even if rebuilding her trust took time.

With a weary sigh, I pushed off from the counter and met Finn's sympathetic gaze. "Well, you've certainly given me a lot to think over."

Finn nodded. "I know it's not easy to hear, but you'll figure this out. Just don't be giving up on her yet." He clasped my shoulder.

I managed a wan smile, gratitude welling for his honesty and friendship, even when it stung. "Cheers, Finn. I needed that boot up the arse."

I couldn't lose hope yet. What we'd started building had been real, I had to keep believing that.

Failure wasn't an option.

One way or another, I refused to accept that we couldn't fix things.

CHAPTER TWENTY-NINE

ROS

"Thanks, Finn." As soon as the door clicked shut behind Jackson, I stepped out of the hallway I'd been hiding in and into Finn's open plan kitchen with a sheepish expression plastered on my face. "For covering for me."

Had it been childish to hide from him? Yes.

But give a girl a break. My heart hurt enough. The thought of looking Jackson in the eye right now made nausea roll in my stomach.

In a few weeks, I'd be able to handle it. Maybe longer since I had to see him nearly every week for events and our trip to London was fast approaching. Every time I saw him and he tried to talk to me, touch me as if nothing had changed, it ripped the wound open all over again.

Finn grunted. "Avoiding him's not going to be any help."

I pulled out a chair at the breakfast bar and dropped onto it. "I know. But how can I face him…?" My words trailed off as I traced the patterns in the marble.

He stared back at me, his brows raised, waiting.

I hadn't even told Abi what happened or why I was hiding out in her guest room begging her to use all her sway over Finn to keep my location secret.

Guess that failed.

"He just does whatever Audra says. I thought this time would be different." The bitterness in my voice surprised even me. I was angry, sure, but underneath it all was this raw, scraping hurt.

"You don't have to tell me what happened." Finn leaned back against the counter, arms crossed. "I know you're mad at him, and you've probably got a right to be. But dodging the problem won't make it vanish into thin air."

"I know." I sighed. "I should talk to him, but it's hard."

Normally there weren't ties holding me to the guy who used and tossed me. Things were much different this time and I didn't have the first clue how to handle it.

Our friends' circles were so tightly woven and our lives bound together by the stupid contract. I couldn't delete him from my brain like I'd started doing with the assholes who had hurt me in the past.

I had to figure out how to live with him without it ripping me in two every time I had to smile at him.

But how?

"Then go have a chat with him. Don't let this stew," Finn said, his tone reasonable like he wasn't asking me to suck on a sour lemon.

But I couldn't. Not yet.

So instead I retreated to my temporary bedroom, locking the door behind me. The silence was comforting, allowing me to drown in my thoughts.

Furious didn't even begin to describe how I felt at Jackson, at Audra. At myself for believing that love meant you stood up for each other, no matter what. A laugh bubbled up, bitter and sharp.

Love, huh?

It seemed more like a cruel joke at the moment.

I paced the small guest room, emotions churning into a ball of pressure I couldn't shake off. The hurt and anger roiling through me threatened to spill over in tears or screams.

How could I have been so stupidly naive?

Of course, Jackson would choose what was supposedly best for his career over me in the end. Audra had been directing his life for years — why would I be any different?

I had allowed myself to believe that when it mattered most, he would be there for me. How many times had he sworn he didn't care what Audra demanded if it made me uncomfortable? How many times had he sworn he would put his foot down for me if I needed him to?

And I'd believed him. Ridiculous.

He was like a sheep, he would always do what Audra demanded, no matter the cost.

You're pathetic, a disdainful voice in my head taunted. It sounded eerily like Dakota. *Did you really think you were special enough to keep him? That he'd throw away everything for you, like you did for him?*

"No," I muttered, swiping angrily at a rogue tear.

I refused to fall apart over any man, even if this betrayal cut deeper than any before. He didn't deserve my tears or the satisfaction of knowing how deeply his choices had hurt me.

I just had to keep reminding myself that his actions reflected on him, not me. I was still the same fiery, determined Ros I'd always been. My self-worth wasn't defined by fickle Hollywood types.

Taking a deep, shaky breath, I sank down onto the edge of the bed and scrubbed my hands over my face. Sitting here wallowing in hurt and bitterness accomplished nothing. I had to resist the temptation to just curl up under the weight of sadness and wallow.

Giving in meant Jackson had won, crushing my spirit along with my heart. I wouldn't let him or any man rob me of my passions that way. Not again.

Jaw set, I crossed the room to dig a battered sketchbook and pencils out of my bag. If I couldn't erase him from my life, I could at least focus the raw emotion somewhere productive.

I settled on the floor, cross-legged and flipped open the sketch-book. My pencil flew as I began channelling all my frustration into bold dress designs.

Absorbed in bringing the visions to life on paper, I barely noticed as time passed and an ache developed in my butt. Shadows slowly shifted across the walls as afternoon faded to evening. For a blissful window of time, hurt and anger faded into the back-ground, my mind wonderfully blank except for fabric swatches and silhouettes.

Eventually a soft knock at the door drew me from my artistic bubble. I glanced up as Abi cracked it open, brow furrowed.

"Are you okay?" Abi asked, her voice tinged with worry.

I attempted a reassuring smile that probably came out as more of a pained grimace. "Yeah, fine. Just working on some sketches." I lifted my pencil in evidence.

Abi nodded, though her concerned frown didn't ease. "Well, don't skip dinner, yeah?" She chewed her lip as her eyes tracked over the explosion of discarded drawings and fabric scraps littering the floor around me. "We're ordering from Geo's."

Which meant there was a generous helping of carbonara on its way. I smiled at Abi, grateful for her attempt to comfort me.

"I won't. Thanks, Abs."

With one last searching look, she pulled the door shut again, leaving me cocooned in silence. My smile faded as soon as she left, shoulders slumping wearily. But after a fortifying breath, I leaned forward again, pencil scratching over paper once more.

Over the next twenty-four hours, I channelled my broken heart into creation, hardly pausing to eat or sleep.

An entire collection took shape on the pages — dresses and tops and jackets infused with all my pain and hope. My hands grew smudged with graphite, fingers cramped around my sketching pencils, but I pushed through the discomfort happily.

Two days later, the guest room looked like a war zone of fabric and thread. I was hunched over my sewing machine, surrounded by a chaos of my own making. Every stitch was a tiny rebellion against the helplessness I felt.

"It looks like a tornado hit in here," Abi said softly.

I looked up, finally acknowledging their presence. Finn and Abi stood in the doorway, their eyes wide with shock as they surveyed the room. I felt a pang of guilt for the mess I had created, but I couldn't bring myself to stop.

"Maybe it did," I said, allowing a half-hearted smile to flicker across my lips. "But it's my tornado. My rules."

"Right..." Finn scratched jaw, looking lost for words.

Abi sighed. "When's the last time you took a break?"

I shrugged, not remembering. Time seemed irrelevant when I was lost in my work.

"You promised me you wouldn't skip meals. I'm worried about you."

The mention of food made my stomach grumble, but I couldn't afford to break my concentration.

"I'm fine, really. Just want to get these designs finished."

I spotted the uncertain look that passed between them, but couldn't bring myself to care about what it meant. Instead, I ignored their concerned expressions and continued to sew, my movements becoming more frantic as if I could force them to leave me alone through sheer determination.

But they weren't easily dissuaded. "We were thinking of ordering brunch from that new place you love. Bottomless mimosas and all."

The temptation of bottomless mimosas was hard to resist, but I pushed it aside. I had work to do.

Finn spoke up, his tone firm. "Abi's right. You need a break."

I made a noncommittal noise, already tuning them out. I had to get these swirling ideas out before they evaporated. Everything else could wait.

❄

"Wow, it's really... coming together in here," Eva said diplomatically the next day. She nudged aside a pile of fabric scraps so she could perch on the edge of the bed.

I'd woken up and gotten straight back to work, barely stopping long enough to chug some water and eat a piece of toast. I was so close to a finished collection, to having something tangible to show when I put my brain to the launching a label part of this challenge.

Abi nodded slowly. "These pieces are lovely, Ros. But don't you think it's time for a break?"

"Can't," I muttered, guiding the fabric through the machine. The needle punctuated my words as if it too agreed: Can't stop, won't stop.

"We get that. Truly we do." Eva gave a pointed glance at my dishevelled state. "But it's like you're on a never-ending loop here."

I shook my head. "I know you mean well, but I'm fine. Just want to get the collection finished."

"When's the last time you—when did you shower last?" Abi's nose wrinkled slightly as she surveyed the fabric battlefield surrounding my station.

"Shower?" I hesitated, unable to recall when I had last stepped into the bathroom.

"You can't keep pushing yourself like this." Abi stepped closer, her voice gentle but insistent. "Talk to us. Let us help."

I couldn't understand why they were making such a fuss. My collection was everything to me, the one thing I could control in the midst of the chaos that had engulfed my life.

They tried to distract me with updates from their lives. Abi's doctor's appointment, Eva's upcoming trip to Bangkok. I answered with a half-hearted smile and nod, my fingers continuing their dance with the fabric and thread.

"That's enough of that," Abi muttered just before the humming of the sewing machine stopped.

"Hey! What the hell are you doing?"

"Saving you from yourself." She stood by my side, the cord in her hand. "You're not dealing with the problem."

"You're burying yourself in work. This isn't healthy." Eva crossed her arms.

"I don't have a problem," I snapped, anger rippling through me. "I'm handling it."

"Sweetie, look at yourself." Eva's tone softened, yet it carried the weight of unspoken truths. "You're hiding behind this sewing machine like it's some kind of shield."

Abi dropped the cord and stepped closer, her expression soft but stern. "You're avoiding dealing with Jackson and everything that's happened. You haven't even told *us* what happened, Ros." Her brows rose. "Does that sound normal to you?"

I opened my mouth to argue but no words came out. They were right.

"Look, we're here for you, okay?" Abi said gently. "But you need to face this. You can't just sew your feelings into these clothes."

I slumped back against the sewing table, the fight draining from me. "I don't know how to go back to before…" I narrowed my eyes, hunting for the right words, but failing.

"Before you fell in love with him." Eva lowered her voice.

I scowled at her. "That is not what I was going to say at all."

"But it's the truth, isn't it?" Abi fixed me with a don't bullshit me look.

I glared at her, her words striking a nerve I didn't want to admit existed. Unfortunately, she was right.

Deep down, beneath the layers of anger and denial, I knew that falling for Jackson had changed everything. It had made me vulnerable in a way I had sworn I never would be.

I held her gaze for a defiant moment before my shoulders slumped in defeat. "Fine. Maybe I did… care about him. But clearly that was a mistake."

Abi's expression gentled. She came over to wrap an arm

around my shoulders. "Oh, sweetie. Caring about someone is never a mistake. Even if they end up letting you down."

My throat tightened painfully as I hugged Abi back, my body almost on autopilot.

"We just want to help," Abi mumbled into my shoulder. "You don't have to go through this alone."

Eva nodded in agreement. "We're here for you, no matter what."

I bit my lip, a swirl of gratitude and stubborn pride battling within me. "I know, and I appreciate it. But... I don't know what to do about Jackson. I thought I could forget and go back to when we were just friends, but how can I?"

I dashed away the tears blurring my vision impatiently as Abi released me and straightened up.

My friends exchanged a loaded glance. Eva asked carefully, "Are you still expected to keep up appearances with him, are you?"

"Unfortunately yes." I grimaced, the bitter taste in my mouth again. "I still have to uphold my end of the contract and now I really need the money if I'm going to launch my own label." I gestured to my growing collection of garments. "So our 'relationship' is still on display for the vultures, per Audra's demands."

Even just saying her name sparked a fresh wave of anger. I filled them in on how he sat mute as a statue taking his marching orders from Audra.

Abi's eyes widened with dismay. "Wait, go back. Jackson seriously just sat there while his publicist planned your breakup?"

"Yup." I popped the 'p' loudly, anger simmering now. "Not a peep of objection from him. Meanwhile I'm sitting there stunned, realising he apparently never intended for us to be more than a publicity ploy."

Eva's expression had slowly darkened into a scowl. "That unbelievable jackass," she muttered. "Please tell me you ripped him a new one after."

My feigned indifference slipped at that. I dropped my gaze, fiddling with my shirtsleeve.

"I... walked out before the meeting ended."

"You mean he hasn't even apologised?!" Abi looked properly outraged now on my behalf.

I bit my lip, feeling a mix of guilt and frustration. "It's not like I've given him a chance."

Abi frowned, concern blanketing her face. "If you don't talk to him, how will you ever resolve anything?"

"I don't need to resolve anything," I shot back, more sharply than I intended. "I've made up my mind. He showed his true colours. I'm not just going to sit around waiting for someone who can't even stand up for me."

I stood up and started pacing the room. If I didn't move, I'd start shaking or seriously break down and no one wanted to see that.

"I thought he was different. I really believed all those things he said about wanting something real." I shook my head, fresh anger welling up. "But in the end he was just like every other self-absorbed jackass."

"You took a leap of faith opening yourself up again after everything you've been through." Eva moved closer, eyeing me like she might reach out and stop my frantic pacing with a hug. I shifted further away. "No one blames you for being hurt."

"Well I blame me. I'm so stupid — I should've known he'd never choose me over his precious image and career."

"You're not stupid," Abi said fiercely. "You're one of the smartest, strongest people I know. I know it hurts, but you'll get through this. And we'll be right by your side no matter what."

Eva nodded, her expression earnest. "Seriously, anything you need — someone to vent to, help packing up his stuff, an alibi for light arson — just say the word."

That surprised a watery laugh out of me. Who knew Eva had developed a bite?

But my brief smile quickly faded. "I appreciate the offer, really. But this isn't something you guys can fix for me." I twisted my hands together, uncertainty swirling through me. "I just need to figure out how to be around Jackson after... everything. But I have no clue how."

My friends shared a concerned look. I could see the unspoken questions in their eyes.

Abi asked gently, "Do you want to try talking to him? See if you can work things out?"

I shook my head sharply, a swell of anger rising. "Absolutely not. I'm done waiting around for him. I refuse to make a man fight for me. If he loved me—really loved me—his actions would have spoken for him."

"Ros," Abi began, but I raised a hand, stopping her mid sentence.

"Please," I whispered, pleading with them to understand. "I can't let a man determine my worth or direction. I won't."

Eva's brow furrowed. "What do you mean? How were his actions not showing love?"

I threw my hands up in frustration. "What kind of man who supposedly loves you just sits there silently while his publicist plans ending your relationship? He'd stand up, make them change the plan. But Jackson? He's too caught up in what's best for his career."

Abi and Eva exchanged glances, their faces showing shock and annoyance on my behalf.

"Don't go getting all worked up about it," I said quickly, not wanting them to start any drama on my account. "I'm fine. Really."

Abi looked sceptical. "You're clearly not fine. You're here, sewing your heart out, avoiding the problem."

"I know it seems like I'm avoiding it, but what else can I do? He made his choice, and I have to live with it."

"You don't have to just accept it," Eva said, her voice firm. "Maybe if you told him—"

"No. I don't want to talk to him unless it fulfils the contract." I stared hard at both of them. "And I don't want you to either. Just let me work. Let me feel like I have control over something in my life, please?"

Abi and Eva exchanged another glance, silently communicating their concern, but they eventually nodded in agreement.

"Alright." Abi's shoulders slumped. "We'll respect your wishes, but don't forget that we're just a call away."

CHAPTER THIRTY

JACKSON

"You've been staring holes into that seat for the past hour," Nathan said from beside me.

Ros was curled up in one of the seats at the other end of the plane, leaning against the window while she chatted and laughed with Abi, Jen, Cat and Mona like nothing was wrong. But I knew better. The tension in her shoulders, the way she occasionally bit her lip, it all gave her away. Our current situation was anything but normal.

Normal.

When had there ever been a real normal between us?

Our entire relationship had been a convoluted mess of pretences, miscommunications, and blurred boundaries.

It had been three weeks since Ros walked out of the meeting. She dodged my calls, evaded my attempts at conversation, and now, as we flew to London, it felt like we were back in October — before the fake dating, before everything.

Somehow we had ended up right back where we'd started —

her avoiding me and hiding behind polite smiles while I agonised over what I'd done wrong.

The past three months of growing closer might as well have never happened.

Eleven hours trapped in an enclosed space with her. If I couldn't get her to talk to me now, it would never happen.

Except I hadn't been able to force myself out of my seat. I just sat there, leg bouncing as I snuck glances down the plane, hoping that this time our gazes would clash and I'd be able to get a deeper read on her.

"I'm just saying there's nothing healthy about this." Nathan bumped my shoulder, dragging my attention back to my friends. "Apologise. Grovel like fuck." He rubbed his eyes. "Just stop with the annoying bloody brooding."

Shaun snorted. "Pretty sure you were just as bad when your girl cut you out."

Nathan glowered at him. "Don't remind me how pathetic I was, please."

Shaun smirked when Nathan shot him a dark look. "What? Clearly you figured it out. Since you and Cat are solid now."

Nathan nodded. "Took a lot of grovelling and honesty from us both. Avoiding the issue just makes it fester." He stared at me pointedly.

"You think I don't know that? I'm trying to fix things with Ros, but she won't even speak to me."

"I know it's frustrating, but honestly, I'd hold off until we land," Shaun said from across the aisle, his voice a mix of concern and caution. "No need to start World War Three on the plane when the rest of us can't escape."

But Nathan was having none of it. "Screw that. You're both miserable. Just get it over with."

"Eh, I wouldn't recommend it." Finn winced.

"And why, all-knowing one, would you say that?" Nathan asked, the words dripping with sarcasm.

I glanced at Finn, hoping for some insider insight, but he only shrugged, a cryptic look in his eyes.

"I'd love to help, but Abi would have my balls."

I scowled. At this point, I didn't bloody care if he fell out with his wife. I wanted my fiancée back.

Ros shifted in her seat, crossing her legs, her knee-high boots drawing my gaze down the length of her jean-clad legs. She was laughing again, her eyes crinkling at the corners.

I couldn't wait any longer. I needed answers.

She was deep in conversation with Jen and Abi, but her head snapped up as I stopped beside their cluster of seats, her smile faltering as she caught my eye.

"Can we talk?"

She eyed me warily, her posture stiffening. "There's nothing to talk about, Jackson."

But I couldn't let it go, not this time. "Yes, there is. We can't keep avoiding this."

"*I'm* not avoiding anything." She crossed her arms and scowled up at me. "You made your priorities clear. They don't include me unless it benefits your image."

I winced at the bitterness edging her words. "That's not true."

"Oh, isn't it?"

"Can we not do this here?" Mona asked, her voice tight.

"Jesus, the pair of you are a tone-deaf disaster," Finn muttered from behind me.

"I wasn't the only one in that meeting."

"Audra barely lets me pick my own clothes! What the hell gave you the impression she would listen to me if I told her we were seriously dating?" She snorted. "That woman hates me. Even if I had told her, I doubt she would have changed the plan."

"That's not —"

"So help me, if you say 'that's not true' one more fucking time I'm going to find a way to push you off this plane."

I sighed. "All I'm asking for is a chance to talk it through."

"And I'd love an original Vivienne Westwood Seditionaries

shirt from the 70s, but hey, we can't all get what we want, right?" Sarcasm dripped from her tone.

"Enough!" Jen shouted.

She stood and Abi followed, both of them stalking towards us with stern expressions painted across their faces.

Before I knew it, they were shuffling us down the narrow aisle of the plane.

"Hey!" I tried to dig my heels into the carpet. But Jen just pushed harder, her face set in a determined scowl that said she wasn't going to take no for an answer.

"Shush." Abi grimaced. "This is for your own good."

"What is?"

"Talk," Jen snapped before she and Abi simultaneously shoved us inside the bedroom and shut the door with a definitive click.

ROS

I rattled the door handle.

"Let us out!" I shouted, pounding my fist against the door. "This isn't funny."

"We're not joking, Ros," came Jen's muffled voice. "You two need to work this out before we land in London."

I turned to face Jackson. A massive bed took up the bulk of the room. We definitely weren't going to be able to pretend we weren't locked in a room together for the next nine hours.

His hopeful expression only made the knot in my stomach tighten.

"I don't understand why you're so angry with me," he said, his voice strained with confusion and hurt.

I lifted my head to glare at him. Was he seriously that oblivious?

"Are you kidding me right now? I'm angry because you sat there like a damn statue while Audra detailed our fake breakup."

Jab. "I'm angry because you let her suggest that you replace me with your ex, *whose bloody engagement ring I'm wearing*." I scowled at him.

"Ros—"

"I'm angry," my voice rose as I cut him off, "because you chose your image, your career, over us. Over me." I jabbed harder. "And it hurt, asshole."

He frowned. "I never chose my career over you."

"Didn't you?" My brows rose in disbelief. "Because that's what it looked like. Letting Audra dictate our relationship while I sat there, feeling like an idiot for believing you might actually care."

He took a step forward, his expression earnest. "I do care. More than you know. But it's not just black and white. There are so many things at play."

"Don't you dare make excuses!" I hated how bitter I sounded. "I'm so sick of you hiding behind 'Hollywood pressures.' Grow a backbone and think for yourself for once."

"I'm trying to explain, not make excuses."

"And that's all I'm hearing. Fucking deal with it." I shrugged. "If you really cared, you would have fought for us. You would have stood up and said something."

"That goes both ways and you didn't answer me earlier. Why didn't you say anything?"

"Because it would have been pointless! The woman doesn't trust me and she'll never take me seriously."

"But you could have tried." His voice rose slightly. "You knew how I felt about you. I confessed my love, for fuck's sake. Didn't that mean anything to you?"

He had confessed his love, and I hadn't given him anything in return which made me as much of an asshole as him in some ways.

"I don't know." I looked away, emotions churning. "I guess I got scared."

Jackson's expression softened. "Scared of what?"

"That it wasn't real. Or if it was, that it wouldn't last." I shrugged helplessly. "I don't have a great record with men, you know that."

He stepped closer, hesitantly reaching for my hand. I should have backed away, stopped him, but I couldn't move, not with that gleam of understanding in his eyes.

"Oh, pixie." His voice was gentle. "I know your past experiences make it hard to trust. Mine do too. But I swear, I'm in this for the long haul."

He threaded his fingers through mine and tugged me closer. I swallowed as my stomach flipped.

"I know you believe that," I said softly. "But when you didn't stand up for me, for us... it was like my worst fears coming true." I blinked back tears. "It made me feel disposable, like you were just biding your time until our arrangement ended."

"No, never." Jackson drew me closer, his eyes boring intensely into mine. "I meant every word when I said I loved you. I want a real future together. I thought you understood that." He grimaced. "And I know how much you hate it when other people fight your battles for you so when you didn't say anything, I thought that meant you didn't want me."

Searching his face, I saw only earnest sincerity. Guilt twisted in my gut. If I wasn't such an emotionally stunted asshole, would the last few weeks of pain have happened? Did I just bring it on myself?

Because he was right.

Fuck, I really was a walking disaster.

Only there was one thing that still didn't make any sense.

"Why didn't you tell me about Bree?"

Jackson let out a sardonic laugh. "Tell you about my ex-fiancée who dumped me right before our wedding? Why would I?"

I looked back up at him. "What did happen with her? With your almost wedding?"

Pain flashed across Jackson's face. "She ghosted me a week before the ceremony. Wouldn't answer my calls or texts. When I finally tracked her down, she threw the ring at me and said she was moving on to 'bigger and better things.' The next day a story ran with pictures of her cosying up to one of the Sanderson brothers."

I sucked in a breath. "God, that's awful. I'm so sorry."

No wonder he had kept it hidden.

Jackson shrugged, but I could see the lingering sadness in his eyes. "I was devastated at the time. But it helped me realise she only saw me as a stepping stone for her career. Was never really invested in us."

I nodded, understanding dawning on me. "So when I avoided defining things between us…"

"It brought up all those old doubts again. Made me question if you truly cared or were just using me too." He smirked. "What a pair we make, huh?"

Shame washed over me. I stepped closer, taking his hands in mine. "I'm sorry I ever made you feel that way. It was never about not caring. I was just scared of getting hurt again."

He smiled, giving my hands a squeeze. "I know that now, pixie. We both made assumptions instead of just talking openly." His smile turned rueful. "If only we'd had this conversation right after the meeting. Could have saved ourselves weeks of misery."

I nodded, but couldn't help feeling defensive. "I know. But I panicked. I saw everything we had crumbling, and I ran."

Jackson led me over to sit beside him on the edge of the bed. "I get it. But running away just made everything worse. For both of us."

I squeezed his hand, the familiar warmth of his skin comforting. "When we started fake dating, I never expected to fall for you. I didn't think you could hurt me because it wasn't real."

His eyes searched mine, looking for something I wasn't sure I could give him. "But?"

"But that's not what happened." The words spilled out. "Being with you, it felt real. More real than anything I've ever experienced. And then, watching you sit there, silent, while Audra planned our breakup… it tore me apart."

Understanding dawned on his face. He tucked a finger under my chin. "Oh lass, I felt the same, I swear it. I should have told you plainly instead of just assuming you knew."

"I guess we both made assumptions." I wiped at a stray tear. "All I could think about was my past relationships and waiting for the next betrayal. I survived by being distrustful, by always expecting the worst."

His thumb caressed the back of my hand, a soothing motion that belied the turmoil I saw in his eyes. "And with me?"

"With you, I stopped looking for the red flags. I let myself just... live. Be happy. And then that meeting happened, and it felt like I was back at square one."

Jackson leaned forward, his elbows resting on his knees. "I thought I was doing the right thing, keeping quiet. I thought you'd take charge if you wanted to change things. But I was wrong. I should have fought for us, for you."

I took a deep breath, the air heavy with unspoken words. "I should have fought too. I should have believed in us enough to stand up to Audra."

Jackson reached for me again, his touch hesitant. "We both made mistakes. But we're here now. We can start over, do things right this time."

I let him take my hand, the contact sending a shiver up my spine. "I want that. But how can I trust this won't happen again?"

"Ros..." His voice was a soft plea, but something in his gaze told me he was searching for the right words, trying to bridge the gap between us.

"I can't do this if it means waiting for the next time the narrative shifts and you stand by doing nothing, all while your publicist decides that it would be better for your image if you were single. It hurts, okay?" The admission tasted bitter, a truth I'd kept bottled up.

"I need you to believe that I'm committed to us," he said, his voice low and insistent. "To you. Give me another chance. To show you, to fight for you, for us." His grip tightened on my hand, grounding me. "I'll prove it. Every day if I have to. Tell me how to fix this. Just please don't give up on us yet. I'll do anything. Except give you space. I've missed you so much, pixie. I don't want to go another week without making you laugh and smile or hearing your terrible singing in the shower."

I scowled. "My singing isn't terrible."

His lips twitched. "Sure, it's not."

My resolve wavered at the raw longing in his voice.

"I've missed you too." I sighed, looking down at our intertwined fingers. His grip was firm yet gentle, reassuring in its steadiness. "I don't want to break up in October."

Jackson's face lit up with a mixture of hope and disbelief. "Does that mean you love me?"

I paused, taking a moment to think. My mind raced through all the happy moments we'd shared — late nights talking, comforting hugs when I was down, the way he made me feel like I was the only person in the world. Compared to the brief sting of our recent fight, the happiness outweighed the hurt.

"Yeah, I do," I finally said, my voice steady despite the butterflies in my stomach. "I love you, Jackson. Despite everything."

The answering grin that lit up his face was dazzling. In a flash he pulled me into his arms, crushing me against his chest as his lips found mine. The kiss was hungry, fuelled by weeks of distance and heartache. I lost myself in it, twining my arms around his neck to pull him closer.

We eventually broke apart, both flushed and panting. Jackson rested his forehead against mine, his eyes bright.

"I've missed that, missed you. These weeks apart have been torture."

I smiled up at him, giddy relief bubbling up inside me. "No more weeks apart. From now on, we talk about everything, no matter how small or insignificant it might seem. Deal?"

"Deal." Jackson grinned. "And now that we're on the mend…" His eyes danced mischievously. "We're alone, in a bedroom, on a plane…"

I laughed, swatting his chest playfully as his meaning dawned on me. "Don't even think about it! Our friends are right outside."

Jackson pouted dramatically. "You're really going to deny a man joining the mile high club?"

"Yup, you'll survive until London." I slipped out of his arms, still chuckling.

CHAPTER THIRTY-ONE

ROS

The limo door opened and I stepped out, the roar of the crowd hitting me instantly. The dress, a concoction of black leather and silver studs that would make Joan Jett nod in approval, clung to me like a second skin. It was daring, bold, and screamed punk rock goddess. It was everything Audra despised.

I smirked as her eyes bulged, her painted lips pinching in disapproval.

Pausing at the edge of the carpet, I soaked up the electrifying atmosphere. Cameras flashed wildly as reporters shouted questions I couldn't make out over the noise. I met their chaotic energy calmly, no longer intimidated by the circus of the red carpet.

Jackson appeared at my side, his hand pressed supportively against my lower back. He speared me with a heated look, one he'd worn ever since I put the dress on.

"You're stunning," he whispered in my ear. "But as much as I'm glad I get to show you off, I'm counting down the minutes until this song and dance ends and it decorates our hotel room floor."

I grinned at him. So what if one of the microphones picked that up? He was mine, his heated words were mine.

It had occurred to me that if I really wanted to piss Audra off, I would have let him rip it off me and made us late.

Shame I had too much sense to be truly vindictive.

I smoothed my hands over his jacket taking him in. As always, Jackson cut a dashing figure in his tailored suit, the dark fabric accentuating his broad shoulders and trim waist. His long dirty blond hair was pulled back in a low ponytail that I never liked on other men, but on him? It made me go feral. All I could think about was pulling the tie out and dragging my hands through it while he pounded into me.

Yes, saying no to a pre-award show reaming was hard.

"Shall we?" With a knowing smirk, he nodded towards the carpet and the waiting horde of vultures.

I slipped my hand into his, lacing our fingers together. "Let's get this show on the road."

With a newfound resolve, I turned to face the sea of cameras, my hand firmly in his. We stepped onto the red carpet and were instantly met with the roar of the crowd and the blinding flash of cameras. Reporters shouted from behind the barricades:

"Jackson, Ros, look this way!"

"Ros, who designed your dress?"

"Are you trying to make a statement with this look?"

"Jackson, how does it feel to have your first independently produced film nominated?"

"Ros! Over here! What do you have to say about the breakup rumours?"

The questions flew at me like bullets, their flashes blinding, but I didn't blink. I kept my polite smile in place, letting the questions wash over me without response.

It all faded into the background. In its place was the sound of Jackson's laughter, the feel of his hand in mine, the look in his eyes that told me I was the only person he saw.

It had taken me too long to figure it out, but I was exactly where I wanted to be — by his side.

Jackson's arm wrapped securely around my waist as we paused for photos. He gazed down at me like I was the most captivating woman in the world, his admiration and love plain on his face. After weeks of distance, that raw openness meant everything.

I leaned into him, soaking up his closeness that I'd missed so much. The gnawing hole from our time apart filled with his touch.

"Doing okay, pixie?" he murmured, his voice barely audible above the shouts.

"Better than okay." My lips twitched into a smile as I met his gaze. "As long as you're here, this circus doesn't stand a chance at getting to me."

An affectionate chuckle rumbled from his chest, vibrating against me and making my heart flutter. The red carpet might have been a whirlwind of chaos, but in Jackson's arms, it was as if we were in our own protective bubble.

"Good, because facing the paparazzi is the easy part, pixie."

After the pandemonium of the red carpet, it was a relief to settle into our seats alongside our friends. Jackson's hand found mine beneath the table, his thumb idly stroking over my knuckles.

I caught him stealing awestruck glances at me every so often, like he still couldn't believe I was really here beside him.

"See something interesting over here, Levi?"

He grinned, eyes crinkling at the corners. He lifted my hand to his lips, pressing a tender kiss to it. "Just the most captivating woman in the room."

My heart fluttered at the openly romantic gesture. I had missed this closeness fiercely.

At our table, Abi radiated an expectant glow in her emerald gown, one hand resting on her just-noticeable baby bump. Beside her, Jen looked regal in royal purple, her intricately braided updo flawless.

Compared to the tension on the flight over, our group of friends now looked relaxed, exchanging eager grins as the show began. This was their element.

"Good evening, ladies and gentlemen!" boomed the host in his polished British accent. "Welcome to the 73rd annual British Academy Film Awards!"

Thunderous applause erupted around us. I took in the lavish decor — glittering chandeliers, sweeping red velvet curtains, elegant place settings.

"Tonight, we celebrate the remarkable talent and creativity that has graced the silver screen this past year," continued the host. " So, let's get on with the show and see which of these fantastic nominees will be taking home the coveted BAFTA statuette!"

The audience cheered, the atmosphere electric with anticipation. One by one, they ticked through the categories, handing out tributes and golden trophies, taking breaks for performances.

"And now, the moment we've all been waiting for," said the host. "The nominees for Best Film…"

I'm not sure I would ever understand why this award of all the rest mattered so much to the guys. They had already swept up a good number of awards for this film and many more on their previous projects. Maybe it had something to do with it being a British award and all four of them missing home to some extent, but they were on the edge of their seats as he listed off the contenders.

The camera panned to each table as their film was named, landing on raucous cheers from our section when Beautiful Lies was called.

"And the BAFTA goes to…" The host paused for dramatic effect. "Beautiful Lies!"

Our table exploded into a deafening celebration. As Jackson hugged me hard, pride and shock played across his features.

Grinning from ear to ear, he, Shaun, Finn and Nathan made

their way up to the stage, clapping each other on the back, awestruck expressions blanketing their features.

Shaun accepted the statue from the announcers while Jackson approached the podium and the microphone.

"This is a moment I've all dreamed of my entire career. To share this with my best friends makes it all the more special." He gestured to each of them.

Shaun leaned over Jackson's shoulder to get closer to the microphone. "And of course, none of this would be possible without our fantastic team and the support of our incredible partners. They're the real stars tonight."

Finn chimed in with a grin. "Especially those who put up with our late-night brainstorming sessions and never-ending edits. Thanks for taking a chance on a fledgling production company, guys."

Nathan's voice was filled with gratitude, "And to our families, friends, and everyone who believed in 'Beautiful Lies' and Kings of Screen Productions from the start — thank you."

Jackson scanned the room, searching for something. Then he found me and his expression softened. "Every story starts with a spark, a moment where fantasy and reality collide. I found that spark in someone remarkable…"

My breath caught, heart hammering against my ribs. It wasn't just the cameras trained on us now; every pair of eyes in the room seemed fixed on our table, the women behind the men of the hour.

"Ros, my love — none of this would mean anything without you by my side. You are my inspiration and guiding light. Your strength, your passion... you're the heartbeat of this project, and of my life."

The guys had started work on Beautiful Lies well before Jackson asked me out, well before we'd started hanging out every moment we could over the summer. If what he said was true then Jackson had cared about me far longer than I ever imagined.

The tears I'd been holding back now freely streamed down my

face. My cheeks felt warm, my hands trembling as I clutched them together to stop their shaking.

"Thank you," he said, and though the speech carried on, everything else faded away. The applause, the hushed whispers, the incessant clicking of cameras — all of it became background noise.

Abi and Jen shuffled around the table, their eyes equally wet. They wrapped their arms around my waist, hugging me while the guys concluded their speech.

This wasn't supposed to be my moment, but Jackson had dragged me into the spotlight with him.

The four of them returned to our table, amongst the applause and cheers of the audience. Jackson was the first to reach us and the girls released me so he could envelop me in a tight hug.

Smiling, he lowered his head and brushed his lips across mine. Our friends around us erupted into a chorus of whistles and cheers, embracing the moment of unbridled joy.

Breathless, Jackson took my face in his hands, staring intently into my eyes. "No award or accolade will ever mean more to me than you giving me a chance. Than your love."

Unable to form words past the lump in my throat, I simply pulled him into another kiss, pouring all my pride and joy into it.

As the celebrations continued around us, Jackson nuzzled my ear, his voice low so only I could hear.

"What do you say we get out of here, pixie?" His suggestive tone made his meaning clear.

I readily agreed, wanting nothing more than intimate alone time with the man I loved. "Lead the way, stud," I whispered, smirking as the final scene of Greece flashed through my mind.

In a way, we were like Sandy and Danny — mismatched souls who had opened each other's eyes. He'd shown me that fame didn't have to change who you were at your core. And I think I'd helped him see beyond the glitz and artifice to what really mattered.

We'd both compromised, blending our worlds together into

something beautiful. Something real. And though the journey had its rocky patches, the destination made it all worthwhile.

Jackson's eyes darkened with desire. He quickly made our excuses and goodbyes to our cheering friends before guiding me out of the hall.

JACKSON

I grabbed Ros's hand and pushed through the exit, eager to escape the chaos of the afterparty. At last, a chance for some privacy.

"Where do you think you're going?" Audra asked, blocking our path, arms crossed and a scowl on her face. "You have a press conference in thirty minutes, not to mention interviews booked all night. Your duties aren't over yet."

I drew a breath and steeled myself, ready to stand up to her once and for all. Ros deserved better than constantly having her life dictated by her ruthless schedule.

"Actually, my priorities have changed for the night."

"What?" she almost shrieked. "Jackson, be serious."

"I am. We're leaving." I lifted my chin, meeting her indignant gaze square on. "Oh and Ros and I won't be breaking up. From now on, she'll do as she pleases and wear what she likes. You'll consult her before making any plans regarding either of our schedules."

Audra sputtered in protest, but I ignored her, leading Ros past.

"Don't be an idiot," she shouted. "You have professional obligations."

I shook my head, squeezing Ros's hand tighter. "Not tonight. We've got a plane to catch to St. Andrews." I glanced over my shoulder, my expression deadly. "Don't need me."

"Jackson Levi doesn't run from his commitments," Audra sneered, standing her ground.

"Jackson Levi is more than a name on a billboard," I snapped.

"He's a man who knows what he wants. And right now, that's to be anywhere but here."

"Your whole life is here!" Audra gestured at the empty foyer of the convention centre we were leaving behind.

"My life is with the person whose hand I'm holding," I said with nothing but conviction in my voice. "Goodnight, Audra."

I didn't wait for her reply. Didn't really care whether she approved or not.

We climbed into the back of the waiting limo. I gave the driver instructions to stop by our hotel so we could grab our bags and then take us to the airfield. Then I fired off a text to the pilot.

The car started moving and I pocketed my phone, glancing up to find Ros staring at me with a shocked gleam in her eyes.

"What is it?"

"You didn't have to do that," she said softly. "Stand up to Audra like that, I mean. I know how much your career means to you."

I pressed a kiss to her hair, breathing in her sweet scent. "You mean more. Besides, it's time I started living for myself, not for the cameras and the fans. If that means taking a break now and then, so be it."

She tilted her head up, her eyes shining. "I'm proud of you."

"Good." I smiled. "There's more where that came from."

*T*he seat belt sign dinged off, and it was like a starting pistol in my veins. I had my belt off and was fumbling with the clasp of Ros's before the sound faded.

She laughed and arched a brow at me. "What are you doing?"

"Making good on a promise," I said with a grin that felt both reckless and true.

Grabbing her hand, I scooped Ros into my arms, striding towards the back of the plane.

"Which promise would that be?" She wrapped her arms around my neck, relaxing into me without a concern in the world.

I glanced back at her, smirking. "The Mile High Club, of course."

"Promises, promises," she teased, but there was a lilt of excitement in her voice that matched my own.

"Trust me, it's one I intend to keep."

"You drive me wild, lass." I nudged open the door to my bedroom and set her on her feet beside the bed, hands sliding to cup her face. "The image of you beneath me in this bed has plagued me all night. I don't think I've ever been this hard."

Her lips curved. "Prove it."

Her challenge sent arousal spiking in my blood. I crushed my mouth to hers, kissing her with a hunger I'd only just begun to tap. My hands roamed her body, relearning her curves as she melted against me with a soft moan.

I pushed the straps of her dress off her shoulders while her hands fumbled with my shirt buttons, tugging them open with impatience. "Dammit, Jackson!" she growled, frustrated.

I chuckled against her neck as the fabric slipped down her body and pooled on the floor, exposing creamy skin and a lacy bra.

She unzipped my trousers and gripped my length through my boxer briefs, squeezing with just the right amount of pressure to make my eyes close in bliss. She grinned as a strangled groan fell from my lips.

The next thing I knew she was on her knees, my boxers were on the floor, and her delectable mouth had closed around the tip, sucking hard. My pulse pounded in my ears as she looked up at me through heavy-lidded eyes.

She moaned around me, her tongue swirling around the head of my cock. I braced a hand on the wall behind her as she took more of me inch by inch into her hot, wet mouth.

Fuck, how I'd missed this.

I groaned again as she hollowed her cheeks and sucked harder.

Her hands joined the party, driving me insane as one caressed the length of me and the other cupped my balls.

"Jesus, Ros..." I panted, my accent thickening as she teased me with her tongue. "You're gonna make me..."

She pulled away, releasing me with a soft pop. "We definitely can't have that," she purred, unhooking her bra and discarding it before climbing to her feet and laying down on the bed. Her eyes were drenched with lust as she spread her legs invitingly. "Fuck me, Jackson."

I needed no more encouragement.

But instead of climbing onto the bed like she expected, I lowered myself to my knees and grabbed her legs, tugging her to the edge of the bed and my waiting mouth.

I kissed her thighs, her hips, and the lips of her pussy, teasing her with the inevitable. She shifted restlessly against the bed, silently begging for more and I gave it to her. Parting her lower lips with my fingers, I flicked my tongue over her clit. Her taste exploded on my tongue, sending a shiver of delight through me.

"Jackson!" she moaned, arching her back.

I grasped her thighs, lifting her higher so I could delve deeper and tease the sensitive bundle of nerves with more force. Her nails scraped my scalp as she held onto me any way she could while I devoured her.

"Oh, fuck," she gasped. "That's... oh... mph!"

I slipped a finger inside her hot channel, revelling in her wet heat as I curled it, searching for that spot that always made her moan the loudest.

Alternate between teasing her clit with my mouth and rubbing that sensitive spot, her moans grew louder, her thighs squeezing around my head as she rocked her hips in time with my thrusting fingers.

"Jackson," she gasped, "I'm... fuck. I'm..."

I upped the pace, sucking and licking and fingering her into a mind-blowing orgasm that had her nails digging into my scalp and her body arching off the bed. She shattered in my mouth, her walls clenching around my finger. My cock throbbed with need as her hips bucked against my face.

As her shudders died down, I crawled up the bed and positioned myself between her legs. Her lips found mine in a hungry, breathless kiss, the taste of her release still on my tongue. She moaned into my mouth, her hands grasping my back, nails leaving crescent marks in my skin. I revelled in the sting, craving every mark she left.

Breaking the kiss, I trailed my lips down her throat, nipping and sucking at the sensitive skin.

"Stop stalling."

"Hmm. I've missed this." I moaned against her ear, teasing her entrance with the tip of my cock. "Your taste, your smell, everything about you."

"Me too," she panted, hips lifting upwards, urging me onward. "Now get inside of me."

"So demanding," I tutted.

Then I plunged into her wet heat with a groan, burying myself to the hilt with a hiss of pleasure. Her nails dug into my back as her pussy tightened around me, enveloping me like a fist around my cock.

"God, Ros," I moaned into her neck.

I pulled out until just the tip remained before sliding back into her silky depths. We moaned in unison, the sound harmonising in the air around us.

"You feel so fucking good."

A hissed "yes" was all the response I received as she wrapped her legs around my hips, encouraging me to go harder.

I refused, maintaining a slow considered pace while my gaze roamed her face, memorising every detail like this was the first and last time I'd get to be inside of her. I'd taken it for granted the last few months and after three weeks without her, I needed this to mean more.

"Stop teasing and fuck me already."

Instead, I rolled my hips, grinding my pelvis against her clit. Her eyes fell shut and her mouth popped open on a gasp.

"Eyes on me, pixie," I growled, stopping altogether as I penetrated her to the hilt.

She opened her green eyes and stared up at me, dazed with lust.

"Yes, just like that," I whispered before resuming the torturous pace.

I plunged my cock in and out of her tight heat, making sure to hit her g-spot every time, but still not hard enough to make her come.

She growled in frustration but didn't break eye contact.

"Jackson, please," she begged, digging her nails into my biceps.

"Please what?" I bit down on her earlobe.

"Oh fuck just... more."

I chuckled before complying with her request this time, thrusting harder and faster, burying myself deep within her core. Her back arched, her nipples hard against my chest.

"Right there," she moaned.

"You're so bloody tight."

"I'm... so close."

I wrapped an arm around her waist, anchoring her to me as I pumped faster and at the same time rubbed her clit with my free hand.

Her breathing hitched and her walls clenched around me as she came again, her cries of pleasure music to my ears. I couldn't hold back any more, each thrust more desperate than the last.

"Oh, fuck, Ros," I growled, my body on fire as I followed her over the edge. I collapsed on top of her and pressed my face into her neck, my cock still buried deep inside her.

"Now that was worth the wait," she mumbled against my collarbone.

"Agreed." I kissed her neck before lifting my head and smiling down at her. "I love you."

"I love you too." She moved her hands to my face, stroking my cheeks as her gaze roamed over me. "I don't know how I ever thought I could be happy without you."

Her lips curved into a small smile before they met mine in a lazy kiss. "I'm glad we finally came to our senses, though."

"Me too."

The sweet ache that came from loving someone settled into my chest as we lay there panting for a few minutes.

"We should get dressed," she said, her voice full of reluctance.

"I know." I sighed before pulling out of her and wincing at the loss of her heat. "But not yet."

A panicked look flickered across her face.

"What's wrong?"

"We're on our way to your family..."

"Yes?"

"I've never... done the whole 'meet the parents' thing before."

My eyebrows furrowed down in confusion. "Okay?"

"What if they don't like me?" Her eyes widened, her serious expression making my lips twitch upward.

"Ros, you have nothing to worry about." I pressed a kiss to her creased brow, trying to ease the worry. "They already love you, pixie."

"They say that but they haven't met me for real and now we're real." She chewed her lip.

I laughed, brushing a stray lock of hair from her face. "Trust me. They're going to adore you just as much in person as they do over the phone. Besides, they're my family — they're insane part of the time but I know they're smitten with you. We Douglases have good taste."

Ros rolled her eyes, though her lips quirked up in a smile. "Alright, put the ego away before your head gets too big."

I grinned, unable to resist teasing her further. "And what if I don't?" I asked, my voice dropping an octave lower.

Her eyes held a mischievous glint as she propped herself on her elbows, looking up at me. "Then I might just have to deflate it myself."

"I'd like to see you try."

She answered me with a laugh of her own, the sound filling the room and wrapping itself around my heart. As I looked into her eyes, this sense of peace settled over me. How had I gotten so lucky?

As we traded lazy kisses, the playfulness between us slowly faded into a tender intimacy. My cock hardened again and I shifted my hips, reminding her that I was still buried inside of her. Her eyes fluttered closed on a groan.

Somehow, I had found my spark, my guiding light, my heartbeat. And I was never letting her go.

ROS

"Just follow my lead," Fraser said, amusement shining in his eyes as the fiddles started up and he positioned me on the dance floor.

We'd arrived in St Andrews just in time for Burns Night. I'd never heard of it until we landed.

Being unfamiliar with Scottish traditions, I wasn't sure what to expect. Fraser grabbing my hand and dragging me onto the dance floor the second I took my coat off definitely wasn't it.

Jackson, the rat, had just laughed and let his brother drag me off, claiming it would be good practice for me. Practice for what?

I took a deep breath, trying to focus on the caller's instructions echoing through the hall.

"Just relax and go with it," Fraser shouted across the music and the chatter of our neighbours.

A couple of turns and I was in over my head. My feet seemed to have a mind of their own, tangling at every step. He tried to guide me, but I couldn't stop laughing at my own clumsiness.

"Seriously, where's your natural grace?"

"Left it back in New York, apparently," I said, finally catching the rhythm for a fleeting moment before losing it again.

He laughed. "Well, at least you're entertaining to watch."

I rolled my eyes, but I'd take all the teasing he wanted to throw at me. None of it would dent my good mood.

I'd spent an entire 24 hours with Jackson's family and they didn't hate me!

What had I even been worried about before?

"Left foot, Ros, not your right." Fraser's grip on my hands tightened as I stumbled yet again.

"I'm trying!" I gasped between laughs, feeling a stitch in my side from the exertion and hilarity. "Scottish dancing should come with a warning label."

He grinned, twirling me around in an attempt to get me back on track. "You're doing fine. Just enjoy it!"

"Easy for you to say." I huffed as he spun me. "I didn't spend an hour a week learning to dance in school."

"Ah, but that's the beauty of it. It's never too late to learn."

I stumbled again, narrowly avoiding a collision with another couple. "At this rate, I'll be ready just in time for the next Burns Night."

"That's the spirit." He grinned.

"Ha ha, you're so funny." I pulled a face, loving his good natured ribbing. "Your brother never mentioned ceilidh dancing was a full-contact sport."

Fraser raised a brow. "You've not seen anything yet. Wait till 'Strip the Willow' starts."

I groaned. "Why does that sound like a threat?"

He just smirked and moved on like I hadn't said anything. Something to look forward to? Probably not.

"Honestly though, you're perfect. I'm glad Jackson found someone who can hold her own. It's refreshing."

"Oh?"

His expression turned thoughtful. "Let's just say Bree didn't do something if it didn't serve Bree. She wouldn't take my mother's constant needling for a wedding date, or agree to let my da read Robbie Burns to her for two hours until she fell asleep on the sofa."

In my defence, it wasn't the poetry that had put me to sleep. I'd been on an emotional rollercoaster for weeks with Jackson and getting the label ready for launch. Sleep hadn't exactly been a regular feature in my life.

Then add a twelve-hour flight, jetlag, an emotional reconciliation, hours of prep for the awards and then the awards.

It was a lot in a short window of time.

"Well, I'm not Bree. And I'm certainly not one to back down."

"That's true." He grinned. "I could tell you had staying power at the Marable gig. No one deals with that level of attention unless they're dedicated."

"Thanks." Warmth spread through me at his approval.

Though would he think the same if he knew that my dedication had been to my friendship and a paycheque at that point?

Then again, wasn't it all the same in the end?

I'd agreed for Jackson. Just because I couldn't admit how I felt at that stage didn't mean I hadn't loved him then.

Before things could get any more serious, I purposefully flubbed my next step to distract Fraser.

"Ros! What are you doing? That was an easy step."

"Me? What about you?" I narrowed my eyes on him, my tone teasing. "Are you sure you're actually qualified to teach this?"

He stared down at me, his lips twitching for a second before he composed himself.

"Absolutely certified," he said with faux seriousness. "I'll have you dancing proper Scottish reels in no time."

I scoffed. "At this rate, you'll be lucky if I don't accidentally fling you across the room."

But despite my appalling lack of coordination, I loved every second. It felt wonderfully freeing to just be myself with Jackson's family. To not worry for a second that I might give us away and cause Jackson an endless stream of questions.

The song ended, and Fraser clapped me on the back. "Well done! You survived your first ceilidh dance."

"Survived is the right word." Panting and sweaty, I backed away from Fraser. One dance was enough, I needed a break. "But that was fun. Even with the near-death experiences."

I left Fraser laughing at my back and made a beeline for Jackson. He stood on the other side of the room, chatting with his dad. He appeared relaxed in a way I hadn't seen him in months, well before our fake dating charade began.

"Ros, darling!" Morag intercepted me before I could take more than five steps, reaching me with a speed that defied her age. "I told Agnes you'd be joining us tomorrow. She's so excited. Don't worry about setting an alarm, I'll knock on your door bright and early."

In my jet-lagged stupor, I'd also somehow agreed to join Morag's walking group at dawn for a sunrise stroll along the beach.

The beach stretched two miles.

You can bet I'd cursed my eagerness to impress when I woke up this morning and Jackson reminded me.

I nodded, trying to muster enthusiasm. "Wouldn't miss it for the world."

Morag beamed. "You'll love it. The sunrise over the sea is breathtaking. And Agnes brings her famous scones!"

I forced a smile, my insides churning at the thought of an early morning on top of tonight's festivities. "Sounds great," I lied.

Truth be told, I'd rather catch my finger in the sewing machine than wake up at the crack of dawn for a beach walk. But I'd do it for Jackson. And his mother.

"And you, my dear, are fitting right in!" she continued, her shrewd hazel eyes assessing me.

I blushed, unsure how to respond. Her praise was like a double-edged sword — validating but loaded with expectations I was ill-equipped to fulfil. "Thank you, Morag. I'm just happy to be here."

It was almost a pinch me moment.

Two days ago, I'd barely been able to look at Jackson without numbing myself to the anger and pain.

Now, I could honestly say I'd never been happier.

Not only had I gotten him back, but he'd stood up to Audra, and his perfectly normal family had embraced me.

Yes, he would disagree with me calling his family normal, but what did he expect me to say when all I had to compare them to was my cheating dad and his bully wife?

"I hope you're not tricking Ros into more of your social gatherings, mother." Jen stopped at my side and threaded her arm through mine.

"Nonsense. I didn't—"

"Take advantage of Ros's jetlagged state and need for you to like her?" Her brows rose in a comical reversal of roles.

Morag's expression turned sheepish, her gaze wandering around the room, anything if it meant not giving in to Jen. "Oh look, there's Fiona. I should catch her before the next round."

Without a backwards glance, Morag rushed off. I gave up biting back my laughter at the absurdity of Jen, a twenty year old student and assistant scaring her fearless mother off.

"Sorry, she can be a lot, I know." Jen released my arm and turned to face me. "I can get you out of the walk if you want."

"No, it's okay," I said before my brain could catch up with my mouth. I grimaced. "Not that I want to get up at the crack of dawn, but it's kind of nice, the motherly vibe."

Jen laughed, but it quickly petered out when I didn't join in. "Oh my, you're serious."

I nodded.

"If you value your sanity, do not let her hear you saying that." She shuddered. "You'll have her calling you at all hours, night and day. She does not check the time."

Her words, meant as a warning, only made me smile. "That bad, huh?"

"I love her to bits, but she's relentless. If she decides you're part of the family, there's no escape."

That should have been intimidating, but honestly, it was kind of refreshing. My family situation would never stop being complicated. Having someone like Morag fussing over me, even if it was a bit much, was comforting in a way.

I nudged her. "Sounds like you've got your hands full managing everyone, not just Jackson."

She rolled her eyes, a wry smile tugging at her lips. "You have no idea. Between Jackson's schedule and my mother's calls, I'm surprised I have time to sleep."

"Speaking of managing things, how did you get that restaurant in LA to shut down half their rooftop for Jackson and me?"

"Oh, that?" Her cheeks tinged with a faint blush. "I just... know the chef."

"Sounds like there's a story there."

She waved her hand dismissively. "It's nothing, really. Just called in a favour."

If she wanted to keep her secrets, she shouldn't have clammed up on me. "Come on, Jen. Spill. There's clearly something you're not telling me."

"It's not important." She shrugged, then her gaze wandered away, just like her mother. "We should... Jackson!"

I frowned. "What—"

Strong arms wrapped around my waist, squeezing me back against his chest. "How are my two favourite lasses enjoying the night?"

The old Ros would've baulked at the idea of being so openly affectionate in front of others. But now, I couldn't bring myself to care, to stop snuggling into Jackson's chest.

"Great. It's been... enlightening so far." I directed a pointed look at Jen.

Something was up with her and this mysterious chef. I made a mental note to dig deeper into this later. Jen deserved a bit of happiness, especially after everything she'd done for us.

He chuckled, his breath tickling my ear. "That's one way to put it. You holding up okay?"

"Better than okay." I turned my head to look up at him, a smile curving my lips.

It felt right. Being there with him, with his family. I wouldn't want to be anywhere else.

His eyes softened, and he kissed my forehead. "Glad to hear it."

I glanced around the hall, seeing the smiling faces of Jackson's family. This was what it meant to be part of a loving family. To belong.

JACKSON

I hadn't expected introducing Ros to my family to feel like this. Ros genuinely seemed to be enjoying herself, embracing this glimpse into my roots. Her laughter and smile never seemed forced or for show.

It was evident in the way she listened to my dad's stories about the wild haggis, her eyes wide. She didn't roll her eyes or scoff at the absurdity of it all. Instead, she seemed to be hanging on to his every word, as if she were genuinely buying into the idea that haggis were real creatures.

"Aye, the haggis is a shy wee beastie," my dad said in his gruff brogue, eyes twinkling. "That's why you hardly ever spot one roaming the glens. But if you're lucky, you might catch a glimpse of their furry hindquarters disappearing into the heather."

Ros's brows drew together, lips pursed as she considered his serious expression. "Their hindquarters? Why only those?"

"Well you see, lass, the haggis' legs on one side are shorter than the other," he explained matter-of-factly. "So they can run in circles around the mountains without falling over the edge."

Around us, my siblings tried and failed to smother their

laughter at Ros's bemused expression. She was too sharp not to see through dad's ridiculousness. But for now, she seemed willing to play along.

We sat at one of the dining tables that had been laid out for the feast portion of the Burns Night celebration. The ceilidh band had laid down their instruments and soft instrumental music played from a speaker instead while everyone dug into their haggis, neeps and tatties.

"I'll have to keep an eye out for these elusive haggis creatures while we're hiking."

"Aye, dinna fash yourself too much searching," dad said with a wink. "They're speedy wee buggers."

"Hmm." Then she stared down at her plate. "And it's okay to eat them if they're so rare?"

My dad leaned in conspiratorially, a twinkle in his eye. "Oh, we only eat the ones that get too dizzy running in circles and fall off the hillsides. It's very sustainable."

I bit my lip, trying to suppress the laughter bubbling up. Ros looked from my dad to her plate of haggis, a genuine look of contemplation on her face.

"Really?" she asked, her tone a mix of disbelief and amusement.

"Aye, really." Dad nodded.

I couldn't hold back any more and let out a chuckle. "He's pulling your leg, Ros. Haggis isn't a real animal."

Her face broke into a wide smile, and she shook her head, laughing. "I can't believe I almost fell for that."

My dad joined in the laughter, patting her back. "You're a good sport, lass."

As the laughter died down, I looked around the room, taking in the warmth of the community I'd left behind to pursue my career. There were people in this room who had taught me to swim, to spell. People who had witnessed the first time I awkwardly tried to ask a girl out or remembered my complaining when I'd broken my arm.

At any moment, one of them could approach us and give Ros a reason to leave me for good this time. Objectively, that was an unfounded fear.

Still, it felt surreal, this sense of ease and rightness.

I'd been so worried about my family scaring her away, but I hadn't accounted for Ros in that equation. She was fearless and could roll with any surprise they threw her way with grace.

My chest ached just watching her laugh and joke with my family.

"Are you enjoying your first Burns Night?" I asked her, reaching for her hand under the table.

"Yes, considering you threw me in the deep end with no preparation." She smirked at me.

I chuckled and squeezed her hand. "You're handling it like a pro, though. You might be an honorary Scot before the night's over."

"Honorary Scot, huh? Do I get a certificate for that?"

"Maybe." I nodded at her untouched plate. "But you have to try haggis first."

She picked up her fork, but made no attempt to cut into it. Instead she eyed it warily.

"It's just sheep's heart, liver, and lungs, minced with onion, oatmeal, suet, spices, and salt. All mixed with stock, and traditionally encased in the animal's stomach." I watched her reaction closely, half-expecting her to recoil.

Instead, she took a deep breath and speared a small piece on her fork. She lifted it tentatively to her mouth, tasting it. Her expression was priceless — a mix of surprise and uncertainty.

"It's... not bad."

I laughed, relieved. "See, nothing to fear."

"**G**etting back on that dance floor is a terrible idea." Ros stared at my outstretched hand with trepidation. "I'm a terrible dancer."

"Come on, it'll be fun. I'm a better teacher than Fraser." I wiggled my hand, trying to look as tempting as possible.

She glanced at Fraser, who was busy chatting up a group of locals. "You hear that, Fraser? Jackson claims he's a better teacher than you."

Fraser chuckled and waved us off. "He might be, at least for ceilidh dancing. Go on, give him a chance."

She hesitated for another couple of seconds and then gave in with a muttered, "If you let me fall, I won't be so nice to you tonight."

There had been a couple of overzealous rounds already. Usually they were reserved for the final dances of the night but our local band had never been one for following the norm. She'd already seen one or two women in heels trip in some of the fast spins.

"I promise I won't let you fall."

She took my hand, still grumbling beneath her breath. I positioned her in the line directly opposite me with a reassuring smile. The music started, filling the hall as the caller announced that the next dance would be 'Strip The Willow.'

Everyone but Ros and I grinned at their partners, promising to not go easy on each other. I bit my cheek trying not to wince at the chances of my first dance with her being this one.

She stared at me from across the divide, questions in her green eyes.

"It'll be okay, just listen to the caller and follow their instructions."

Thankfully, the caller took over before she could give voice to the murderous expression on her face.

"First couple, start with a right-hand turn!" the caller announced.

Her eyes lit up as she watched the first pair begin the dance, spinning around with a right-hand turn, the lady weaving her way down the line of men.

"Just you wait, Jackson." Ros fixed me with a gleeful look. "We'll consider this payback for dumping me in the deep end."

I laughed. "Whatever you say, pixie."

As the first couples made their way down the line, her excitement grew. She bounced on the balls of her feet, eagerly anticipating our turn.

The room was alive with the sound of stomping feet and clapping hands, the rhythm of the dance driving us forward.

"Here we go," I said as the caller announced, "Next couple, start your turn!"

I grasped her hands, my wrists crossed, and we began our own spin. She laughed, a bright, joyous sound, as we twirled around each other. She wove her way down the line, spinning each man with a laugh and a glint in her eyes that I wanted to see every day.

Each time she returned to me, she was breathless and beaming. The pattern continued with me spinning her before handing her off to the next man and taking the hand of the next woman in line. A whirl of movement and laughter, as we worked our way down the line.

The music picked up pace, and the spins became faster. Ros threw herself into the dance with abandon. The joy in her face was undeniable, and it warmed me to see her so free and happy.

Then it was our turn again. Only this time, we both threw extra energy into the spin. The sheer force of it tore her hand from mine. I careened backward, landing with a thud on the wooden floor. A burst of laughter echoed around the hall.

Ros appeared above me, her eyes wide with surprise and amusement. "You okay there, Big Shot?"

I grinned up at her, the embarrassment overshadowed by the hilarity of the situation.

"Never better."

"At least you kept your promise," she said, her eyes dancing teasingly. "You didn't let me fall."

I stood, brushing myself off, still laughing. "Well, I had to save someone from hitting the deck, right?"

Around us, the dance continued, the hall filled with the vibrant energy of the ceilidh. I took her hand, leading her back into the fray.

I wish I could say we were more careful with our spins this time, but I'd be lying. She had well and truly embraced the fun of 'Strip the Willow', and careful wasn't it. We travelled down the line, spinning each other harder and harder, relying on each other to keep us from getting dizzy or falling again.

As we moved together, I couldn't help but think how moments like this were what life was really about. The raw, unscripted laughter, the shared experiences, the genuine connection.

With Ros, everything felt more authentic, more meaningful.

And now I'd get to experience it every single day. I couldn't have asked for a better end to our fashionably fake arrangement.

Loved Jackson and Ros? Dying to spend a little more time with them and the whole Kings of Screen gang? Then turn the page to read the moment Ros finally gets a "new" engagement ring…

I usually reserve this for my mailing list but this is easier in print. Plus, it's just nice to have it all together, right?

BONUS EPILOGUE

 *hree months later...*

JACKSON

"Where are you taking me?" Ros asked for the fifth time.

The car stopped on Melrose Avenue, outside one of the most exclusive vintage jewellers the city could boast. It had taken Jen weeks of research to find this place.

That delay might be the only reason I'd found the patience to wait to do this.

Only the absolute best would do for my pixie. Jen and the owner had assured me that this was the perfect avenue to fulfil that.

But time was running out.

In a week, we would leave for Romania, and I refused to get on another plane with her wearing that ring.

I'd considered it beautiful once, but pink would never suit Ros.

"Just wait and see," I said as the driver opened my door. I shot her a grin. "You trust me, remember?"

She glared at me and I chuckled, stepping out of the car.

"The longer you keep up this guessing game, the more debatable that fact becomes," she grumbled as she shuffled towards me, a glint of annoyance mixed with curiosity in her eyes.

"I promise you'll like this surprise."

I took her hand and led her towards the entrance of the jeweller. Stepping into the shop felt like entering another world. The interior was a blend of rich velvet and warm colours, showcasing an array of vintage jewellery that sparkled under the lighting. Each piece seemed to tell its own story, a history waiting to be discovered.

Ros's eyes widened as she took in the surroundings, her initial hesitation giving way to awe.

"Why are we here?" She glanced at the display cases, her fingers twitching at her side as she held herself back.

"Welcome to Timeless Elegance Vintage Jewellery," the owner, Eleanor Grayson, called out from her spot behind the glass display cases. "It's nice to meet you in person, Jackson." She moved around the cases, her hand extended to shake mine.

I shook her hand, her grip stronger than I expected for a woman who appeared to be in her seventies.

"Thank you for pulling out all the stops at such short notice." I gestured to the blissfully empty shop. Something Jen had orchestrated with Eleanor a week ago.

"No need to thank me. This is normal protocol for us when dealing with someone of your calibre." Then her shrewd eyes shifted to Ros. "And this must be your bride-to-be."

Ros's gaze shifted between us, something akin to panic flitting across her face. Things had gotten a wee bit confusing between our private and public lives since London. I'd had to start prepping her before every outing, almost reminding her what the public thought our situation was.

Today, I would fix all of that.

If she said yes.

"Yes." Ros eventually nodded, a polite smile claiming her lips. "Nice to meet you."

"I spent the week going through my collection, and I think I found some wonderful options." She tilted her head, meeting my gaze with a knowing smirk that would be driving Ros insane as she tried to figure out what we were up to.

I nodded and she pulled a velvet-covered tray out from beneath the counter. Ros followed her movements like a hawk stalking prey.

Eleanor set the tray down on top of the glass counter and pulled back the cover with a practised flourish, unveiling an array of vintage engagement rings. Each unique, design telling a story of a bygone era. I didn't need to see her reaction to know she would love all of them.

"These are beautiful, but why do I need a new ring?" Ros's question cut through my thoughts. "Our engagement is for the media and fans, Jackson. What does it matter if I'm wearing Bree's ring?"

I took a deep breath, feeling a mixture of nerves and excitement. This was the moment I spent three months planning for, the moment I wanted to change everything between us for real.

"Because I want to ask you to marry me," I said, my voice steady despite the rapid beating of my heart. "For real. Not for the media, not for the fans, but for us."

Her eyes widened. "Are you serious?"

"Never been more serious in my life." I held her gaze, willing her to see the truth in mine. "I love you. And I want to spend the rest of my life with you, not as a publicity stunt, but as your husband."

Her hand trembled slightly in mine, and for a moment, I worried I had misjudged the situation. Maybe it was too soon. Maybe she wanted to wait until she was absolutely sure of us...

Then, she smiled, a genuine, radiant smile that lit up her entire face and set the rumblings of old doubts to rest.

"I... I don't know what to say."

"Say you'll marry me. For real."

She looked down at the rings, then back at me. "Yes."

"Yes?"

Hope like nothing I'd ever felt unfurled in my chest, but I needed her to be clear.

"Yes, I'll marry you for real."

I blinked at her, almost unable to believe those words had left her mouth.

"Quit staring at me like that." Ros crossed her arms. "I'm not going to change my mind. I'm not going to throw the ring at you. I said yes, jackass, so get your ass over here and kiss me!"

Snapping out of my dazed state, I pulled her into my arms, closing the small gap between us. My lips met hers in a kiss that was a mix of relief, joy, and a promise of a future together. It was a confirmation of everything we had been through, a seal on our commitment to each other.

As we broke apart, her cheeks were flushed, her eyes shining with unspoken emotions. "So, which one of these do you think I should wear?" she asked, gesturing to the tray of rings Eleanor had laid out.

Each ring was unique, carrying the essence of its era. But there was one that stood out to me, a ring that seemed to echo Ros's spirit — bold, unapologetic, and beautiful. It was a vintage Art Deco, with geometric lines and a bold blue sapphire surrounded by a sleek circle of diamonds.

"That one," I said, pointing it out. "It's as unique and captivating as you are."

She tugged off the pink monstrosity and replaced it with the sapphire, twisting her hand beneath the shop lights. She couldn't tear her eyes from it as the light refracted.

"It's perfect," she whispered.

And I couldn't agree more. It fit like it was made for her, echoing the same vibrant, unyielding charm that defined her.

"What are we going to tell them when they notice the ring's different?" Ros peeked up at me from beneath her lashes. Then her attention shifted to Eleanor. "And why are we discussing this in front of outside company?" she whispered.

Eleanor chuckled. "A certain level of discretion is needed to do business in this town, especially with the calibre of my clients. You don't need to worry about me selling your secrets."

She stared at her, her lips pursed. "That's all great, but doesn't really make me feel any better."

"She signed an NDA, pixie." I wrapped an arm around her, pulling her back into my chest. "No one is going to find out."

"You're sure?" she asked, turning in my arms as she bit her lip.

"Yes. Absolutely sure." I smoothed my thumb across her lower lip, freeing it from her torture. "Now, what do you want to tell the press? We'll make up a story, but I think you're creative enough to come up with something convincing for us both."

She laughed, a sound that filled the room with warmth. "Audra would never have let me handle that, but—"

"No buts. Audra's gone. It's our lives. You pick the story."

A month after we got back from Scotland, she'd pushed too hard on the new rules I'd set for her. Somehow when I said 'my relationship with Ros comes first,' she heard 'full steam ahead on the breakup plans.'

I couldn't say I was surprised, honestly.

But Jimmy supporting the decision and having a list of replacements ready for vetting shocked me. He even let Ros help in filtering through them. Which of course earned my agent brownie points, like he intended.

"Alright." She grinned up at me and I bit back a groan of despair.

"What are you going to say?"

"You'll find out when I decide."

It sounded reasonable enough. Only the glint in her eyes made my stomach twist with dread. I loved her, but she didn't half scare me when she got an idea in her head.

❄

ROS

"Guys, this is just too much!" Abi said, holding up a tiny pair of knitted booties. Her eyes were shiny, holding back tears. Pregnancy had turned my strong, independent friend into a sentimental mess.

I leaned back in my chair, a smile tugging at my lips as I watched her sort through the baby shower gifts. Laughter and chatter filled the room, a warm, comforting buzz that made me feel at home.

Everyone had turned up at Finn and Abi's house for a very late-in-the-game baby shower. And I mean seriously late—— Abi was due to pop any day now.

Add to that the fact we had just a couple of weeks left before the Kings of Screen and their partners flew to Romania to start filming Rogue Squad 6? Life had gotten a little stressful for Abi.

But we were all here, supporting her in any way we could.

Even Eva had tuned in via video call from Hoi An in Vietnam, her smiling face displayed on a tablet propped up on the mantle, despite the fact it was the early hours of the morning for her.

"Those booties are adorable, Abi!" Her voice echoed slightly in the spacious living room. "Who made them?"

"Mona." She rubbed her swollen belly. "Can you believe it? She knitted these herself."

Mona, sitting across from me, just waved her hand dismissively, but her cheeks turned a shade of pink. "It was nothing, really."

"But they're perfect," Abi insisted, carefully placing the booties back in the gift box. Her gaze met mine, and I could see the mix of excitement and anxiety in her eyes. "I can't believe I'm going to be a mom soon."

"You're going to make a fantastic mom," I said sincerely.

Abi's smile wobbled a bit as she folded a blanket carefully. "I hope so. I'm just... it's all becoming so real, you know? Any day now, there's going to be a little human here who's completely dependent on me."

I reached out and squeezed her hand. "You're going to be amazing. You've got this incredible maternal instinct. Eva can attest to that."

"Don't remind me," Eva groaned, her tone and expression teasing.

"Plus, you've got Finn, and all of us, to back you up."

She nodded, taking a deep breath. "Thanks, Ros. That means a lot."

The rest of our group was scattered around the room. Finn was deep in conversation with Shaun, both of them laughing about something. Nathan, Jen, and Charlie, Finn's agent, leaned against the breakfast bar, nursing glasses of wine, chatting and watching Cat coo over Emma and Charlie's five-month-old baby. Nathan had this slack-jawed look of terror on his face that would amuse me for days.

Jackson joined me on the sofa and leaned in, his warm breath tickling my ear. "Thinking of getting any of those for our future kids?" His voice was light, teasing, but I heard the underlying note of hope.

I rolled my eyes. "Let's not get ahead of ourselves. We've got a wedding to plan first, remember?"

And I had a story to concoct.

He chuckled, his hand finding mine and giving it a gentle squeeze. "Right. One step at a time."

As Abi continued opening gifts, her eyes suddenly widened, a hand flying to her mouth. She pulled out a tiny onesie, the front reading 'Daddy's Little Co-Star.'

Finn glanced over, a proud grin spreading across his face. "Couldn't resist that one," he said, winking at Abi.

The room erupted in laughter.

"Did you get yourself a matching one?" I asked.

Finn kept a straight face, nodding solemnly. "Of course. What kind of father do you think I am? Can't have my kid out-styling me."

"Wait, wait," Nathan cut in, his grin wicked. "Are you telling us you're going to parade around in a onesie too?"

"Only on weekends," Finn said, deadpan.

Abi shook her head, but her eyes were bright with amusement. "He's kidding... I think."

I couldn't help but join in the laughter. "Well, that's one paparazzi shot I can't wait to see."

"I bet he'd do it too, just to make Abi laugh," Jackson said.

I glanced at him, seeing the affection in his eyes as he watched Finn and Abi. It reminded me of how he looked at me sometimes, like I was his whole world. It warmed me from the inside out.

"Okay, but Finn, you know they make dad versions of those, right?" Jen said.

"I'm way ahead of you, Jen." Finn winked at her. "Got the T-shirt and the matching mug."

"Talk about being prepared." Charlie laughed. "You're going to be one of those dads, aren't you?"

Finn shrugged, a mock-serious expression on his face. "Got to embrace the role, you know?"

Abi, still holding the onesie, chuckled, rolling her eyes lovingly at Finn. "I can just imagine you two wearing those on your Sunday strolls."

I couldn't help but laugh along with everyone else.

"Ros, is that a new ring?" Eva's voice broke through the chatter, her tone a mix of curiosity and excitement.

Everyone's attention turned to me, and the burn of a blush crept up my cheeks.

"Yeah, it is," I said, lifting my hand for everyone to see. The ring glinted, a beautiful contrast against my skin.

"Do you want to tell them, or shall I?" Jackson asked.

I glanced at him, smirking. "Why don't you take the honours?"

He cleared his throat, a proud smile on his face. "Ros and I are getting married."

"Yeah, yeah, we know that already," Nathan muttered.

"For real," Jackson said, his tone dead serious.

For a moment absolute silence fell around us. Then a chorus of excited gasps and congratulations filled the room.

Abi was the first to jump up and tug me to my feet. She wrapped her arms around me in a tight hug. "Oh my God! That's amazing!"

"Congratulations, you two." Finn clapped Jackson on the back.

As the initial wave of excitement settled, I smirked at Jackson before announcing to the room: "I've got the perfect story to tell the press about the ring change too."

I turned to Abi and Mona, a playful glint in my eye. Jackson groaned.

Mona leaned forward, her interest piqued. "Do tell."

"Well," a mischievous smile claimed my lips as I snuck a peek at Jackson, "I thought we could say Jackson was so swept up with wedding fever, he got ahead of himself and bought me a ring right after Finn and Abi's wedding. Before he really knew me."

He chuckled, taking it all in stride. "If that's what you want the narrative to be, I'll go along with it."

I stared up at him, almost struck dumb. Say what now?

"You're okay with that?" I asked, touched by his easy acceptance. "But it makes you look like a lovesick man."

He shrugged. "Who said I wanted to deny that I was?" He smiled, a smile that spoke volumes — of love, commitment, and a shared future. "Anything for you, pixie."

His willingness to let himself look a little silly for my sake was touching. It was just so him — putting me and my feelings first.

I leaned against him, a sense of contentment washing over me. This was right, us being together, planning a future. It felt like everything had finally fallen into place.

Eva's voice came through the tablet, breaking the moment. "So, when's the big day? Have you set a date yet?"

I exchanged a look with Jackson. "Not yet, but we're thinking sometime next year. We want to make sure it's perfect."

In that moment, surrounded by friends and family, with the man I loved by my side, it was impossible to ignore how far I'd come. From letting fear of things I couldn't control rule me and keep me from any meaningful connections beyond my two best friends, to the comfort of knowing I could rely on Jackson and the people in our lives.

It made the ups and downs of the last eight months more than worth the pain and heartache.

ALSO BY MORGANA BEVAN

True Platinum Series (Rock Star Romance)

(Rhiannon)

Chasing Alys – Ryan (Resistant to Love)

Charming Daphne – Matt (Force Proximity)

Winning Nia – James (Second Chance)

Enticing Mel – Dan (Secret Baby)

Needing Emily – Emily (Accidental Marriage/Runaway Bride)

Defying Ella - Jared (Close Proximity / Snowed-In)

(The Brightside)

Braving Lily - Lily (Opposites Attract)

Daring Ceri - Alex (Second Chance)

Marrying Olivia - Lewis (Accidental Marriage)

Kings of Screen Series (Hollywood Romance)

Between Takes (Enemies to Lovers)

Married Blind (Marriage of Convenience)

Acting Counsel (Close Proximity, Forbidden)

Fashionably Fake (Fake Dating)

Lights, Camera, Baby! (Accidental pregnancy)

Sign up for Morgana Bevan's mailing list: https://morganabevan.com/mailing-list/